# The Cattlewash Assailant

## BRIAN J E SKINNER

Tellwell Talent
www.tellwell.ca

ISBN
978-0-2288-2538-8 (Hardcover)
978-0-2288-2537-1 (Paperback)
978-0-2288-2539-5 (eBook)

# Table of Contents

**SUNDAY**

Prologue .................................................................... 3

**MONDAY**

Chapter 1:    Her Arrival ............................................. 15
Chapter 2:    Who's Missing? ..................................... 19
Chapter 3:    Flying Fish Cutter ................................. 25
Chapter 4:    Escape, then Run ................................... 31
Chapter 5:    Call the Police ...................................... 37
Chapter 6:    The Interrogation ................................. 46
Chapter 7:    Wade Barnwell ...................................... 55
Chapter 8:    Gathering Clues .................................... 64

**TUESDAY**

Chapter 9:    The Incident .......................................... 77
Chapter 10:   Some X-Rays ......................................... 86
Chapter 11:   The Contract ......................................... 98
Chapter 12:   Derk Warrows ....................................... 105
Chapter 13:   The Bus Tour ........................................ 113
Chapter 14:   Pleasure Cruise ..................................... 123
Chapter 15:   Crisis Team ........................................... 136
Chapter 16:   Cinnamon Scent-Bomb ........................ 146
Chapter 17:   Hector's Heart ...................................... 157

Chapter 18: Snacks And Alcohol ............................ 162
Chapter 19: The Chase ...................................... 169
Chapter 20: Rescue Challenges ............................ 180
Chapter 21: Tucking the Duppy ............................ 188
Chapter 22: Rayna's Notes ................................. 197

## WEDNESDAY

Chapter 23: Cloudless Sky .................................. 207
Chapter 24: Malibu Rum .................................... 215
Chapter 25: Many Aliases .................................. 224
Chapter 26: Sapphire Beach ............................... 232
Chapter 27: Evening Festivities ........................... 244

## THURSDAY

Chapter 28: Tourist Attractions ........................... 255

## FRIDAY

Chapter 29: Girl Fight .................................... 269
Chapter 30: Alessio's Partners ............................ 280
Chapter 31: Two Teams .................................... 289
Chapter 32: Plan B ........................................ 299
Chapter 33: Sweet Goodbyes ............................... 306


Acknowledgements ......................................... 313
Author's Note ............................................ 315
Photographic Credit ...................................... 317
Next Novel Excerpt ....................................... 319
Book Club Questions ...................................... 327

With
love to
my parents
Eustace "Toby"
Theodore Skinner
and
Norma Mary Elson
Skinner

# SUNDAY

# Prologue

"Well, hello there," Captain Evanson Springer greeted the approaching man with a firm handshake as he prepared to board the catamaran. "Welcome aboard." He watched his passengers board and beamed a warm and welcoming grin, his salt-and-pepper soul patch catching the evening light. *It's a beautiful evening, and this is going to be fantastic.*

"I'm Byron Glenning, and this is my wife Kennedy," Byron introduced, guiding her forward with a protective hand on her back, his stainless steel briefcase clutched firmly in the other. He took the gangplank steps cautiously, balancing his cargo with his sandaled feet.

"You'll really enjoy this trip. Evanson and I are the best crew. We'll make your time aboard beyond compare, and I bet you've heard about our rum punch," Akeel, the first mate, grinned as he completed final preparations to launch the *Dingolay*. Akeel worked swiftly, deftly untying ropes and returning gear to the boat's hooks. He always loved the water from a youthful age and took immense pride in helping Evanson build a successful small business over the years. The two of them were solid business partners, popular with private charters. Akeel's youthful face was easy on the eyes, and Evanson's charm was genuine.

Hopping aboard and hoisting the anchor, Akeel accidentally bumped into Byron's case; motioning to the captain to suggest stowing it securely—in the secret compartment—by the captain's deck, where high rollers or celebrity tourists kept their valuables.

Byron noticed the bump and couldn't resist sharing about its valuable contents. "This case holds the most revolutionary advancements for automotive tires, set to be a worldwide game changer. It's my latest R&D project, perfecting the rubber compound for all sorts of tires, and if we're lucky tomorrow," he wrapped his arm around Kennedy's waist, "we'll be rolling with an eight-figure bank balance!" He looked for the crew's expressions, but they weren't as enthusiastic as he was. His voice hushed, "I didn't want to leave it in the hotel, in case there was a break-in."

Both Byron and Kennedy were exhausted from their vacation's final stretch. They had tried to keep the trip strictly business but decided to sneak in a little relaxation the night before their big offer. With two professional incomes and no children, Byron planned to retire after this deal and enjoy the fruits of his life's innovations. Kennedy would become a consultant part-time, looking forward to spending more time at their California timeshare and on sunny golf courses.

Evanson often delighted at the stories each passenger told. As a retired high school teacher and a people person, he and Akeel preferred taking out their small catamaran with peaceful business or celebrity couples over the college students their competitors chartered. He softened, "That's quite an accomplishment and it's lovely to have a mature couple on board. You can place your case down here sir. It's waterproof and you can set a code to lock it if you'd like. Now on to the next item of business. Fancy a rum punch?" he asked while winking at Kennedy. "And for you darling, what would you like?"

Kennedy sought relaxation, her mind avoiding Byron's mounting excitement. As an e-commerce business owner, she knew the importance of clarity during crucial business moments.

"I don't feel like anything too heavy. Do you have a Malibu? A Malibu and orange?"

"I'll have an XO if you have it. Don't want to get too ahead of my deal tomorrow, but I'm here to celebrate if you know what I mean." Byron said as he closed the compartment. He whispered the code to Kennedy, making her smile.

"I knew you'd pick that one. It's easy to remember our anniversary."

"Isn't this beautiful? The best way to end a great vacation. I can't wait to get this deal wrapped up tomorrow and we will join the millionaire club by Friday. I still can't believe it!"

"Don't worry about it tonight. Just enjoy this view! You've been anxious this whole trip. Come sit with me on the net." Kennedy leaned in for a kiss watching her husband's anxiety melt from her sugary lips.

Byron smiled warmly, cherishing his wife, and feeling elated to celebrate with her after enduring six years of failed prototypes. Coming to Barbados to test his new rubber compound's durability in the hot climate was the decisive step in his proposal. He had spent the entire whole week's vacation creating video clips to highlight his genius work.

Akeel tried not to interrupt the mood, "We've got all the rums of the Island, mate," handing Kennedy her Malibu. "You want the XO straight? With Ice?"

"Sure, or neat with a lime wedge."

As the sun began its descent, they sailed towards deeper waters, the breeze weakening. Evanson kept the trolling motor running smoothly.

Byron had suggested to the crew that a more secluded area, away from touristy chatter, might be lovely, and Evanson and Akeel agreed to arrange the tour. As they spoke, Kennedy admired the ocean's beauty, the sunset draping the water in perfect hues. She held her drink and leaned back on the netting of the catamaran. Out of the corner of her eye, she thought she spotted a fish leap, but it barely registered.

The boat gently turned on the chosen route. Kennedy took in the pleasant panorama of glowing beachfront condominiums and resorts, occasionally seeing a beachcomber or child splashing in the surf. The early evening sun was gorgeous. Byron was right. *This is beautiful*, she thought, getting up to rejoin the men, who were laughing over some Island lore.

"Well, if you will excuse me, I need to replenish our rum, seems Byron here has taken a liking to the extra old." Evanson kidded.

"How many have you had?" Kennedy hesitated. *Could he be drunk*, she wondered? "You better strap a life jacket on him," she called down to Evanson, "I don't want him falling overboard. He needs to sober up too for the meeting tomorrow."

"Akeel," Evanson called up, "Can you get the man a vest?" grabbing another bottle of XO, he peered out the porthole window, looking cautiously at the water. A hollow emptiness settled in his stomach. He could have sworn he spotted a dark, mysterious yacht on the sea, but scanning the horizon again revealed nothing.

Akeel instructed Byron to find a comfortable spot and stay put while he went to the catamaran's bow to retrieve the life vests from their safety tether. Quickly gauging which vest would fit Byron's muscular frame, he was about to untie the larger vests when Kennedy screamed. *Oh Lord,* Akeel thought, hesitating for a moment before grabbing the rescue ring and rushing to the scene.

"What happened?!" both men chanted in unison, their eyes frantically scanning the sea as they arrived at the port side. Captain Springer hoping the catamaran's rigging wouldn't collide with Byron if he fell, or potentially knocking him unconscious.

Akeel tossed the ring into the water watching for Byron to reach it. He opened his mouth to Evanson, "I'll stay here and look for him. I only managed to grab the ring." his voice weak from the situation.

"Promise me you'll get him back on the boat fast and watch the wife! The sun's almost gone. We can't look for both of them if she's not careful!"

Byron was barely above the water but managed to grab the dinghy rope draped off the side of the pontoon. *Somebody reach for my hand,* he thought, arm outstretched, head bobbing through the crest of the sloshing spray.

*I'm going to drown! Ken!* Gasping for air, his wet clothes weighing him down.

"Byron... Byron!" Kennedy wailed, poised carefully at the pontoon's edge above where her husband was drowning. *Please don't let him die. Please!*

"There he is!" Akeel shouted.

Kennedy focused on Byron, "Hold on, they're getting you a vest."

Evanson rushed to the bow, knife in hand, cutting through the brittle rope. *Please don't go under sir,* he pleaded silently. *Please Lord, stop the wife from jumping in.* Imagining the headlines if they both drowned, His hands aching as he fought with the last knot to free the vests.

Looping his arm around the same rope that Byron clung to, Akeel pulled hard to lift Byron's head above the water, easing Kennedy's fears, as she shrieked over the unfolding scene.

"Akeel!" Evanson called loudly from the bow. "Cut the engine! Turn on the hull lights and steer toward shore. If he loses his grip, we can dive in and get him back in shallow water. This area is free of reefs, about two and a half fathoms deep. He'll be safe once we get a vest on him."

As chaos intensified, the mysterious dark yacht— tailing the *Dingolay* the entire time—stealthily pulled alongside the starboard side of the catamaran. Then, it turned sharply to sideswipe the unsuspecting passengers.

*Cut the engine, and steer for shore.* Akeel found the moment to make it happen.

Kennedy pleaded with Akeel, "No don't leave him. Please help keep his head above water. I think he's struggling!" peering over the side, "Byron, hold on! We're heading back to the shore!"

*What the hell was that?* Evanson, was the first to take notice that something had bumped into their hull. Squinting in the pale twilight, he opened his eyes with bewilderment. It was that mysterious dark boat that had come out of nowhere. Before he could say anything, a strange yet extremely sharp pain erupted in the right half of his abdomen. Looking down, he saw he was bleeding, dark blood pulsating down his shirt and onto the deck. *What is happening?*

Staggering, the gentle rock of the sea adding to his disorientation. Evanson felt a second, then third sharp, searing pain in his neck and chest. They were gunshot wounds from a silenced gun; he heard no gunfire over Kennedy and Akeel's frantic cries. Losing his balance, vision darkening, Evanson toppled into the sea. As the sun set, Captain Springer breathed his last, succumbing to the once-romantic pleasure cruise's depths.

The mysterious yacht remained unnoticed, even though its sharp turn had caught the captain's attention. A crew member of the dark vessel was able to hop aboard and expertly aimed his silenced gun towards Akeel, as Kennedy moved to get a better view of her near drowned husband, blocking the assassin's mark. Adjusting slightly, he fired a shot into the back of Akeel's neck.

Kennedy's head was down towards Byron, essentially unconscious, water pooling into his ceased lungs, his heartbeat barely a murmur.

Akeel fell into the water, appearing as a clumsy rescue dive. Floating lifelessly at first, the weight of his clothes quickly pulled his body deeper.

Seeing both Akeel and Byron slip beneath the water's surface, Kennedy called out to Akeel, who failed to respond—his muscular body now lost below the waves. Frantically shifting on the railing's edge, she slipped on the deck, hitting her head on the bar's side, vodka bottle crashing as it fell to the deck. Alcohol seeped into her fresh gash as her head began to throb. Looking out at the dim sky, Kennedy saw a figure approaching, harpoon gun in hand. *Who the hell are you? Don't come near me.* The figure hesitated then bent down, close to her face. A smirk formed as Kennedy's vision darkened.

"Your husband's case where is it?" the figure hissed.

Kennedy made no reply and lost consciousness.

As the assassin's vessel secured itself to the *Dingolay* and began towing the boat deeper, the crew member quickly scanned for signs of a breach and the briefcase. Calmly, he lifted Kennedy, to the dark yacht's hidden mechanical cabin. As the rope guided the crewless catamaran back to deep water, the crew member returned to the captain's deck.

"She's unconscious, but I tied her up as usual."

"And the briefcase?" the callous Captain asked.

"I didn't see it on the deck. I doubt it flew overboard during the job. I'll search for it once we're back in port."

"No, get back on that boat and check again. It wasn't in the hotel room earlier. I want it in my hands within the hour."

Exiting to the starboard deck, the crew member ran towards the stern, carefully leaping onto the *Dingolay*, at once beginning the search for the case.

The bodies of Akeel, Evanson and Byron rolled gently in the waves like tall grass swaying in the breeze. It would take a few hours for them to reach the shore, and this quiet route in the evening, meant witnesses would be scarce. Under the moonlight, the two boats silently navigated, carrying with them the plight of three lives lost beneath the sea's surface.

# MONDAY

# Chapter 1

# *HER ARRIVAL*

## 1.

Klara Hockley leaned forward to peer out of the airplane window as her plane descended for its final approach into Barbados. She smiled and settled back, adjusting the armrest button to return her seat to its upright position. Closing her eyes during landing was a thrill for her, guessing the exact moment when the plane would touch the runway.

Klara had never been to Barbados before but had visited the Cayman Islands when she was young. She loved seeing the Turtle Farm and the Sting Ray City attraction and longed to do some scuba diving while travelling to Barbados. First a career high school teacher and geography department head, she longed for helping people before trouble started. Now a graduated recruit in law enforcement Klara was free to travel for the summer break before selling herself to a division.

The plane landed smoothly after a quiet five-hour flight. Klara stood up as soon as she could, nursing her old hip injury that would flair up if cramped for too long. She nearly bumped her head retrieving her carry-on from the overhead compartment. Traveling light was her norm, partly due to her name sometimes causing issues at customs. Her doppelgänger's lifestyle contrasted sharply with her own uneventful existence, leading to frequent stops and luggage checks by K-9 units.

"Those teenagers…" Klara muttered to herself, recalling about her carry-on that obnoxious teenagers sprayed at the Toronto Airport while shooting a TikTok video. She took a connecting flight from Calgary, which she would never do again if she could. She almost missed her flight due to the ruckus from the Calgary Stampede Rodeo tourists. With her checked bag of books to donate to local schools and her carry-on with the essentials, Klara planned to be by a beach before sundown.

Handing her in flight magazine to a flight attendant, Klara joined the queue to exit the plane. A friendly Bajan woman paused the line, allowing Klara and the other passengers to disembark efficiently.

The burst of heat, the hot tarmac, and the short fragrant walk in the Caribbean air to the gate, really got Klara in the mood. Scoping a luggage carrier for her large orange suitcase, she made her way into the gate and fished her passport out.

Customs was straightforward, with disciplined yet courteous agents staffing the booths. Klara passed through without any issues, her face betraying none of the excitement she felt at her smooth entry into the country. She looked around the airport, taking in the beautiful terrazzo floors and the refreshing airflow. Finally spotting a baggage cart, she quickly fetched it, wheeling it towards the baggage claim area.

"There's a free cart over there," Klara pointed out to another traveler, smiling as she watched the person grab it and head towards the carousel.

"How was your flight, ma'am?" a passing airport staff member asked, noticing Klara's relaxed demeanor.

"Smooth, thank you. I'm here to see if my sister wants to come to Barbados. She's looking for a destination wedding hot spot."

"You've found it. We are known as the island in the sun. We'd love to have her get married on the rock. Lots of views of the beach and sea make a perfect backdrop."

*Hmm. She was so friendly. That doesn't happen in a Canadian airport.* she thought and replied with a polite nod, her mind already planning her itinerary in Barbados. The wedding of her sister Marcy would be in a year, and Klara was to arrive first, before the maid of honor would join her on Wednesday. As with all destination wedding trips to scope the perfect beach, the maid of honor always wanted the final say. Klara tolerated Marcy's friends. But Florence—or Flo—Wickworth wasn't worth much. It was funny Marcy chose a two time divorcee for her party planner.

Two youth approached Klara as she was waiting for her luggage. "What have you got there?" the first boy asked.

"Um, I don't have... are you talking to me?" Klara puzzled. Looking toward the second boy for a lead. He stared at her with a blank expression.

The first boy smiled. "I asked, what have you got there? You are supposed to say..."

The other boy chimed in, "Just a bit of Peter Piper's unprinted pickle pepper printer paper for the printer." His face broke forming a childish grin.

"Preposterous! Peter Piper pickle pepper printer paper for my Officejet Pro Laser Printer?" his young voice never missing a beat. Klara was amazed that nobody was recording this performance.

"Well, the Peter Piper pack of pickle pepper printer paper can be put or placed pickle pepper print side up so Peter Piper's perfectly unprinted paper can finally get printed!" the first boy stopped with his hands outstretched.

Mr. Stoneface replied, "Perfect!" then both boys took a bow.

Klara was stunned. "That was amazing boys! Quite the tongue twister!" wishing she had recorded the skit; she would send it to Marcy. She saw her orange suitcase and smiled when a muscular cricket player pulled it off for her.

Moving to the hired-car area, Klara loved the fragrant scents from the duty-free boutique as she exited. She smiled as she watched birds fly through the open airport. With her phone out, she recorded when a small flock of birds swooped down to eat crumbs at the delight of children's laughter. She savored the moment, knowing this trip would be memorable, despite the occasional challenges of collecting her sister's wedding details.

Klara moved towards the exit, her thoughts wandering to the adventures awaiting her in this Caribbean paradise. She glanced at the airport's bustling surroundings, noting the warmth in the air and the promise of sunny days ahead.

# Chapter 2

# *WHO'S MISSING?*

## 1.

"Right this way, straight to your hotel, and just in time for the beach! Where are you from? First time to the Island?" chanted the cabbie, lifting the luggage with care and opening the door for Klara.

"Thank you. I'm from Canada. Have you heard of Edmonton?" Klara asked.

"Oilers hockey and there were some roaring wildfires up there in McMurray, Fort McMurray, right?" the cabbie said, moving around to the driver's side and motioning to the other drivers he landed a fare.

"Yes, that's right! Wow, the news traveled all the way down here?" Klara muttered to herself, "they know about those wildfires in Fort Mac."

"And that heroic story of the skateboarding boys in Calgary stopping that girl from being assaulted in a back alley. I have a CTV news app and my brother-in-law works in Calgary. I'm sure crime is not an issue up there. We're trying to get rid of the crime issue here on the Island. We just passed our 50th anniversary of being free, and by our 55th anniversary, we hope to be fully independent of

Britain. Where are you staying?" the cabbie asked, setting up the fare.

"Yes, those boys were a ray of sunshine for that woman. They won an award for their bravery." Klara replied, spotting a roadside beach bar, and feeling at ease, thinking that within a few hours she'll sit on the beach in paradise. "It is not too far from here. It's called the Stingray Cove Apartments, in Rockley, I think?" Klara began digging in her bag to see if the GPS unit she brought would reach a satellite signal. She had the hotel saved if she decided to rent a car with Flo later on and tour wedding destinations. She read that Barbados was touristy, safe to drive around, and fun to explore.

"That rental is in Maxwell Hill. Haven't you heard anything from your travel agent? Did they call you before you left Canada?" the cabbie continued.

Klara's eyes shifted to the rearview mirror to see if the cab driver was serious. "What happened? Fire?"

"Two tourists went missing yesterday from their other hotel. Just never came back from their evening cruise."

"Maybe they went out later, got a bite to eat?" Klara offered. "Or they are sobering up on a beach. Those mini cruises have an open bar, do they not?"

"Tourists eventually show up, but when the police are involved, it must be serious. Two others went missing a few days earlier from that resort too. Hopefully, they have your room with a view of the sea, and the A/C on when you open the door. Don't go missing yourself!"

The driver competently honked whenever he knew the other drivers, or a car swerved into their lane and swiftly used the roundabout to get onto the Spring Garden Highway.

*Missing.* Klara turned to look out the window. *How can you go missing on an island party cruise?* She pressed her hand to her chest, and gasped, "You don't think they drowned, did you?"

"I don't know, but I'm sure they will turn up. I don't know the first couple, but the others are British, from what I've heard," the cabbie said.

"That's weird," Klara thought. *Brits don't usually get so crazy drunk they sleep it off on some beach.*

"I hope they are okay. Missing! That would be awful." Klara looked out the window at the various resorts and rentals. Sometimes, a run-down chattel house would catch her attention, and she could feel the sadness ebbing from its rickety walls.

The cab arrived at the sight of several police units in the parking lot when one officer approached the cabbie.

"Are you picking up?" the officer side-stepped to the shade of a palm tree as beads of sweat wept from his forehead in the afternoon sun.

"No sir, just dropping off. I told her the rental would be busy. Anything turn up about those tourists?" the cabbie replied.

"I shouldn't be telling you this, but this is the second set of tourists that have been reported missing this week. We were just beginning to piece together the first case, now this?!"

"Can I get out? I'd like to use the washroom. I'll grab my suitcase." Klara offered a twenty dollar U.S. bill to the cabbie, then opened the door and stood at the curb.

The cabbie pushed the hatch button so Klara could get her luggage.

"Thanks, girlie," he chimed.

Wheeling her suitcase up the sidewalk ramp and through the front lobby door, Klara felt the burst of air conditioning while greeting the front desk worker. "I bet you're tired of all this crime stuff happening?" Klara queried.

The desk attendant, who seemed quite shaken up over the police units and their flashing lights, just stared toward the street.

Looking at the young woman behind the desk, Klara sensed that this sort of Monday afternoon action was not the usual affair in this area. She opened her mouth to speak but turned when a muscular police officer entered the lobby.

"Well, we can't seem to see any sign of forced entry, nothing is stolen or in disrepair. So, if they turn up, give us a quick call and we'll come back for a statement." He turned to Klara and reassured her, "I wouldn't worry. These sorts of cases are rarely unsolved. Please enjoy your stay in Barbados."

"I'm not overly worried Barbados is safe. It's my first trip here. My sister would like to get married next year and I'm thinking that she'll choose Barbados. I'm really looking forward to…" she caught the look from the desk attendant. "Is something wrong?"

"I'm incredibly sorry, but your room will not be ready since this incident with the guests in twelve. My room staff also don't work on Sundays, and we are doing renovations, so your room is not ready for you to check-in. I could put you up in our sister suite in Welches. It is not on the beach, mind you, but it's near the Oistins fish fry."

"Wait. The tourists in room twelve are missing, and you are sending me to where the other set of tourists are missing too." Klara pained, "I really need to use your bathroom."

"I'm terribly sorry. Down the hall to the right." She turned to the officer as Klara left the lobby, "I don't believe this. I come to work and now it's a crime scene."

The officer replied, "Take it easy. Don't fret, there is nothing you can do. Try to make this new guest comfortable. We'll get it safe around here again real soon." He gave her a courteous nod and exited the lobby to his SUV in the parking lot.

"You are running low on toilet paper," Klara said as she resumed her stance, awaiting the new room's information. "Will there be any price difference between the two hotel rooms?"

"I was able to give you the manager's special rate, and you have air conditioning in the room, as well as a fan overhead. In the night chest, you may find a green coil and some netting for the mosquitoes if they bother you. Here is the address, and I will call you another taxi, free of charge. I hope this is to your satisfaction?"

"Oh, no, it will be fine. I'm flexible. I'm a Canadian."

"Are you a teacher. We could use some more Canadian teachers here. Most schoolteachers are overworked, and the children are acting up more and more. In the future, please come back to Stingray Cove. I'll get you the honeymoon rate that comes with early morning room service."

"I'm almost a police officer. Just taking my summer off before I hit the pavement and go job hunting. Thanks for all you have done. I can't imagine how difficult all this extra attention is. I love how friendly everyone is in Barbados too. Klara gave the desk attendant a warm smile and went out to watch the sunset.

With the new directions in her hand, Klara began texting Marcy while listening to the officers.

**Klara:** It was a great flight. My hotel got switched though.
**Marcy:** Oh, why?
**Klara:** Some tourists are missing. I don't mind. The airport had some boys that melted my heart. They did this tongue twister thing that was amazing. I should have recorded it for you.
**Marcy:** Do you think Barbados is the one?
**Klara:** Half a thumb up so far. I'll keep you posted.
**Marcy:** KK.

Klara watched the officers lecturing the common tourist locations for sober entertainment to a drunk tourist who was severely sunburnt. Marcy would probably text back in a while as Klara knew she was busy watching *Suits*. Her phone needed a charge and since her feet were tired, she wanted to relax tonight. She peered around at the tourists walking along the street, picturing their adventures. The evening was about to start. Klara sat on her suitcase tilting her face to the late afternoon sun.

# Chapter 3

# *FLYING FISH CUTTER*

## 1.

"So, you are getting moved..." a voice said from a parked tow truck. Klara cautiously shifted her head to see who spoke. The driver's door opened and an average sized man with a boyish stroll moved towards her. "It sounds like a break-in or kidnapping from what I've overheard. I was listening and as usual they told me I could get in trouble if I interfere with their official police business. New to the rock? You can't wear any camouflage clothing down here. It's illegal, just saying! Did you see the tourist map of all the cool island bits? I could show you..." the man looked at her and stood a foot from her suitcase.

Klara's expression looked drained but on guard, and her posture at first suggested she wanted to find a beach and relax. She looked toward the man, tilting her face from the sun's glow.

"Most of the people I've met today have been courteous, friendly, and kind. You sir are none of those. Would you please step back!"

Her phone began to vibrate in her purse, and she quickly answered it, wondering if it was a message about the room arrangements. The name on the call was familiar.

"Hi Marcy," she chimed. "No, I haven't moved yet... Flo wants me to text her tomorrow, sure. I'll call you back, I'm waiting for a taxi, and someone is trying to pick me up." She turned to the man and returned the phone to her purse, "I'm not interested."

"No worries. The name's Jones, and I was just trying to keep you company before your cab arrived. Oh, if you ever get in trouble and need to get picked up, call this number." He offered his business card, which opened up to a square showing his truck at night.

"Thanks, but I won't be renting a car. Next time you approach someone, tell a joke, or offer some sunscreen. To be honest, I didn't read a helpful vibe from you at all." Klara stretched quickly then wheeled her suitcase to the cab entering the parking lot. She gave the cabbie the Sandy Wharf address and watched Jones lurch back to his truck.

The trip to Sandy Wharf, the Stingray Cove's secondary, less elaborate complex, was along an uneventful route. Lots of times the cabbie nearly hit women walking with sacks of laundry perfectly balanced on their heads. The cabbie could see that Klara was tired and skipped the chatter but did say that the Breezes restaurant was a wonderful place for a hot meal.

Klara thanked the cab driver and smiled when he said he'd bring her suitcase to the lobby. She entered the front door and had a short wait behind a young family. Seeing the toddler hop over the cracks in the concrete floor recharged her. When she got to the desk, her room keys and a food voucher for a Mount Gay rum punch and Flying Fish Cutter at the Breezes beachside restaurant were presented with a bottle of water. Conveniently, she now would get the much-needed rest that she deserved, free of charge. She dragged her suitcase to her room, splashed some icy water on her face and plugged in her phone.

Due to the past few hours, Klara felt a little concerned over the unknown that would unfold before Flo arrived. Both Marcy and Klara orchestrated this one-week holiday to be a creative and adventurous experience, as it was carefully planned months in advance, leaving a few elements to be decided on once they arrived. So far it has been mixed, but a hot meal as the cabbie said might fix the evening. After a quick gulp from the bottled water, Klara strolled to the restaurant.

Breezes Oceanview Bar was partially crowded, with a steel pan song harmonizing with the smooth rhythmic southern sea's waves. As she followed the host to her table, servers were gossiping about some highly athletic man's chiselled abdominal region at the rowdy corner table by the bar.

The table that Klara arrived at had a cliffside view and a tiki torch casting an amber glow on her face. Klara imagined how she must look spent, in need of some frolicking in the surf or laying in the sand, feeling its therapeutic warmth.

"Good evening, and where are you coming from today?" The server sang, a musical calypso pitch to her voice.

"Well," Klara pained, "I was supposed to be staying at the Stingray Cove, but there is an investigation going on. Before that, I arrived from Canada."

Her voice shifted to a whisper, "I heard about that. Those poor folks. They were here," she slightly turned and pointed to a table two seats away. "Just yesterday I remembered them coming in and ordering. The man was in trouble from his lady over spending too much time making videos on their vacation, and boy were her eyes roasting him."

"They are missing," Klara mentioned. "What do you think could have happened?"

"Let me take your order, bring some drinks. It's not too busy here, I know what might have happened, but I don't want to go to the police. Rum punch, juice smoothie with a little coconut rum? What will you have?"

"I have a coupon for a free meal. Is it a big plate? I don't eat very much." Klara said, placing the voucher in the server's hand. "Can I just have orange juice? I'm not in the mood for a big alcoholic drink right now." Klara hesitated. "And a big glass of water too, thanks."

The server read the voucher then asked, "What I suggest is the Cutter with a side of macaroni pie. That will go well with your orange juice. Sound good?"

"Sounds delicious. I haven't eaten since this morning.

"Girl you'll waste away in this heat. I'll be right back with that juice," the server hurried off to fetch her beverage and place the order.

Klara leaned back and stared at the violet sky. She concentrated on the soothing rhythm of the waves sloshing across the sand below. *I really wished I made it to the beach today.* Klara sighed, "Tomorrow."

"Here we are, orange and your cup of house salad. I also brought you a little jigger of our rum punch. I heard you on the big glass, so here's a sample, with one of those umbrellas. Your meal will be right out. And in other business..." the server took a hasty glance to gauge her time. "The couple you say went missing; I think they might have not held their liquor. The man, I think Byron was his name, or something to that ring, was hitting the drinks quick, his lady not impressed." She leaned in and whispered. "He may have drowned if he not sober up too quick if he went for a sea bath. We have a saying on this Island, that the beach be beautiful by the day's sun and treacherous by nightfall. He may have gone in the water with his girl, struggled and pull her down with him. It will be a crying shame when a little one playing on the beach see their bodies wash ashore, bloated like a ripe fish."

Klara had a strong stomach, but when she inserted the image of a bloated fish into her head, looking forward to the Flying Fish Cutter might not be the most delicious dish of her day.

"It looks like your Cutter is ready, oh and I forgot your water..." She seemed almost animated when she rushed off to fix her error.

The jigger of rum punch looked refreshing, a hue like grapefruit and guava. The little sprinkle of Nutmeg reminded her of cozy fireside eggnog, but the thought of frigid winter temperatures was distant in her new island paradise. Klara twirled the cocktail umbrella reading

*Barbados famous rum punch! Make it at home with one sour, two sweet, three strong, and four weak.*

The server brought her water, a galvanized mini bucket of condiments, and her meal. The sizzling Cutter discharged the rich aroma of Bajan curry. Klara loved local cuisine, especially the most popular dishes that returning customers would rave about on social media. Klara's first bite was filled with the opulent flavours of both spicy and savoury. When it came to West Indian, garlic and curry were staples in every Bajan's spice rack.

# Chapter 4

# *ESCAPE, THEN RUN*

## 1.

Kennedy Glenning's headache subsided as she opened her eyes to see she was in the berth of a boat. The sounds from the fire room hissed and stammered as she let her eyes come into focus. She heard movement on the top deck and vague murmurings that she figured were the crew or her captors.

At present, the tears that she had withheld for her husband Byron would keep her silent and give her time to think. She was unclear about what happened, but in seeing her surroundings, her mind raced to seek a solution to escaping the capture, hopefully contacting the police for her protection. She figured that she would not be able to leave due to the police interviewing her for statements, and the police would question Kennedy during an investigation. That all didn't matter now as she wanted to escape and get on land.

The berth was small with a slant roof, so she had to crouch as she looked around to see what had shacked her wrist. Thankfully, it was just a heavy nautical rope, which shed fibrous shards of brittle twine into her skin from the salty ocean water. She fumbled around for any sharp object but winced when the rope's knot would slice into her tender skin.

She found a pillar supporting the central bow thwart, bare and unpainted throughout the top half-section. Finding a barbarous edge where she could begin tugging the rope across, she shifted to her knees. The rope was quite old, so it would take a few solid pulls to penetrate the main strands, to slide the knot-free. She began to stretch the brittle cord up and rub the raw edge to start the fraying.

Within the first five minutes, the rope's knot shaved sections of dead threads, and with enough room to begin back pushing the knotted area, she would be free. Kennedy's wrist was bruised and littered with tiny glass-like shards, piercing her at the slightest movement. The pain was severe, but the adrenaline kept her in pursuit. She didn't hear footsteps cascading down the stairs, steps away from the fire room.

The crew member who lifted Kennedy stepped down to the room beside where she lay to clean his gun. His head felt torn between the shots fired on the *Dingolay* and the lack of luxurious finds he could sell in his territory on the underground markets. The briefcase was handed to the captain and not much else. He was tired from stripping the *Dingolay* registration numbers and dumping the catamaran in the Saint Lawrence Gap harbour.

He opened a small box of gun brushes and lubricants and began cleaning the gun's firing deposits. After completing dozens of jobs, this routine was second nature. His other gun was tucked into his shorts, safety off.

There were only two men aboard the *Assailant* when it sailed to wreak disaster on the sea. The dark hull and topside, engineered to propel silently, would blend into the upper waves of the onyx waters at twilight.

At the helm was Captain, a ruthless man who lived a highly secret and untraceable life. His accent suggested deep European roots, and his tact at sailing, paramount, from the vast experience and naval exercises. He was the mastermind over the selection of contracts and the executive in handling the arms dealings. Rarely did he have to finish the job as his henchman Wodan was highly accurate.

The capture of Kennedy Glenning and the two tourists' deaths from last week began to make Wodan uneasy. They have never been this sloppy in the past; it was only a matter of time before the police would gain enough evidence to link them to the murders.

Wodan reassembled his gun and placed it alongside the other silenced pistol in the rear of his shorts, flipping his shirt over to cover the gun heels. Remaining on his list is to visit their guest to see if she woke. Pulling the bandana up to cover his nose he inserted the key to open her door.

Kennedy had managed to work herself free and found her cell phone and purse in a box of random belongings from other assumed victims. Her cell phone was corroded with dry, salty markings from the saltwater exposure and would not turn on. Equally disastrous, her cash and room key were both gone. If she could get out of the room and back to the hotel or the police, she could get her passport and get the aid she required. She grabbed a metal pen from the collection of trinkets and laid back down where she awoke. Now that the boat was motionless, she figured someone would come for her. Her head cocked to the side; she looked towards the door. There seemed to be movements from her view of the slit at the base of the frame. Clutching the pen, she closed her eyes and waited for the door to open.

Wodan turned the handle and opened the door slightly ajar. His experience taught him that you received the upper hand if you waited long enough. Sensing the woman was more fearful than forceful, he opened the door and entered the fire room. Noticing that she had shifted from her back when he tied the restraints to her side, he reached around his hip and took hold of one of his silenced pistols. Taking a cautious step forward to see if Kennedy was still tied, Kennedy shifted her leg as if asleep. Wodan paused, turning his muscular frame's weight to allow for a steady stance if shots would warrant it. His eyes fixated on Kennedy's next move.

"Hey! Get up. I see that you are untied."

Kennedy had positioned her leg to loop the pen in the folds of her island braided anklet, and in shifting her leg while Wodan was watching, she had now concealed her weapon. "You'll never get away with the murders and killing me will only make it harder for you too."

"Shut up!" his voice as stealthy as a narc enforcer. "On your feet. Captain has orders for you."

Kennedy wasn't sure how this would play out as he was blocking the route to the stairs, and she knew that there would not be much light on the top deck, so she could try and stab him in his neck and then disappear into the night. She figured the time must have been close to midnight, and if she were lucky, she could at least catch a taxi or hide in a shadowed alleyway. Her heart was racing, but she figured that this was her only opportunity for escape. She took a step forward and glared right at Wodan's masked face as she crossed into the hallway.

Wodan watched her movements, puzzled at how confident and fearless she was.

When she had reached the stairs, he barked, "This gun has your bullet ready in the chamber. Try anything and you're finished."

Kennedy took her first step with her anklet partially hidden from both their shadows in the dimly lit hallway. She reached out to the railing and began to shake her arms, pantomiming the illusion of fear for her life. Taking another step, she soon peered around the upper deck of the boat. Noticing that there was an accessible area to the starboard side, she lessened the quiver in her arms and pulled herself up to the deck while positioning the pen to be in her immediate grasp, if required. Wodan began to ascend the staircase, and after performing a triple check for another crew member or the Captain, Kennedy removed the pen and held it in the pit of her hand.

She envisioned where the pen would go, his eye, his throat, neck, chest. She only had one attempt, so when his gun holding shoulder became apparent, she swiftly aimed to pierce his neck but stabbed his shoulder in haste.

In the pale shimmer of moonlight, she saw the gun in his hand, forcefully ripped it from his fingers, and threw it overboard.

Wodan stumbling back and eventually fell down the short flight of stairs, removed the pen from its gruesome site and reached around for his second silenced gun.

Taking an overly cautious double head bob to see if she was a shooter, he realized that she had vanished. He bounded up to the top deck and scanned the shore. Squinting, he noticed frantic footprints leading to a grove of palm trees.

He took out his phone and speed-dialled his partner. "The witch stabbed me in the shoulder and stole my gun. I'm on it."

"I'm only going to allow this mistake once. Next time I'll do the job myself and put a contract on your head," was the reply.

"There won't be a next time. Once we split the cut from this load, I'm out." He ended the call, and with blood dripping from his shoulder, he took off after her.

# Chapter 5

# *CALL THE POLICE*

## 1.

"How is the Cutter miss?" checked the server shifting her posture to her hip.

Klara, with her mouth still chewing, raised a finger for a moment, "this flying fish is delicious! The macaroni pie is mouth-watering too. Like a spicy mac and cheese." She was glad to finally consume something local, as the flight snacks were too reminiscent of cardboard cuisine.

The Breezes had died down, and several servers were splitting tips and clocking out.

"Did you see that?!" the server stood tall, eyes darting to the dimly lit shoreline. "It doesn't look like a jogger this late. That woman is running! Hard! Look!" she felt it necessary to point down to the beach, and in rising abruptly, she drew attention from the wait staff.

"Is everything alright?" another server inquired, worried a lizard or snake crossed the table or Klara's lap.

"I think someone down there is in trouble. I can't see anyone but, oh… there on the stairs!"

"She's definitely spooked. There are no sharks here are there?" Klara turned her head to ask the server but gasped. "What's wrong?"

"That is the lady... the missing tourist who was here. No husband. I'm sorry, your meal was no charge from your ticket. Try and have a good night, I need to call the police that she has been found." She darted back to the bar, bumping a few tables with her hip.

"What! That's the missing tourist!" *Where's her husband?* Klara was standing now, trying to look down at the beach, surveying the surf if there was a drowning incident. As she turned back to watch the server on the phone, her eyes barely missed Wodan's silhouette crossing the coast.

"I want to leave a tip. But I want to see if she needs some help. She's frantic!" Klara mouthed to the server.

She put her hand over the receiver, "Tip yes, help her? Are you crazy? Stay a tourist yourself and leave the police work for them!"

"What if her husband did drown?" Klara caressed her chest. "I don't know what I'd do if I was married, and my husband drowned."

The server understood. Another tourist would be less intimidating than a police examination room. "Miss, if you think that you will be able to help her, you are a gem. Father help you!" Klara knew that although this was an exhausting day, she'd have trouble sleeping if she missed the chance in whatever situation this was going to turn out to be. *I'm just going to talk to her.*

"Thanks for the supper." She left and ventured toward the Sandy Wharf, thinking she might be able to catch the mysterious woman before there was too drastic a scene.

Wodan left the beach and was nearing the top of the cliff rock staircase, where a long dark alley meeting up with a side street was still with abandonment. His shoulder wept blood in varying locations while on the focused pursuit of his target. He figured, if he stopped her from talking, the DNA evidence trail that was breadcrumbing back to the docked *Assailant* would be precluded, set apart as a wild animal fight or a fishing accident. He raced through the alleyway and caught the tail view of her hair as she ruptured around the building's corner and towards the office. He crossed the street and bought some cover near a concrete wall in a neighbouring parking lot. He moved a bougainvillea planter outward to squeeze behind and poised the gun on the sill of the barrier wall, so his shoulder was comfortable. Once she came out of the office, one clear shot would finish the hunt.

Klara checked for a break in the oncoming traffic, seeing headlights spaced further apart for a chance to race across to join the panting woman in the office.

"Call... the Police!" Kennedy screamed, tears flowing down her cheeks and sinking to her knees. Her back appeared hunched yet carefully shielded from the glass door. She shivered and jerked away when Klara put her hand on Kennedy's shoulder.

"I am so sorry. How can I help?" She said as soft as a grandmother, then turned to the office attendant, "why aren't you calling the police?" Klara turned back to Kennedy, "Are you bleeding?"

"The police are on their way. I'm going to fetch some water and some fruit." The attendant transferred into an adjoining room and then returned to the desk, "keys. I'm sorry."

"He's dead… Byron… gun," Kennedy sobbed.

*Gun?!* Klara pondered. *There is more to this than I thought. Should I get involved?*

Kennedy spoke, "Is he out there?" Turning her neck to peer out the glass door.

"Who?!"

"There was a man… I tried to stab him in the neck but managed to hit his shoulder. He had me downstairs…" she choked up, "Oh Byron!"

"There is nobody in the parking lot. Even when I just came across the parking lot, nobody was chasing you." Klara looked for the attendant. "Maybe we can lock the door until the police come." She turned back to Kennedy, "My name is Klara. I hope you don't mind me helping you."

"Thank you, Klara. We were just ending our vacation, Byron, my husband," her voice squeaked. "He booked this evening cruise with this guy named Akeel. I had my suspicions at first, then asked this hotel's front desk clerk if she trusted him. She went to school with him, so what could I do? I had no idea."

The attendant returned with a couple of bottles of water and a large granny smith.

"Byron fell overboard," she continued, "and we were trying to find him. I don't know where Evanson was, he went downstairs for more rum. That's when Byron wanted to move on the boat and lost his balance." Kennedy took a large drink from the one-litre water bottle. "Thanks for the water."

"My pleasure, ma'am."

"We should lock that door, at least until the police show up. What is taking so long, I mean it's close to midnight."

"I'm sorry miss, but it is house policy, that we must leave the door open, for emergencies." She frowned, understanding that their policy should be under review over the current situation at hand. "I will bring it up at the meeting on Wednesday."

"Can I use the lounge bathroom, please? Freshen up." Kennedy shuffled across the tile floor, exhausted. The desk attendant buzzed her in.

*Hopefully, the police come, I want a cool shower.* Klara's mind raced. She glanced at the tourist shelf filled with day trips and activities that she could most certainly add to the wedding portfolio. She couldn't stop thinking, *I wonder if her husband's body will be found. I couldn't imagine this misery on vacation so far from home.*

Flashing lights cascaded through the room. Klara noticed it was only a road construction vehicle.

## 2.

Wodan could feel a lizard crawl across his foot but remained as a mannequin, his gun comfortable in his palm, still ready to fire at a moment's notice. Squeezing one shot off without witnesses would finish his work for the evening. His wound had ceased its drip, so his only pain was Kennedy's beating heart pumping her lifeblood.

**3.**

Kennedy came back to the front desk. "Is there any way to get my passport and luggage. I don't know where I'll sleep tonight, but the police can hold my stuff at the station. I have to tell them about the gun."

"I can give you another key, and all your stuff is in a missing kit, but you are found now, so I guess you can take it with you." The attendant looked drained, but what a story she would tell the overnight partner when she took over in fifteen minutes. "Here you are Ms. Glenning."

"Thank you."

"The parking lot is still clear. Nobody's around." Klara took hold of the door handle and pushed it open.

Kennedy took the room key out of the holder and turned to Klara, "This man with the gun, I don't know his name, but he threatened to kill me. I'm fairly sure he had something to do with our catamaran boat ride too. He had a red bandana over his face and brown eyes and one of those silencers on his gun. When we went up the stairs of this dark-colored boat, he didn't see that I was ready for him. There was this box full of things, phones, jewelry, some IDs, one passport. I figured he was a thief and a murderer by the way he was talking."

They made their way towards the room. Kennedy turned to Klara and thanked her for her comfort and time. She fit the key into the slot and tried the handle. Nothing blinked. Kennedy tried again, flipping the card around and over; nothing.

## 4.

Wodan realizing that they were gaining access to the room, took steps to shift his view between two planted palm trees. Still hidden, he made himself comfortable and nursed his wound. Later the shirt would have to be tossed overboard in deep water or burned in a pit fire to avoid suspicion. He had other shirts from the previous foul-up in the back seat of his Nissan, so after destroying them tonight, the evidence would be scarce. Wodan fixed his gaze on his target and returned his aim. Klara's neck was in constant violation of a clean shot to kill Kennedy. Realizing his predicament, he checked to see if he had at least a few bullets in the clip. Ironically, it was just that, two in the clip and one in the chamber. If events are required, it could be lights out using all three.

## 5.

"She said this key was ready." Kennedy yawned. "I guess I'll just wait in the lobby." She turned to move back to the office, still looking for the police SUV to arrive; failing to see Wodan's location.

"Did you want to wait in my room until the police come? It might make you feel a bit better. I'm sorry about your husband. Did you want me to go to the police station with you?" Klara offered. "I won't be able to sleep tonight."

"The *Dingolay* was the boat's name, I think. I know you want to help, but it's okay."

Klara went to open the door, leaving Kennedy wide open.

"You're so kind. I hope they catch that thug." Kennedy's last words.

From Wodan's only shot angle he squeezed the first shot that nearly missed Kennedy's neck and hit her collar bone. Kennedy fell spraying blood over the wall and towards Klara's torso. There was no time to scream, as she fell and grasped at her neck. She was convulsing, her eyes rolling back and blood pouring out over her hands.

Klara finally let out a short scream and ran through the door. The phone nearly flew off its base as she dialled 211, the emergency number printed near the phone keypad. Klara barely waited for the call to connect, and then screamed, "She's been shot at the Sandy Wharf Hotel!" She turned to the desk attendant, "Don't hang up the phone, they will come now. Kennedy was just shot in the neck! Oh God!" Carelessly she ran out again to return to the scene.

As soon as Klara left for the desk, Wodan moved quickly from the palm planters and kept his aim on Kennedy. He moved closer and saw that she didn't have much time left, drawing rapidly to her end. She lay hunched over, trying awkwardly to keep the blood from escaping from her gory neck.

Wodan bent down and watched the light leave Kennedy's eyes saying, "Go to Hell." then left the scene before Klara returned. He leaped over the pink concrete wall, placing the spent gun back in his shorts' waistband and disappeared into the night.

Klara rushed back on the scene and fell to her knees. Her face froze in horror, seeing the body of the woman who, moments ago, was trying to open her room. She went to Kennedy and checked for a pulse. She was gone. *Rest Kennedy. I will help find the bastard that did this.* She thought, then shut Kennedy's eyelids and placed her matted hair across her face for dignity until a sheet was available. She retreated to the curb and bowed her head between her knees. She hardly heard the police officer say to raise her hands. Only when she saw the baton in his hand aimed to strike her did she acknowledge. Two other officers helped her to her feet and began to pull her away from the scene.

"Where were you? If you were here twenty minutes ago she would be still alive." She tried to pull away but struggled; their grip was unshakable. "I have done nothing wrong! I was only trying to help. I'm a cop back home. I know we are going to the station."

"It will all get straightened out at the station. We'll get you cleaned up, and you can have a splash of water to feel better. Whether you are a cop or not, you must cooperate fully. Do you understand?" The constable fixated in a deep stare. "Why so quiet?"

She was led to the police unit's back seat, handed a moist towelette to clean the blood off her hands and face for her police booking. She watched through the window as a body bag containing her new friend, whom she tried to comfort; zipped up and hoisted in the back of the ambulance. Placing the used towelette on the seat beside her, she bowed her head and started stitching clues.

# Chapter 6

# *THE INTERROGATION*

## 1.

Wodan checked the scene once he was safely over the concrete enclosure. The strobe lighting from the ambulance and the police units gave him an adrenaline rush, and he grinned menacingly in the darkness.

Seeing his main target removed in a body bag and the other woman, obviously shaken up over the entire ordeal by being escorted to the back of a police SUV, gave Wodan the needed satisfaction of moving on with his evening worry-free.

Due to the bullets being untraceable and purchased off the illegal markets, Wodan breathed easy knowing the police could begin to investigate the Canadian-sounding woman to the death, as she travelled from the crime scene as the only witness. They would be interviewing her for what she knew about the murder. Suddenly realizing his mistake, he pulled out his phone and speed-dialled his partner. "Hey, the job is done."

"Excellent. I appreciate the speed in catching her before the police were involved. I'm watching a news alert of screams in the Maxwell Hills district. You didn't cause a panic by completing your work in public?" he sounded careful, as if the police may trace the line.

"No, but one woman got picked up, Klara. Sounds Canadian or American. She was trying to help, and the fusty witch that stabbed me told her everything. Once my aim was set, I completed the hit but didn't have time for the other. She's in police custody so I'll suit up."

"Make her your next mark if she is a threat. I have a lead for our next job. There is a mixed group of law students and investment brokers sampling with heavy quantities of experimental drugs, and I overheard them booking a private night cruise for the west or south coast. The job will be quick with the nerve agent, but the timing must be critical. Each broker knows when the payloads arrive, so I'll need you to be wet and on surveillance."

*Another hit with nerve gas, what is he thinking?* "Look, don't you think we should lay easy for a week? Let these five deaths cool down, buried thick in crime profiles and paperwork before we jump on another one?" Wodan hoped these questions would not bring repercussions. He watched as the detective returned to the police SUV with Klara in the back seat.

"Tomorrow at six o'clock on the *Assailant*." ignoring Wodan's requests, his partner ended the call, and Wodan placed his phone back in his shorts' side pocket.

He paused as he saw Klara's unit leave the parking lot and speed down the road. He appeared utterly camouflaged as he stood in the darkness.

He walked back down the dark alley, descended the cliff staircase, and back across the beach. He took out his cellphone again as a man having an e-cigarette walked out from a terrace. Wodan dialled the police station's night desk number, "Hello, I'm calling in regard to a tourist named Klara apprehended by unit nine…"

The stranger noticed the glint silver reflection of the gun in Wodan's shorts. Ignoring it as a harpooning weapon, he took another puff from his e-cigarette and exhaled to the view of the sea.

# 2.

Klara's mind raced, torn, and her body ached in the hot backseat. She felt exhausted on the drive back to the station. Forcing her eyes to stay open, she thought, *Kennedy must have escaped from the shooter… But there was nobody in the parking lot. And I never heard the gun go off!* When they arrived at the police detachment, the night holding cell officer and a detective greeted them at the garage. He opened Klara's door and looked at her, "I bet you are sorry for what you did."

"Excuse me? What did—" Klara started.

"Rakeef, leave her alone. She's just in for questioning."

"What? I heard it was a homicide?" Rakeef choked.

"She was crouching by the victim. She's just a tourist and a victim herself, just look at her."

"Her name was Kennedy. The missing tourist you were looking for." Klara had stepped down from the opened door and shut it quietly. She leaned on her left leg and stretched her hip from the stiffening ride from the tight backseat. She felt a pop in her hip, but the tightness was deep.

"Thanks for the information, but I highly recommend we get you in a more comfortable location, call your hotel as well to let them know you are here. They can send a housekeeper to deliver a change of clothes for you as we might need that shirt for evidence." Detective Nelson commented, his face stern but his heart soft for the ordeal Klara had encountered.

"I'm a fellow member… of law enforcement. How long am I going to be detained for? I didn't do anything to the vic." Klara said out of pure exhaustion, not realizing her tone sounded non-compliant; she knew if she was on their good side at the start, she could sleep in after the questioning, then go to the beach before mid-day. "Have you looked for her husband? She told me he drowned." She looked at both officers, judging who could offer her more information.

Detective Nelson opened the security door, holding it open for Klara, and mentioned, "He will be found. We have coast personnel that watch for overnight incidents. Are you injured at all? Do you need a doctor?"

"My hip is a bit stiff."

"The Bayview Hospital is just up the street. You should check it out tomorrow if it gets worse. Our first responder is out right now on the happy hour route."

They had walked through a large hallway with a restraint chair and several charging law enforcement electric scooters.

"Please wait here for a moment, I need to see what room is free and get my notebook." He turned to the desk sergeant. "Any messages?"

"Just one. It has been a quiet night. A man called saying he was the lawyer for the girl with you, Klara it seems. I told him that we don't have anyone booked under that name Chand." She handed the message to Detective Nelson.

"Did he sound familiar?" he asked, placing the message in his left shirt pocket.

"No, but you know these lawyers' offices, they pick any law student up to save a few dollars. Her lawyer back home probably connected with a law office down here to help her."

"Is there anyone in exam room two? I'd like a bottle of water and a coffee. She looks pretty tired." Chandler shot a glance at Klara, who had collapsed on a chair, head tilted to one side almost asleep. Stale tear trails had moistened her cheeks. She looked like a teen who had partied too long at an all-night rave beach party but with someone else's blood on her shirt from a beach bar brawl.

"Yes Chand, room two is open."

"Thanks, Gladys." He turned to Klara and bent down to her face. "Miss? Miss?" he deepened his voice. "Miss!"

"Wha— Yes, what is it now?" Klara said in half a daze.

"We are going to transfer you to examination room two. I have coffee and water coming over. Have you had anything to eat in the past few hours?"

"Just a fish cutter at Breezes." She looked at the clock. "That was about two or three hours ago."

"Do you mind barbeque chicken? We are going to order a meal for you as this questioning may take some time."

"Sure, that would be great, with a salad, in case it's spicy." Klara softened. She could tell he was a kind man.

"I'll meet you at exam room number two. Washrooms are on the right, please make yourself comfortable. Detective Thomas will be joining us to take notes. We are working on a lead in a supposed double homicide from last week involving another missing couple. Anything you can tell us, we would appreciate." He walked off towards an officer reading the paper, passed on some instructions to pick up Klara's food order, and the officer took off through the door like the lottery service was calling his name.

Klara's reflection in the mirror convinced her to wash her face. The booking officers must have seen that her face wreaked sorrow, but she felt rejuvenated and awake upon a fresh splash of water. Remembering that the faster she told them everything, the quicker she could find sleep and tell her sister tomorrow from a beach lounger.

Chandler joined Klara as she waited by the door, "Would you mind grabbing this?" handing her a vending machine coffee.

"Just milk no sugar. Thank you, ah..."

"Detective Nelson." He opened the door and gestured with his free hand for her to take a seat before barking to Rakeef to join them.

"Is this going to be recorded? I'm not sure if you do that here." Klara was trying to get comfortably close to the table, but the metal chair legs securely remained bolted to the floor.

"Rakeef is bringing the audio equipment, but I assure you these are just formal procedures." Chandler took the pen and wrote Klara on the top left margin, then asked her what her purpose for the trip was to try and ease her uncertainty if she had any.

"I'm Canadian, here to scope out my sister's wedding details for next year."

"Sorry, Chand. It was missing the microphone." Rakeef had brought in a folding chair and set it up to the right of Chandler. "Okay, Miss, when this red light is flickering it means you are too quiet. Please check your volume as you speak and—"

"We've understood. She's one of us," he whispered. Let's begin; it's late." Chandler turned to Klara and pushed the mic towards her, adjusting the angle.

"I checked into the Stingray Cove and was told there was a problem because guests were missing. I got moved to another hotel that they own—"

Rakeef chimed in, "What other hotel?"

"Uh... the Sandy Wharf. The desk attendant gave me a voucher for a meal at The Breezes, which is walking distance to the Sandy Wharf. I checked my room and plugged in my phone then went for my meal. The server saw a woman running on the beach at the bottom of the cliff." *Why are they taking notes already!* Klara thought.

"That was the server who made the first call right?" Rakeef whispered to Chandler.

Detective Nelson wrote down his lead.

Klara continued. "We decided that she was running not jogging, and the server told me that she was the missing tourist's wife." Klara took a sip of the coffee. "I'm trying my best."

"Perfect so far," Chandler commented without looking up from his notes, adding subject notes in the margin.

"Your volume is great too," Rakeef had whispered, with his hands gesturing a thumbs up.

"Okay because this is when it gets really crazy." She let out a nervous laugh, placing the coffee back on the stainless-steel exam table.

Klara had never been to an international police station before, let alone an examination room for a homicide investigation. She gestured with her hands, "I should have left it all alone… I guess it might be my fault I'm here, but I figured it might be comforting for another tourist to help instead of a local person or the police. Just a thought." Klara sighed.

"Go on," Chandler spoke. He sensed that the witness might get upset and began scanning around the room for the box of tissues.

"I crossed the lane and went over to the hotel as she ran right into the office. She was terribly upset and said there was a man with a gun trying to catch up to her and kill her." Klara felt a tear roll.

"Rakeef get some tissues." Chandler turned to Klara. "Can you try and remember exactly what she said, to the best of your ability if you would? I know this is hard. Please be as descriptive as you can."

"I made a split second decision. If I had my phone, I would have tried to seal her wound, but I had no idea where the shooter was. I checked for a pulse after the office dialed your detachment, but she was already gone."

Chandler had drawn arrows to connections with the other unsolved case and circled around possible leads at the mention of the gun.

# 3.

Outside the police station, Wodan had stepped out of his car and straightened his suit jacket and tie. His bleeding had ceased, as he had applied medical tape after soaking the wound with a quick splash of witch hazel and placing a hotel tea bag on the site. The clot had begun to solidify, and as Wodan taped his shoulder closed, his skin would start to knit as early as the morning, fully coagulating the puncture. His walk was purposeful, but he felt apprehensive. He hoped they would let him in at such a late hour, but he figured the Canadian woman's conversation would add fodder to the police reports and muddle the previous evidence on the murders of Johnathan Redding and his girlfriend Andrea Lopez. Wodan chirped the lock on his car and prominently sauntered to the after hours night door. Gladys looked up at the window as he knuckled the glass. As she thought this was the lawyer on the phone call wearing a suit this late at night, she buzzed him in. Hearing the locking pin release, he opened the door.

# Chapter 7

# *WADE BARNWELL*

## 1.

"Excuse me, Chand?" came a muffled shout from outside the room.

"Klara, it appears your food is here." Chandler rose from the chair and glanced towards Rakeef to stay seated as he left the room.

"Here is the chicken and salad. I hope she likes Chefette." the officer announced.

"I'm sure it will be fine. Thanks." Chandler opened the exam room door again and noticed a suited man was approaching him. Holding Klara's meal, he turned to Wodan, "Can I help you?"

"I am Ms. Hockely's legal representation. I find it quite against protocol to begin questioning the witness before she has had the opportunity to consult her legal rights." Wodan had come close to Chandler but kept a professional distance, as a lawyer would.

"She hasn't divulged any incriminating evidence in her responses, we have them on tape as well, so I assure you, everything has been quite professional with the protocol of this interviewee." Chandler passed through the door, leaving Wodan outside the exam room. When the door was closing, Wodan wedged his foot across the door's threshold, preventing it from locking.

"Here is your order, Klara. Can I have your coffee refilled?" Chandler turned to Rakeef, "What?"

"What is he doing here?" referring to Wodan, who had now entered the exam room.

"I am the legal counsel for Ms. Hockley. I would like to inform you that she has not been able to seek legal advice before the beginning of this meeting. Therefore, I must ask you to leave, until such a time has passed, then I will come to find you where you can continue your interview."

"I don't think—" Klara began, Wodan cutting her off.

"Ms. Hockley, it is in your best interest to remain silent until they have left. I am bound by the attorney-client privilege, so anything you say is between you and me. I can help you here, as I have seen you in the back seat of their SUV, and at once called to enquire if you had sought legal counsel." He turned to Chandler, "Before any more protocols are violated, please leave this room immediately."

Rakeef had looked to Chandler for his reaction, but he merely opened the door and began to lead Rakeef out.

"You have thirty minutes, and I will be right outside this door." Chandler stepped back and let the door shut, its lock clicking.

Wodan placed his briefcase on the table and opened it to provide a little privacy from Chandler's view, then handed Klara his business card. He then moved to the recording equipment, switched it off, and unplugged the microphone, moving it out of the way. To Klara, this all seemed legitimate, like a lawyer, which had years of practice. She looked at the card again.

"Wade Barnwell, divorce attorney?" Klara looked at him.

"Yes, I specialize in divorce, but I am trained in handling all sorts of situations and caseloads. Currently, I have only one other case over a little money embezzlement, but that is nearly finished. Do you have any small bills on you, to make this official, that you have bought legal representation? One dollar will suffice." After setting up the table to cloak the fallaciousness that he was not a lawyer, Wodan sat across from her and waited.

"I don't have any pockets in these pants, but my purse has a few Bajan dollars in it. Would that be, ok? I don't have any small U.S. bills." She was a little skeptical thinking maybe he was on her side.

"I assume they have your purse outside this room?" Klara nodded. "Ok, we can do it later." Wodan offered his hand to her.

Upon shaking Wodan's hand, Klara felt uneasy. Why was a lawyer wanting her as a client when she didn't have any involvement in the homicide. She asked him, "I haven't done anything, so I don't know if your services are required?

"Twenty-five minutes," came Chandler's muffled call from the other side of the glass.

"I assure you there may be a technicality that might ruin your vacation, I assume you are here for pleasure. Also, since you had no premeditated involvement with the event I would imagine they won't press any charges. Now please, we need to begin. What exactly did you tell them? Any names? Weapons? Detailed descriptions?" Wodan was purely professional; Klara only had the slightest inclination that he was suspicious.

"I told them the name of the woman who died and explained that she was running from a man with a gun."

"What makes your think she was being chased?" Wodan stared as he waited for her response.

"She wasn't jogging to burn off her cocktail from lunch, she was being chased. I could tell, and she told me she was.

"And that is absolutely everything you have said so far?" still sounding casual.

"I believe so, yes." Klara opened her bag of Chefette. "Do you mind if I eat this? I'm trying to wait, but I am getting hungry. The smell of this chicken is wonderful." She looked at Wodan.

"Please," he gestured his hand in approval.

"I can still talk or listen. We can keep going. I want to get out of here as soon as I can and try to get back to my bed before sunrise. It's been a long day." She took a bite of the chicken, her eyes animated at the burst of flavour she was experiencing.

"Alright, if you would, please walk me through what you are planning to tell them." Wodan took out a notepad like the one that Chandler had written on before. "Can I trust that you will not keep anything from me as your legal counsel?"

Outside the exam room, Chandler was watching the actions and movements of Wodan. Thinking he was too calm for a law student, he motioned to Rakeef to return.

"Yes, Chandler?"

"Ask Gladys for the list of all the law students currently enrolled. Also, the current record of all the lawyers that are registered in Barbados. This guy seems too calm for a student, but I've never seen him come in before. You can also call the Northern Division, and have them check on the lawyer..." He glanced at the business card on the table by Klara's wrist. "Wade Barnwell."

"Sure thing." Rakeef rounded the corner.

*Something's not right here*, Chandler thought. *I'm going to find out*. After a glance at his wristwatch, he banged on the glass door, "Fifteen minutes."

Klara had finished her meal and carefully boxed up the remains in a neat pile. Wodan had received nothing damming from Klara's responses to his questions. He felt that whatever she told the police, they would not be able to link him to the murders, and without seeing the gun, they would have to go on the cross-matching of the spent shots pulled from the body. If he could reach the hospital in time to retrieve the bullet, that could stall the investigation and remove any doubt of the ammunition used in Andrea Lopez's death. Wodan would not make the same mistake a second time. He had to work fast, and with his energy level beginning to crash, it would have to be soon.

"Wade?"

"I'm sorry, I was thinking of the actions you were involved in this evening. Must be a terrible start to your vacation. You said it was just a week?"

"Yes, that is the only time I have, my sister wanted a destination wedding and I'm to tour around here for a bit and gather some fun wedding locations. I've heard of Harrison's Cave so far."

"Five minutes, wrap it up." Chandler was precise.

"Well, we have a good solid place in this questioning session, I have all the confidence that the statements you divulge, will not hold any incriminating evidence or actions on you. Remember you are a victim here, and when they bring whoever did this to justice, then you can hopefully return to your normal schedule of wedding planning." He rose from his seat, and plugged the microphone back in, arranged the papers back into the briefcase, and offered his hand to Klara again, "Please try and get some rest as well. There are lots of areas on this beautiful island for you to explore."

He clipped his briefcase after they had concluded their meeting with the handshake and walked to the door as Chandler was opening it.

"Your time management seems too perfect for an amateur lawyer. Which law office are you practicing with Mr. Barnwell?" Chandler whispered.

"I'm not an amateur. I am setting up my own practice. Look for Barnwell and Associates if you feel the need. I'd give you a card, but you're not my client." Wodan returned the stare Chandler was showing and then passed through the door and exited the building. He had spent the last hour cloaked in his facade, and they had not caught him. He returned to his car, started the engine, and in staring at the police station, told himself, "Alright Wodan, let's get to work."

Chandler went back to sit with Klara. Rakeef had not returned yet.

"Did you give him any money?"

"Oh no I forgot. I told him it was in my purse, and I forgot to pay him." Klara looked at Chandler, "is something wrong?"

"We did a check into this Wade Barnwell. He's not a lawyer." Chandler watched Klara's expression change almost at once.

"I knew something didn't sit right. What does that mean?" Klara folded her arms.

"We checked all the names of the law students at the University of the West Indies, and all the law offices' names on the Island. His name did not appear on any of the lists. Then we cross-referenced the name Wade Barnwell in other law programs in America or other reputable schools across the world. Nothing from a Google search. His name didn't come up on any of our profile systems either."

"I got the fingerprint kit, Chand. So, the microphone, and the tape recorder?" Rakeef began opening the kit.

"Those were the only places he could have left a print." He turned back to Klara. "Did you see him touch anything else? As he gave you the business card, he just held the edges, so he knows what he is doing."

"I can't believe I was so naive. I must have been tired. Forgive me, I can't remember what he touched. I'm sorry." Klara watched as Rakeef dusted the microphone and tape recorder, and Wade's fingerprints were lifted and sealed in their protective films.

"I'll take these to the lab." Rakeef sounded almost excited, as if he had not been able to perform detailed police work lately. He left again, Chandler returning his gaze on Klara.

"These things don't usually happen around here. I hope that what he is up to will not jeopardize this investigation or your safety. Please remain calm, it may be nothing, but it seems a little too carefully planned that a lawyer would show up without you calling him, and this lawyer does not exist on paper in any law school we can access. What did he ask you to do? Anything feel out of place?"

"No, he just wanted to find out what I was going to say." Klara sifted through her thoughts and suddenly realized, "Do you think he is involved? Could he be the killer?!"

Chandler looked up to her shocked face, "It would be equally convenient, as we need a suspect for the other unsolved case. You'd make a good detective. You have the mind for it."

"What should I do? He may be out there. Should I go back to the Sandy Wharf?" Klara was sweating, her mind thoroughly shaken from its fatigue.

"This late in the morning, he won't do anything. Once the results come back from the lab, we can file a full report to launch an island-wide chase if necessary. I don't want any other visitors or tourists getting hurt."

"I'd like to help as much as I can. I don't want to get in the way, but I want to find out as bad as you do who killed Ms. Glenning. She was so brave." She stood up and grabbed the bag from Chefette, "she did not deserve to die from that killer! I will be back tomorrow; with a list of any other facts I can remember."

Klara began to walk away but then turned back to Chandler and sheepishly muttered, "Ah... can you call me a taxi?"

"Let's go for a drive. I need to check that crime scene again."

# Chapter 8

# *GATHERING CLUES*

Both Wodan and Chandler were travelling to find clues, but for obviously distinct reasons. Both drivers' temperament was with an increased purpose, and when they arrived at their destinations, they exited their vehicles with the same thought. *I need that evidence.*

Wodan parked in a far-off space of the parking lot and walked through the emergency doors.

"Good morning. I am Wade Barnwell, a lawyer on the single homicide case of the missing person that is under current investigation. I spoke with Gladys at the Hastings detachment, and I am here to check for the entry points of the bullet wound to evaluate the possible case against my client, Ms. Klara Hockley." Wodan stared at the nurse, who was trying to process what exactly she just heard.

"So, you are working for the police on this case?" She was still confused.

"No, ma'am. The client I stand for is a victim in this case. She is involved as a witness and based on the location of the bullet wound I need to examine the angle of entry. I would like to view the body, to see how the police could hold any responsibility against her innocence." He hoped these lies would gain him entry to the body of Kennedy, for he had to find the bullet.

"Well, the medical examiner won't be in until seven o'clock, so as long as you just take pictures or write notes and do not touch the bodies, I'm sure it will be fine."

Wodan could not believe how easy it was to convince her. "Do I need to sign in, or…"

"Yes, there is a clipboard on the outside of the door to the exam room. This visitor key will let you in. Please make sure to keep it in your pocket and return it to me. I don't want it to get soiled with any matter from the examination room."

Wodan was amazed, thinking this nurse would surely lose her job from such gross misconduct over the hospital etiquette rules. *Her loss not mine*, he thought, then took the key and headed down the hall.

He removed a pair of latex gloves from his pants pocket and placed them on before signing in and touching anything. *How could I be so stupid?* Wodan realized that he had left fingerprints on the microphone in the exam room with Klara. *They won't find very much on me, though. I'm not in their system.* He signed in with gloved hands and fitted the key into the exam room lock. He would have to work quickly if the nurse changed her mind and had someone go with him during his search.

He saw three body bags on the steel tables and inspected each for what each bag held—the middle one, imbued with an Asian male labelled with two close-range gunshot wounds to his back. The far body bag was said to have a Caucasian woman with ballistic trauma to the neck. Wodan smiled, taking pleasure in reading the descriptions of his execution handiwork.

Looking around the lab, Wodan saw the instruments tray over by the sink. He took the scalpel and forceps, then went over to the portable lamp and wheeled it to cascade light in the critical area. He carefully unzipped the bag to expose Kennedy's face. Moving the lamp and positioning himself for the extraction, he received a chill when he overheard hospital night cleaning staff wheeling their custodian cart towards the door.

Wodan worked, hoping the medical examiner would not catch his negligence, but had no time to worry. He folded the bag back to cover Kennedy's head and quickly moved the matted hair beside her face. Whisking the metal zipper with a thumb over the teeth he reduced the rezipping sound of the bag. He shut off the light and stood in a shadowed area as he saw the exam room door open, and the custodian changed the garbages. He replaced the box of nitrile gloves and placed a stack of clean towels in the cupboard. He listened to music audibly, streaming from the external speaker on his phone, and didn't notice Wodan or anything that was not in its usual location.

When the lights were back off and his eyes readjusted to the lab lighting, Wodan moved back to Kennedy's bag.

## 2.

"I will be just a few minutes. If you want to go to your room I understand. I hope you can get some sleep." Chandler circled his vehicle, opened the trunk, and took out an evidence bag, a pair of gloves, and a flashlight. He lightly slammed the trunk door as not to wake the other guests at the Sandy Wharf.

Klara quietly got out of the SUV and gave a kind wave to the detective.

"I'm sorry for keeping you up so late Klara, please get some rest, and if you still want to make that list for the case, take your time to collect your thoughts." Chandler yawned near the end of his comment, signalling that he, too, was ready for sleep.

"I will. Thank you, detective." Klara shut the door and walked down the dimly lit sidewalk to her terraced room. Chandler waved with a gloved hand to bid her good night. He walked purposely towards the crime scene, which looked drastically different from five hours prior. The Investigation Unit removed the spilled blood from the walls and sidewalks. They rinsed grass and removed the police evidence markers. Chandler carefully navigated through the police tape and, in lifting the flashlight, switched it on to illuminate the wall directly behind where the shooter hit Kennedy's neck.

Looking closer into the wall, he saw a few metal fragments. Reaching into his shirt pocket, he removed a barreled metal pen and flicked free whatever pieces of metal were uncollected from the first pass of the crime scene. He opened the evidence packet and brushed the filings into the sealable bag. Although he didn't have the bullet, he had a few metal pieces to send to the lab for testing.

Chandler checked the ground beside the wall for other debris and chuckled when he caught the shine off one of the metal shell casings, fully intact by the bougainvillea.

Reaching down, he reopened the evidence bag and flipped the first solid piece of evidence into it. Rising again, he switched off the light and headed to the SUV.

"Rakeef, I got a casing. I'll see you in the morning." Chandler left the voicemail on his phone as a familiar face approached his window. "Hi Derk." He said as he lowered his window.

"Lot's of action around here. So glad I'm not a cop. Who's the girl Chand?" Derk Warrows inquired.

"A member tourist from Canada. Not sure how many years of service but she's smart. Hey Derk, I think we've got a situation on our hands here. Can I ask you for a favour? Maybe Jones too?" Chandler smiled.

Derk smiled back. The history between them as professional friends could be a museum exhibit. Derk was the Island's main private investigator that helped the police from time to time on tough—sometimes off-record—cases. Jones the tow truck operator and Derk would often be at every crime scene to haul away the wreckage and share a first responder observation.

"Jones is itching for some action. What do you need?" Derk leaned in on the sill of Chandler's door.

"That Canadian girl is here at the Wharf, and she's been through a lot. The guy we're looking for is still at large and I'm uneasy about her safety especially if she starts her own investigation. She's keen. If it's not too much to ask, can you keep a look out if she gets in trouble?"

"Rest easy, and hey, if I catch him, I'll give you a call, so you can get the arrest and make the paper." They shared a chuckle. "What's her name?"

"Klara Hockley. She's nice Derk. Thanks, I'm headed back before the cells are full of happy hour hooligans."

"Sleep tight. I'll keep a lookout." Derk winked and leaned off the SUV, patting Detective Nelson on the shoulder. He returned to his idling truck and waved as he drove off.

Chandler quickly checked his phone for messages then steered to the road. The night was still with only the sounds of his yawn and the left turn signal. It would be a long ride to his house after returning to the Hastings detachment to drop off the little evidence bag that could very well bring both unsolved cases to their conclusion.

## 3.

Wodan unzipped the bag holding Kennedy. At first glance her neck was more swollen. The bullet wasn't where it should have been and had moved from the pulsations pushing her artery walls apart. Finding the bullet would be a more complicated and tedious endeavour. Fearing that the next interruption would be more severe than a custodian on their rounds, he began digging through her neck flesh like a surgeon under a crucial timeline. Unclear, due to his near ten minutes of searching, he was unable to find the bullet. Wodan's forceps eventually sent vibrations that he had struck something solid, and upon further care, he removed a chunk of concrete that had lodged itself in the wound from her collapse against the wall.

*Where is it?* Wodan paused, then placed the concrete on the table beside her shoulder. He resumed his focus on finding the bullet for a second pass. In his haste, he did not notice that the chunk had slipped off the table and fallen to the floor, rolling under the wheels' supporting bars. As he looked for the bullet, the medical examiner opened the door to the lab. He was early and wanted to do a preliminary observation since he had three bodies in his lab. He stood at the doorway with a coffee in his hand and a shocked look on his face as he was about to turn on the lights.

"Stop! What are you doing?!" he roared, then retreated to the hallway and shouted, "security! Kate, someone is defiling one of the bodies in the lab!"

Wodan's heart was about to explode, adrenaline flowing to every cell of his body; he worked at an accelerated fury, promptly resetting as much as he disturbed. He quickly zipped up the bag, threw the examination tools into the sink, and peeled his gloves off, hand in hand. Reaching for one of the lab coats, he took off his suit jacket and almost tore the sleeves as he raced to dress in hospital attire. Finding a biohazard bag, he shoved his suit into the bag and turned the handle of the door with his elbow. He sprinted down the hallway and into an unlocked hospital supplies closet, using a foot to swing open the door. He waited for his heart to cease its violent rhythm, dropping the biohazard bag to his hip. He slightly opened the door to spy on the collection of hospital employees now gathered around the examination room.

"Who let that guy in?! Who?!" screamed the medical examiner, his supratrochlear artery bulging in his forehead. "This is a professional establishment, and I have never felt so indignant over the malpractice of letting the general public waltz into my lab and help themselves to whatever they please!" He tore the sign-in board off the wall and screamed at the nurses, "Who the hell is Wade Barnwell!?" He then slammed the clipboard to the floor, discharging the sheets of paper in all directions at everyone's feet.

Wodan saw that the nurses were all focused on trying to solve this catastrophe, then he slipped as flatly as he could out of the closet and retreated to the darkened hallway away from the coterie.

## 4.

Chandler's cell phone vibrated. He pulled his sport utility vehicle over into a parking lot and accepted the call. "Rakeef, can't this wait till I'm at the station?"

"We just got a call from the Bayview Hospital."

"And what happened?"

"That lawyer, Wade Barnwell," Rakeef replied.

"What did he do?" Chandler was growing impatient.

"The medical examiner tore a strip off his team when he caught Wade in the exam room leaning over one of the bodies."

"How did he gain access? Didn't they have someone in the room overnight? What were they thinking? We haven't even begun the investigations yet! Did he take anything?" Chandler was so tired but wanted to keep receiving the information. He was going to put Wade away.

"They said he was digging in the woman's neck and left a pretty gruesome sight. Her neck was mangled. I heard them say something about a bit of concrete on the floor under her tray."

Chandler closed his eyes and leaned back. "Was the concrete painted green at all?"

"A little bit. How did you guess?"

"He was digging in her body for the bullet. Wade is covering his tracks."

"So, he did it?!" Rakeef exclaimed.

"Either he did or he's collecting the evidence for the killer. Because of this, I know he is involved with the murders. Put the coffee on," he took out the evidence packet.

"Aren't you going home?"

"No. I've got something in my hand that might tie this Wade to the murders. I'm coming in." Chandler dropped the bag on the passenger seat and shifted into gear.

Crane Beach walking path. A cabbie mentions this foot path of steppingstones to Klara in chapter 8.

# TUESDAY

# Chapter 9

# *THE INCIDENT*

## 1.

Klara woke up extremely stiff and with a cramp in her left thigh. She hobbled to the bathroom, had a shower, and felt a bit more relaxed. *Maybe I should get checked out before heading to the beach*, she thought, *after the police station.* With a towel wrapped around her hair, she unzipped her suitcase and took out the stack of used books to get her crocheted beach bag. *Maybe I'll meet someone on the beach that knows the closest library,* she hoped. Throwing the towel on the hook she immediately went to the writing pad by the phone and began jotting down the most damning evidence that could help the police catch Wade. Twenty-five minutes later, she stood outside the Sandy Wharf with a continental croissant, watered-down coffee, and a giant fresh banana. She saw the taxi pull up.

"Take me to the Hastings police department."

"And now what be happening to you last night girlie?" the driver called out, his voice rich with a Bajan accent.

"Trust me. You don't want to know. Plus, I don't know where to begin." The taxi did not have the air conditioning on, so Klara rolled down the window, letting the sea's breeze flow through her damp hair. She figured it would be best to help Detective Nelson and his team try and catch Wade as she still felt abused by his charm.

"Have you been to the Island long? Tis beautiful this time of year. All the beaches are public around the Island, and some are free of coral, like these ones coming up on the right. You look like you swim... So, you swim?"

"I do, but I need to help the police today. I might find a sunny beach with some waves this afternoon for some sun and a swim. I heard the Crane Beach is beautiful."

"That's a pleasant beach, good waves, some tourass, but the sand is good. There is a little walkway of cement circles that the locals cross, and there be someone there to help you down. Lot's of tourass too scared of the steppingstones though," he changed the subject. "Have you had Chefette?"

"That barbeque chicken was so delicious! I had it last night. Your flying fish is great too. My hip is very stiff so no stairs today."

"You been to Oistins fish market? There are little shacks by the Boatyard that cook up fish cakes and serve it with a rum. You like it there, many tourass in that spot. Do you want me to wait? You be long at the police station?" The driver was turning into the detachment's lane, at the roundabout.

"I might be a while. I was a witness last night by the Sandy Wharf Hotel. So please don't wait for me. Thanks for the ride though and the conversation." She handed him a U.S. twenty.

"This is too much for the fare. I don't have change, only beewee."

"It's all right keep it. Thanks again." Klara waved and headed towards the detachment, hoping Detective Nelson or Rakeef would be there to greet her.

## 2.

At the Bayview Hospital, a call over the incident has prompted an emergency meeting. The hospital board executive was in attendance, with the medical examiner, the nurses on the shift between midnight and six in the morning, and the overnight hospital security guard. The nurses were all gossiping about union representatives not being at the meeting, and the one nurse who gave Wade the key was trembling uncontrollably.

"Ms. Mayers. I am having a challenging time understanding your professional opinion over the decision made during your last shift. We had security breached when the individual you let in, began using tools to extract tissues from one of the three bodies. Please explain yourself!"

"He... he was dressed in a s...s...suit and spoke to me in lawyer language. I had no idea he was going to touch the bodies." June choked out. "He didn't seem to me, the type to mess around in the lab or using tools on them." She occasionally would look up to the men across the table but then returned to her bowed head and slumped posture.

"Seems to you exactly. You had no authority to make such a decision. Giving him the key unsupervised could set the police back months in their investigation." he paused for emphasis. "And then for him to vanish. Who knows what else he helped himself to out of our supplies? I am just beside myself over this. You leave me no choice."

"I made one mistake, no more. Please, sir, it won't happen again. I will work with the police and help them as much as I can." June had stopped trembling and grew some of her confidence back. One nurse from the group stood.

"How dare you Chair! How was June to know anything about what was going to happen? She is an excellent nurse. She does a superb job of running the night desk. You should take a shift with us dealing with the drunkards that come in." There were several shouts from the other nurses, "Yeah," the prime chant.

The Chairperson raised his voice, "Enough everyone! My decision was a suspension with pay for one week, with full counseling if needed, not a nursing revolution. No one's job is in jeopardy."

June took a sigh of relief, "Thank you, sir."

The nurses lightly cheered and murmured, "That's right. We stick together."

The medical examiner stood, "Chair, I hope your decision doesn't affect the wellbeing of this hospital. The behaviors from the nurses should all be under review by their next performance appraisal, if not I'll work elsewhere. I have a hospital in Aruba begging for me to transfer. Good day to you sir. Now I have a mess to clean up." He walked out.

"May we go?" a nurse asked loudly from the crowd of chattering nurses, some crowding around June.

"You all are dismissed. Please head back to your zones, and let's make sure that this situation never happens again."

As the nursing staff left, June shot a glance at the Chairperson, but he was writing notes on his pad.

## 3.

Klara walked to the front desk looking for Detective Nelson, but the secretary asked her to sit as she paged him. He just stepped out of the office. She looked around the front desk area, organized with papers and forms, suddenly glancing outside as she heard a scuffle occurring in the parking lot. A man was resisting the two police officers carrying him into the detachment. There were shouts and shoving, then the one injured officer took out his nightstick and tapped the back of the man's knee, causing him to fall on the cement floor. When he fell, Klara noticed a little bag of powder fly under her seat, and the man glared at her, suggesting that she not say anything. She casually flexed her foot, crossed her legs, shifting her weight to cover the package.

"What the hell is going on?" Chandler's voice boomed throughout the office area. He helped the officers lift the man off the floor and into a chair. He looked at Klara, "Good morning. It's a little busy as you can see. Happy hour was more like happy hours last night."

"It's ok, I can wait for a bit." She flashed the little piece of paper that had her substantiation on it. When they were gone, she watched as the secretary left to refill her coffee and flicked the little packet from under her foot, back out to the floor where the arresting officer had just detained the man.

"Ms. Hockley, Detective Nelson will see you now," the secretary had returned with her mug of coffee steaming up from behind the desk hutch.

"There seems to be a little package on the floor there," Klara motioned to the packet as she adjusted her purse and walked to Chandler's office.

"Detective?"

"Ms. Hockley, please come in. It has been a helluva morning already. Did you sleep at all last night?"

"It took a little while to sleep from the frogs that were chirping last night, and the heat, but when my head hit the pillow and the gentle breeze floated through the room, I was out like a light. I was able to write down a few things that I remembered. I hope they can help." She pushed the paper across his desk.

"Thank you, I'm sure it will. Sorry I wasn't able to get to the desk to greet you this morning, I had a team extract that bullet casing from the Wharf."

"So that means you can charge the shooter?"

"The lab is testing the metal, so I should have results this afternoon. I hope that this case is linked to the other case from last week." Chandler paused and then looked at Klara. "You should find a beach, not get meddled up in this police stuff. You're on vacation."

"Chand!" Rakeef yelled from the hall. "Chand, have you heard?"

"What is it, Rakeef?!"

"Some fishing boat found a body."

"What? Where?"

"Oh sorry, I didn't know you were occupied." Rakeef came around to the back of Chandler's desk, whispering, "They said it was pretty bloated, might have been on the sea for a few days. The sun was starting to rot the flesh on his back."

"Another tourist from the other missing persons case you think. Did he have any wounds?"

"They said that there were rope burns around his wrist. No ballistic trauma." Rakeef retreated to the door, "Do you want me to get a crew together?"

"Sure. Just let me have 5 minutes to wrap up with Ms. Hockley." Chandler turned to Klara, "I'm sorry but something has come up. I can call a taxi for you, and here," he rifled through his desk drawer. "I have a couple of tickets for a bus tour around the Island. It might let you get to know the good sides of Barbados. It takes you to the Morgan Lewis Sugar Mill, and the Barbados Wildlife Reserve. They are usually surprisingly good tourist attractions." He handed them to her.

"Thank you, I'll save the other ticket for my sister's maid of honour who arrives tomorrow." She put them in her purse.

"And find some time for a beach today. The sea is warm like a Jacuzzi."

"I've got my suit right here." Klara stood showing off her handmade beach bag and extended her hand. "Thank you, detective."

"I hope this concludes our meetings, but if I see you on the beach, please, just call me Nelson. I may be under cover." he winked.

Chandler gently showed her to the door, then went out to join Rakeef at the parking lot.

# 4.

Wodan flipped through his recent calls and dialled his partner.

"Yeah?"

"We have a problem."

"What do you mean, we? What did you screw up on this time Wodan?"

"Hey man, I'm trying to tie up the loose ends here, while you sit on your yacht and rant about setting up a new hit. I almost got caught in the Bayview Hospital when the M.E. was screaming his head off that there was a security breach."

"You're slipping up bad, Wodan. The next job must be flawless, and if you screw this job up, I'll make the call you don't want."

"You know, I'm getting tired of these threats. You should watch out for the law yourself. There is a tourist working with them, Klara, I'd be careful, she'd turn you in in a heartbeat if she found out your involvement with any of the crimes. She's a do-gooder."

"What are you saying? You killed your target, you pulled the trigger, you got caught! It's you who should be looking over your shoulder. This is the last job you and I are working on together. You said you wanted out; when this job is over, you and I are finished, paid up in full, and split!" Captain ended the call.

Wodan threw his phone against the bedframe with such force the phone rebounded hitting the floor and sliding under the bed.

He was fuming, tossing the chair from the corner of his room against the wall, and then head down, feeling the rage subside; he let his heart rate cease, grabbed his keys, and drove off. His phone lay under his bed dead, in recovery mode from the impact. No tracking or no cellular signal would broadcast. In his wrath, he did one of the most brilliant things he could have done to buy him some time to save his life.

"I need an order, pickup for one, male, armed. Wodan. 26 Ocean Reef Drive…" Captain listened closely for the response, "Payment tonight after 11 p.m. after photo proof of the body." He ended the call, then went to the garage, grabbed the *Assailant* key, and pushed the button to engage the engine on his Mercedes. Listening to the audible chimes upon start-up, he thought how he would set up Wodan to take the fall tonight after he processed the tourists and their drug stashes. Captain fastened his seatbelt, clicked the garage to close, and began to reverse his Mercedes out of his driveway. He would not appear threatened, and after this job, tonight was looking to tie up any loose evidence and get off the Island.

# Chapter 10

# *SOME X-RAYS*

## 1.

Klara stepped out of the Hastings police department, the warm sunshine cascading through some palm fronds making zebra stripes on the concrete. Looking around and deciding to walk to the beach just up the street to check the water and catch a little morning sun. She took a few steps and then her hip seized up. *Crap. I can't go to the beach like this. Flo is not going to like me slowing her down.* She peered through the palms, and in seeing the beach was already bustling, she slowly headed towards the bus shelter.

"Can you tell me if this bus will take me to Bayview Hospital?"

The woman sitting in the bus shelter ceased fanning herself and stared at Klara, "See that sign? It say *out of city*, which mean the bus be going all round the Island. It take you even to the top of St. Lucy parish, but if you get off, you can cross the street and hop on a *to city* bus, and you'd be right to go down to Bridgetown Market." The woman eyed Klara suspiciously, not knowing which nationality she was at first, then softened when she found out she was Canadian from the Canadian flag badge sewn on her beach bag.

"So, I should go to that bus stop?" Klara pointed to the other side of the busy street, five houses down from her current location.

"Yeah, that be the one to take you to the Bayside. Why do you need to be going there? In trouble?"

"I have a stiffness in my hip. I just want to check it out." Klara figured it wasn't worth trying to re-explain everything to every one of the friendly locals; it was easier to keep it simple.

"A rum will fix that. You'd better hurry, your bus be coming, look."

"Thanks!" Klara shot a look down toward the bus, *a giant mechanical bumblebee in blue and yellow*. It appeared several houses up the street, so she had time to navigate a path through the traffic. Klara saw a family beginning to hustle up to a quieter area of the road, with the bus stop sign displaying to the city directly across from her. *C'mon legs.* Clutching her purse and awkwardly jogging over to where they were, when the traffic stopped, she was able to cross with a limp. She smiled as a few local men waved at her as they saw she was in discomfort.

"How much is the fare?" she asked the driver.

"Three Bajan dollars. Fifty cents. No U.S."

"Oops, I'm sorry. I only have a five." She started digging in her purse frantically, assuming she was holding up the schedule or the traffic behind the bus.

"You can pay more, but no refunds. Exact amount only. Hold on." The driver closed the door and honked his horn, re-entering traffic. "Keep looking in your purse;

if you don't have the money, I'll let you off at the next stop. It's the Bayview Hospital. They have a gift store and restaurant there you can break your bills. Next bus will be pretty quick."

"I'm sorry, next time, I'll have the money, I just arrived yesterday, and had a crazy night last night."

"I figured, many tourass that ride the bus, always ask the fare when they're new. Welcome to Barbados. On holiday?"

"Yes, first time to Barbados." She found the bill. "Just take the five." She placed it in the box as the bus honked and veered to miss a tourist jogging.

"You have to find a beach miss; you light as a duppy!" He chuckled, "a ghost."

"I'll check out the Crane beach later, is it crowded after lunch?"

"We, the local people of Barbados, go to the beach in the early morning, and the late afternoon, so the sand not burn you when you walk. You find many tourass sunning themselves all day long. Don't burn yourself girl. Here's your stop. You'll have to exit near the rear."

Klara looked around, the bus was packed, and several people were standing up to leave. She thanked the driver for his kindness and advice, then gingerly made her way through to the rear bus doors. A little girl dropped her doll at Klara's foot and began to fuss. Klara bent down, picked the hand-me-down—from three generations or more— off the floor, and handed it back to the girl. She smiled a half toothless smile, which bloomed Klara's mood.

"Here you go, she would be very lonely if you left her here." Children began looking at her, smiling, admiring her hair, jewelry, and sandals. The rear door opened, and the passengers politely filed off the bus and wandered off in different directions. A teenager was limping with a crutch at the side of the street, trying to navigate a safe passage to the hospital, and grew increasingly more stressed as the traffic thickened.

"Can I help you cross?" Klara's voice soft, like her outside supervision first aider voice. She had helped many kids with their playful bumps and bruises in her years as an elementary school recess supervisor, so help and kindness were traits still ingrained in her personality years later.

"Thanks, my leg…" he shifted his weight, "cricket."

"Mine too but not as bad as yours. I've seen it. It's a wonderful team game. What position did you play?"

"Deep cover sweeper. I can throw fast. It's in the field, way out."

"Do you see that black Mercedes car; we can cross then. Are you ready? Here comes a break on the other side of the traffic." Klara positioned herself beside the young man, and they hobbled across the break in traffic. A muscular sports nurse was coming out with a wheelchair to greet them.

Captain in the Mercedes had no idea that this woman helping the intern with his new patient was the girl Wodan was looking for. When they crossed, Captain continued his route back out to the docked *Assailant*, preparing it for the nightly seizure and plundering of the partying students' treasures.

"I saw you were having a tough time. Are you, his coach?" the nurse said, wheeling the chair behind the cricket player.

"Oh no, I'm here just to check out my hip. I just wanted to help him cross. Does the traffic ever slow down around here?"

"No, but you find breaks like the one you just did. Easy now, I'll take the crutch back here. Cricket injury?" The nurse took the player towards the door, conversing about the match and score. Klara found the main entrance and headed in its direction, hoping for some stretching advice.

## 2.

Wodan watched from his car; the few police littered around a body that had been reported, washed up on the beach. He had been putting together an anonymous package with Captain's picture on the *Assailant*, a written confession signed by Wodan explaining that Wade was not a lawyer, and the reasons for collecting the bullet from the Bayview Hospital morgue. He had secretly printed transaction receipts from Captain's laptop to the arms dealer in buying the ammunition and guns involved in the robberies. He dropped a bracelet from Andrea Lopez into the package; the girl with ballistic trauma shot one week prior when he broke into her hotel room and stole her luggage. The police recovered a few clues to help solve that case, but with the evidence that Wodan would release to them in this package, Captain—his boss—would take the fall for all the crimes. He sealed the box, and with gloved hands, he opened the door of his car. Leaving the car idling with the air conditioner blasting, he placed the box on the front hood of one of the Police SUV units. He went back to his car, removed the gloves, and quietly half shut his door. He reversed the car and drove away undetected.

"Hey, Nelson! Is that a box or a bomb on your hood?"

"What? Where did that come from?" Detective Nelson reached for his radio and moved guardedly toward his unit to be a safe distance if the package would explode and to avoid embarrassment if the box was a hoax. "Did you put a box on my hood? It's a brown one, fruit sized box…" He waited for their response.

"Don't know what you are talking about, Chand."

"Have you heard of any bombs targeting the police SUVs?"

"Does it look like a bomb?"

"Don't want to take the chance on that Piper." Chandler looked at the box closer, then moved in to see if it gave off the suspicion of an explosive device. "Never mind, not a bomb. I'm opening it."

"Be careful. Use your knife to cut the tape, then use your flashlight, baton, or the windshield wiper to try and open it. Saves your fingers in case it's live."

"Thanks, Piper. I'll be careful." Chandler unclipped his flashlight and carefully lifted the flaps to find that the box held a clear bag of evidence. He put his flashlight back, reattached the clip, and then took out his phone.

"Derk Warrows please." He looked back to the group by the body on the beach as he took a pen from his pocket and tenderly inspected the box's contents. "Hi Derk, another body, and I have a box with… It looks like some evidence and a picture of a guy on some yacht. Don't know if it is related to the two tourists that got killed, Redding and Lopez. I might not need your services unless this yacht owner is shady."

"Does this body have the same rope marks by the wrists?" Derk asked.

"No, but this one has a couple of bullet wounds. The flesh is quite marred. I know you will want to know about the bullets, but they might be corroded." Chandler replied.

"Once the body is processed, let me know. Did you find any connection to the stuff you found at the Sandy Wharf shooting yesterday?"

"Just a small evidence bag's worth. Ok. I'll keep you on the file. They are zipping up the body now." He changed his tone, "what is happening here, Derk? It's like a couple of gangs are dumping their garbage and hoping the evidence doesn't wash to shore."

"If it's all from one or two killers, once we get linking evidence to pin this case to the other two, we can stop these murders from continuing. I don't think it has anything to do with our locals."

"Here's hoping. Thanks." Chandler ended the call and traded the phone with a pair of gloves from his pocket. Careful not to smudge the edges, he grabbed the box from the center of the sides and slowly placed it into a substantial evidence bag designed for a limb or vehicle body panel. Seeing that the officers were back at their SUVs and leaving, he took off to the Hastings detachment.

## 3.

Approaching the front reception desk the triage nurse barked at Klara, "Are you injured?"

She glanced back, assuming the nurse was talking to the person behind her but noticed that she was alone. "Not terribly. I have a very tight area in my hip that is not getting better. It seized up twenty minutes ago."

"Hold a moment." She left the desk and went to talk to the other nurse behind a wall of files. She returned with a very stern posture, "Miss, this is the emergency area of the hospital where people who are injured will be seen first. We have no time for jogging injuries or girls who drank too much last night. You are risking your entire day for something a sea bath or a stroll along the beach might loosen up."

Klara stood at the reception desk, feeling a pang of frustration at the nurse's dismissive tone. She took a calming breath before responding, "I understand, but I want to see someone. It might get worse from what happened last night at the police station."

The triage nurse's expression softened slightly, though her tone remained firm. "Who advised you to come here?"

"A detective. I'm involved in an ongoing investigation," Klara explained, hoping this would convey the urgency of her situation.

The nurse glanced at Klara with a mix of curiosity and skepticism. "Wait here."

Klara waited anxiously as the nurse disappeared behind the wall of files again, to consult with someone. A few moments later, she returned with a different demeanor, a hint of apology in her voice. "I'm sorry for the misunderstanding. Please fill out these forms and have a seat. We'll get you checked over as soon as possible."

Relieved, Klara nodded gratefully and took the forms, quickly jotting down her information. As she began the forms in the waiting area, she couldn't help but feel a wave of exhaustion wash over her. The events of the past day had taken their toll, and now, with the hospital's clinical atmosphere surrounding her, she felt a mix of apprehension and determination.

She glanced at her watch, realizing that the day was only beginning. Despite the nurse's earlier words, she knew she couldn't dismiss her discomfort as easily as a walk on the beach might suggest. Deep down, she sensed there was more to her pain than simple muscle tightness.

As she waited for her name to be called, Klara took a moment to collect her thoughts. She knew she had to focus on her health and her sister's wedding details, but her mind kept returning to the interaction she had with Kennedy, wondering what Chandler and the police were uncovering, and whether they were any closer to solving the mysteries that had unexpectedly entangled her life.

The minutes ticked by slowly, each second punctuated by the distant sounds of hospital activity. Klara closed her eyes briefly, hoping that whatever the examination revealed, it wouldn't further complicate the already tangled web she found herself in. After waiting anxiously in the hospital's emergency area, Klara's name was finally called. A young doctor with a friendly demeanor greeted her and led her to an examination room.

"Hi Klara, I'm Dr. Patel. What brings you in today?" he asked kindly as he reviewed her forms.

Klara explained about the discomfort in her hip that hadn't improved despite her brief sleep from the night before. She mentioned quickly that she was involved in a police investigation, which prompted Dr. Patel to listen more attentively.

"Alright, let's take a look," Dr. Patel said, motioning for Klara to lie down on the examination table. He began the physical examination, palpating her hip joint and testing her range of motion.

As he worked, Klara couldn't shake the sense of unease that had been lingering since the previous night's events. She wondered if her hip pain was merely stress-related or if there was something more serious causing it. The doctor's focused expression didn't give away any clues, and Klara's mind raced with thoughts about not getting enough for finding finding areas for Marcy's wedding and the danger that seemed to lurk around every corner.

After completing the examination, Dr. Patel stepped back and reviewed his notes. "Based on what I've observed, it seems like you might be experiencing some inflammation in your hip joint, possibly due to overuse or strain. I'd like to order a quick X-ray just to rule out any other underlying causes. I don't think there is anyone waiting. It won't take up too much of this sunny morning."

Klara nodded, feeling a mix of relief and ease. She knew the X-ray was necessary to understand the full extent of her new condition, but she also dreaded the potential for a slow recovery. She pondered; *Flo will want to get going right away. I hope she understands.* Dr. Patel reassured her,

"Don't worry, Klara. It's standard procedure, and after a quick X-ray, you will back on your vacation."

Soon, Klara was escorted to the radiology department where she underwent the X-ray procedure. The technicians were efficient and professional, and within a short while, she was back in the examination room waiting for the results.

Dr. Patel returned with a small smile on his face. "Good news, Klara. The X-ray shows no signs of fractures or serious joint issues. It is acute inflammation but in a tricky spot, from the stress and strain you've reported on your forms. I also think you may be having feelings of stress from the episode you experienced. The mind is a strong organ, and it gets to boss the rest of your muscles around. Have you thought of post traumatic stress that you may have, because your mind hasn't rested? You had a horrendous first day. I didn't see you write any rest on a beach chair or by the pool on your forms. My advice is simple, that should be the first priority for your vacation."

"I like that advice. Beach rest from a doctor in Barbados." Klara smiled. She hadn't thought about the crimes, or Wade for the past hour.

Klara breathed a sigh of relief, grateful that her condition wasn't more severe. Dr. Patel handed her some anti-inflammatory medication and advised on the gentle stretching exercises to help alleviate the discomfort. He also encouraged her to take it easy, find a beach to prioritize rest to allow her body time to recover.

As Klara left the hospital, she felt a weight lift off her shoulders. The reassurance from the doctor was comforting, especially given the tumultuous events she found herself caught up in. Her focus shifted to more wedding planning before Flo arrived.

Reflecting on the day's events, Klara resolved to stay away from the investigation as Chandler had said, while also prioritizing her own well-being. She knew there were still unanswered questions and dangers lurking, but for now, she would focus on relaxation and recapturing her vacation.

# Chapter 11

# *THE CONTRACT*

## 1.

Wodan failed to notice that there was a white car with onyx tinting following him two cars back. He ran through the evidence that he put in the box, the confession, and Captain's picture before the *Assailant*'s dark panels, taken when they were simple cruising partners before the cloak of assassin gunfire and plundering for pleasure and profit. As he pulled into a gas station, the white car drove past and snapped a lucrative picture of Wodan as he stepped out of his Nissan. Within the time he uncapped his gas tank, the image would upload to the Shandwick Trust of hired executioners that would bid on this evening's job of his slaying. Split seconds later, an email from a cleaning service front confirming the disposal of the order would arrive in an undetected and natural fashion. Captain received these notices in his inbox in the past, assuring him that the job was quick, clean, and professional.

Wodan inserted the nozzle into the tank and leaned his hip against the rear fender. He looked up at the flies buzzing around the halogen lights painted in fly eggs and cobwebs.

Captain heard his phone chirp in his Mercedes on the Southern Coast as he exited near the Eastern Shore. The job was assigned and confirmed; a shooter and driver team had won the bid to work Wodan within the eleventh hour that evening after their arrival on a private jet two hours from now. "That team? It won't be undetected after they're done." He chucked to himself. "Good luck Woden." Captain's phone dimmed then blackened as he thought his troubles would be all over in less than twelve hours.

Wodan replaced the gas cap and proceeded to the station's lobby as a motorcycle drifted towards the air pump. He paused and turned to the cyclist.

"I bet that's a joy to drive." He said, watching the long blond hair fall from under the helmet.

"Thanks," the cyclist flirted as she rested the helmet on the seat, showing her tight jeans flexed against her muscular rear. She then strolled to him and said, "It gets great mileage, especially on a pursuit."

"Shoot, you're a cop?"

"You betcha. Now give me some space and watch my bike. It's my day off and I don't want to see anyone messing this perfect afternoon up."

Wodan watched as she entered the door and then noticed a white car with very dark windows stopped across the road in a liquor store parking lot. He wondered if that car was a nightclub owner's, completing a liquor order, or an undercover police unit following him from observing his departure after placing the box on officer Nelson's SUV. He was overtired from all the excitement and stress from the recent *Dingolay* job and murdering

Andrea Lopez and pushing her boyfriend over a balcony a week prior. He figured the afternoon sun was weakening him as well, as he hadn't eaten in several hours.

The female officer returned and shot a quick smile at Wodan as she returned the helmet expertly over her golden hair. Mounting the bike, she called to Wodan, "You look like you aren't feeling right. You drunk?"

"Sorry, no, I guess I'm stressed. I'm going through a bad break up."

"Maybe you need some space, your car is full, take a drive up the coast. You should clear your head, take a dip in the sea, or just relax under some palms." She lifted the kickstand and began walking the bike back. She paused and looked at him. "Take some time for yourself and loosen up. You'll either fix your mistake or move on." She smiled and drove off. Wodan watched her leave, then turned back to the parking lot where his search for the white car came up empty. Realizing it was gone, he quickly concluded his gas payment and purchased a few bottles of water. With moderate haste, he returned to his car and sped off towards the Western Coast. Moments later, the white vehicle resumed its tail behind him, cautiously at a safe distance.

## 2.

Captain smiled as he boarded the *Assailant* carrying a steel case loaded with Wodan's fishing equipment. The charter of college tourists would bring a large load of tech, and drugs, as the tip-off reported rowdy behaviour in a beach bar from several of the men showing off to their girlfriends. The ladies posing for selfies, dripping with jewelry, with the hottest superphones on the market. In his mind, Captain would use the fishing gear as evidence linking Wodan to this final job and leave him safe and clear of the police investigation. His gloved hands opened the lid of the steel case and checked the shaft's fitment for the speargun, comparing it to the opened box of new bolts delivered with last night's shipment. Satisfied that the fitment looked exact, he loaded the spear, aimed at the wooden dock twelve feet below the deck, and fired the speargun.

"Hey that's a great shot, but next time aim for a swordfish." chuckled Hector Gubbs, a dock man who usually spent his time net fishing off the side of the longest pier.

"These are some new spears that I ordered on the Internet. Just checking to see if they would hold in the shaft on a downward aim without creeping loose or jamming." Captain thought for a moment that now there was a witness who had seen the spear, but he figured that it would be hard to identify from afar due to its gunmetal colouring. He would have to make sure that the injuries on tonight's plunder would identify as a harpoon accident from a scuba spear. Glancing down at the dock, he saw that the spear had been forceful enough to penetrate clearly through the other side of the boards and the metal ring with the line were now the only visible remnants of the spear.

"They any good?"

"I'll try them tonight before sunset, and let you know when I see you next. You going to be net fishing tomorrow? There are higher waves in the forecast, so your fish will swim farther out to the reef."

"I'll be going to church in the morning, but I'll be out here again by midday. There will still be some fish in the shallows. Good day to you, happy fishing."

Captain waved, then crossed the gangplank to retrieve the spear. It had made a definite hole in the dock but was easy to remove. The point was titanium and barely scratched. The manufacturer had boasted over their tips to ably spear any fish no matter their size, which pleased him, that a few drunken bodies would be insignificant to withstand its piercing thrust. Returning to the *Assailant* and checking the yacht instruments, Captain was ready to set sail in the late afternoon and be finished, collected, and back before eleven o'clock to receive confirmation that Wodan's termination concluded.

## 3.

Across from the hospital, Klara finally made it to the sandy shore and found a beach lounger under a palm tree. Admiring the picturesque scene for a moment, it resembled a postcard straight out of a travel agency brochure. "This is what I should have done yesterday," she sighed contentedly, feeling the warmth of the sun on her face as she settled onto the lounger.

"Hey lady, braid your hair for a dollar? You can even pick the beads!" a cheerful voice interrupted her moment of relaxation.

"No thank you, I'm just here for a short while. I don't want to burn," Klara replied, eyes closed, soaking up the sunshine.

"I could tell you a joke instead, or offer you some sunscreen," the voice persisted.

"Hold on, what did you say?" Klara sat up, pulling down her sunglasses to get a better look.

"Jones mentioned you gave him that advice," the voice continued. It belonged to a tall muscular man wearing a black mesh shirt and ripped jeans, who leaned in closer as Klara adjusted to the sudden conversation. "I'm Derk. Chandler briefed me about your first day."

Confused, Klara tried to piece things together. "I'm sorry, I don't understand. Is Jones the tow truck driver and your friend? How do you and Detective Nelson know each other? Are you a cop?"

Derk smiled reassuringly. "A private one. I specialize in off-record assignments. Let's just say I'm here to show you the better side of Barbados. With your hip, the hospital visit, and that sleepless night, Chandler thought you could use a friendly face."

"Wait a minute! Have you been following me?" Klara's tone grew more skeptical. "Jones is kind of creepy, and now you are...?"

"Klara, trust me," Derk interrupted gently. "Chandler asked me to keep an eye out for you since last night, especially in case the shooter tries to track you down again. Think of me as your personal security detail, minus the red carpet. Don't worry about Jones. He's the strong and silent type."

"I don't need your protection, if that's what you're offering," Klara retorted, reclining back into her tanning position.

"Jones mentioned you're a tough one. That's a good thing," Derk remarked with a chuckle. "I'll leave you be, but here's some sunscreen just in case. Can't have you turning into a Canadian maple leaf on your first day at the beach."

"Who are you?" Klara asked, still unsure about Derk's sudden appearance. She waited a moment before stealing a glance in his direction, but he had already disappeared. After twenty minutes of hearing the surf and feeling her skin start to sweat, Klara packed her bag, and stood brushing the sand off her legs. She placed Derk's sunblock bottle in her bag and gingerly carried her sandals to the sidewalk. She dusted her feet from the loose sand and as she slid into her sandals a lizard stopped right by her foot. "Aren't you a cute little guy. All I see are magpies and crows on my yard."

She walked across the hot pavement and heard a concord jet roar as it began to fly around to land. She watched it like it was an air show. Miles from where she was standing, two critical passengers were about to land and start their contract.

# Chapter 12

# *DERK WARROWS*

## 1.

Klara hopped off the bus and walked to the Sandy Wharf. Once in her room she fished out her phone. Disappointed by the lack of text notifications from her sister, she fired off a message to Marcy.

**Klara:** It's been a wild ride! Police car, jail, fake lawyers, hospital…

She flinched at what she wrote and quickly tried again.

**Klara:** Actually, made it to the beach today.

With Marcy's response likely delayed, she pocketed her phone and stared out the window.

The hospital and brief beach visit had brought some much-needed relief. Craving another dose of calm, she took her medication with a gulp of icy water from the fridge.

Digging into her beach bag, Klara found Derk's number scrawled on the sunscreen bottle. Curiosity piqued, she decided to text him.

**Klara:** Hi, it's Klara from the beach earlier. Got a quick question for you.

**Derk:** Hey there, done the beach already? What question?

**Klara:** You seem to know a surprising amount about me. Can I trust you?

**Derk:** As you know Chandler and I wouldn't want any harm to find you, especially with everything going on.

Klara hesitated, still unsure about Derk's intentions.

**Klara:** So, any plans this afternoon? I've got a bunch of young adult novels I'd brought with me to donate. Any schools or libraries in the area?

**Derk:** How many novels?

**Klara:** Just a small stack. Enough to fill a bag.

**Derk:** I know a school that would love them. By the way, Chand mentioned you were given a bus tour ticket. Thinking of going? It's about to leave in an hour.

**Klara:** Maybe. Just took a pill for my hip.

**Derk:** I can swing by, and we can go together. Think of me as your personal tour guide. I'll meet you at the lobby.

Klara pondered for a moment, then sent her reply.

# 2.

"Rakeef get in here!" Chandler called out, his voice echoing through to the next office.

"Yes, boss?!"

"This is unbelievable! Have you read this confession?"

"I took a quick look at it, seems legitimate. Did you find anything?"

Chandler moved some loose papers on his desk, making room for the notes he had scribbled in the last few minutes, "This guy is the mastermind behind the whole operation. This yacht seems unfamiliar too. It's dark grey like a military warship's coloring." He looked at Rakeef, pointing to the picture of the sizeable multi-million-dollar yacht. "Why would a person want a dark-colored ship? Other than for seedy behaviors and illegal activity." Chandler moved a written note towards Rakeef, "we recovered the bullet from Andrea Lopez in the hotel room's bathroom wall and cross-referenced it with the casing found in the Kennedy Glenning murder. They match and appear to be from off the Island. I have no idea from where... Europe. Not from around the islands. The bodies that have come from the sea, Evanson Springer, and the rope burned tourist, they were both on Evanson's charter when this man attacked them," pointing to the confession, "and the hit was ordered from this guy," pointing to the yacht owner's picture.

"Did you think he is here on the island, or is it the fake lawyer that steers the operations?"

"He may be in Europe. Piper's running the search." Chandler rose to his crime corkboard, overpopulated with notes and clues, and stood there for a moment with his hand resting under his chin. "But why kill Kennedy and not Klara?" Chandler stood for a moment with his hand on his chin, scanning the dozens of theory notes and collected statements and evidence. He turned to Rakeef, who had moved beside him, also peering at the corkboard's array of the biggest crime they had seen in decades. "Rakeef, let's go back to the night we brought Ms. Hockley in after the shootings. Wade wanted to talk with Klara, to get information, right?"

"I think so, Chand."

"So that means that Wade is the shooter, and I bet he only had three bullets left on him when he took out Kennedy Glenning."

"What about Jonathan Redding? He wasn't shot first before he fell?"

"No, he must have witnessed Wade in the hotel room, and they fought where Wade tossed him over the balcony, then shot the girlfriend. I can't believe it; it is all coming together!"

"So, you think Klara is safe? They won't try anything with her?"

"I bet, that because she is hanging around us, they have lost interest in her. Her vacation partner is arriving tomorrow, and she has nothing of value with her."

"Hey Chand, wasn't there another worker with Evanson on his boat. A Jabar, or Aaron?"

"It starts with an A for sure. Andrew. Why?"

"Is he missing? Or in a hospital? He would be a star witness."

"Check with Gladys if Evanson Springer had any priors, maybe you'll find his partner's name." Rakeef moved to the door, "Hey Thomas! Where is his boat? Docked at a port or was it dryland stored recently? Check that too."

"Sure, thing Chand!"

Chandler sat in his desk chair and closed his eyes, replaying the case with muted distractions. *Andrea Lopez went on a boat charter, came back, and probably saw Wade push Johnathan off the balcony. They must have struggled and fought, where Andrea must have hidden.* He opened his eyes and reached out, taking a sip from his morning coffee mug. *She must have hidden in the bathroom, where he shot her.* Chandler gasped. "He used a silenced gun!" He wrote on his notepad again, then leaned back in his chair. *Then he joins the yacht owner or an accomplice on a dark grey yacht, and they go after Evanson and his guests Kennedy Glenning and her husband.* Chandler lunged for the phone on his desk. He dialled the airport and inquired about the other passengers on the flights within the last month for another Glenning on the passenger manifest. While he waited, Rakeef returned.

"Chand? Sorry; are you on the phone?"

"On hold; what did you find?"

"Evanson worked with a guy named Akeel and they run a deep-sea fishing charter on their boat called the *Dingolay*. It was seen a few days ago, but now the usual sailors on his part of the southern deep-sea fishing areas say they haven't noticed the *Dingolay* out on the water."

"I wonder if it sunk?"

"Could be, especially if they were out deep, we'd never find it with the currents. Nobody dives in the deep-sea fishing areas, but a fish finder might pick it up. There are no sites of choice for divers in the southern areas except Mount Charlie and Highwire and I doubt the boat is resting there."

"Check the Digicel records for an Akeel and see if he has a phone contract. There shouldn't be too many results with Akeel as the first name. If it is an alias, we will have to forget it."

"I'll check back soon," Rakeef left as Piper crossed Chandler's office.

"Piper, thanks!"

"You called me Chand? Thanks for what?"

"For almost solving the case! Once you find out who the owner of the yacht is, I'll take you out for supper!" Chandler leaned back in his chair again and produced a smile suggesting a sigh of relief that he was finally able to weave the tendrils of this case together and apprehend the yacht's captain. The phone automated message chimed on for the fourth time. It reminded him that the airport staff was doing everything in their power to complete his call, courteously and with compassion, then cut out, interrupting the background music with a live woman's voice. "This is Detective Chandler Nelson calling. I would like you to do a passenger manifest search from last month to today on a Kennedy Glenning, yes, Glenning. And can you tell me if there was another Glenning traveling from the same airport with her to Barbados? We are looking into the identification of a middle-aged man who was spotted drowned in the water by a local angler. We think he is her husband, but I just want to clarify any errors. Thanks, I'll hold." Chandler leaned forward in his chair and studied the notes before him on the desk. *Kennedy used her credit card to book the Sandy Wharf room but paid cash; I wonder if he is her husband*, Chandler thought as the airport attendant came back to the call.

"So, his name is Byron Glenning. Thank you so much! Have a great rest of the afternoon."

Chandler quickly navigated through the hallway and found Alessio Sufaletta, the bomb squad officer, who regularly checked surveillance and any wiretaps. He was standing and munching on his sandwich from the platter while he waited for a background check on a new daycare chef as Chandler approached.

"Hey, Chand."

"Al, I need you to do a background check and credit card pull for a Byron Glenning from England. See what he was up to on the Island. The airport confirmed he did not make his flight back to England, and we have a body fitting his description on the slab in the Bayview morgue."

"You want dental and blood records too? I've got a mate in the Britain office that knows a thing or two and is good at releasing information for overseas investigations."

"Sure. I'd like to clean that morgue out, there seems to be quite the pileup of bodies in there."

"I'm on it, Chand." Alessio dusted his fingers from crumbs and began typing and clicking his way into police and Interpol databases.

Chandler went to the front reception desk, checking if there were any messages and holding the calls for him. He wanted to look at where the docked yacht known as the *Assailant* was and, hopefully, find any loose evidence or the captain of the mysterious yacht.

# Chapter 13

# *THE BUS TOUR*

Derk arrived to greet Klara with her bag of books at the lobby entrance to the Sandy Wharf.

"I'm trying to get it out of my mind, but this is where Kennedy died." She motioned to the new plaster over the damage in the wall.

Derk softened. "The bus tour will help heal your mind. You only knew her for a few minutes, but you had such an emotional connection to make a recurring memory. As an investigator, I've seen things that I can't describe but there is nothing I can do for the victims."

He grabbed the books and placed them in the back seat of his truck.

"Hop in, this bus tour isn't going to wait."

The route was littered with tourist rental cars with music blaring and girls screaming when they would squeeze by a taxi or bus. Derk let Klara off, so she didn't have to walk too far and found an oversize parking space.

As Klara approached the bus terminal office to hand in her voucher, she noticed the waiting area had an interactive sign to poke your face through. She saw a similar one at the Cayman Island Turtle Farm when she was a child. Appreciating the artwork of the cut-out characterizing yourself to be a pirate with a peg leg and a parrot at this location made her smile. A few children played around the sign with their mother heckling them to stay still and pose a pirate face. Klara waited for Derk then handed in her ticket when he bought his pass, breezed through the gift shop, and boarded the bus on the left passenger side so they would see the land in the afternoon sun and the ocean in the rich oranges and pinks at the beginning of sundown. She sat in her seat and didn't mind sitting beside Derk, hoping the tour trip would ease her grief. She had put on a powerful face and appearance yesterday, but she thought of Derk's earlier advice. *It is out of my control.*

She felt the bus begin the tour, then heard the conductor welcome them aboard with a thick, warm, and rich calypso Bajan accent. Within minutes they were on their way and touring the southern area of the Island. Derk would point out the little histories that the conductor wouldn't mention. Their route would take them up towards the northern tip of St. Lucy parish, with brief stops at the major tourist attractions en route, then to finish with the quaint surfing and fishing areas of Cattlewash and Bathsheba. Klara took several pictures that she texted to Marcy and snapped a few of her and Derk for her own memory. As the sun was casting warm hues through the bus, Klara would sneak a glance at Derk. At first she was unsure, but after the tour with him he eased her mind and made her feel safe.

The tour took roads that Klara wished were a bit wider. At times, the bus would squeeze past a corner with the friendly honk from a passing car warning of a collision. Klara held her breath often and leaned into Derk, for the air was a tinge of foul sweat, mixed with Bajan curry from someone snacking on fish cakes and from the near misses of motor vehicles zipping by. She loved to drive but being on the other side of the road than she was used to and on some of the narrowest roads in the Caribbean, she was glad she was riding a bus. Derk pointed out the classic windmills, ripe sugarcane fields, and weathered rock cliffs risen in the middle of a local farmer's goat field. She loved his stories and the fairy tale qualities each landscape provided, with the quaint chattel house homes, the Purple Heartwood houses, and the wild cotton puffs blossoming on the occasional roadside tree. The Northern tip of the Island was windy with large seawater spray through roadside blowholes. The bus driver narrated the lore and historic landscape features as if on recording, occasionally waving with a brief honk to walkers on the curbless roads. The Morgan Lewis Mill was breathtaking, and although it was not in operation the day the tour was on, Klara marvelled at the majestic shadows it cast over the rugged terrain at the foot of its stone base. Standing by the base of the windmill with Derk she closed her eyes and took in the sounds and heat from the late afternoon sun.

"You're right Derk." Klara leaned into his shoulder.

"It's getting your mind well again, isn't it. Barbados is beautiful." Derk had his arm around Klara's shoulder. A passer-by could mistake them easily as a couple.

The bus honked as Klara was envisioning the beautiful landscape and ancient architecture set before her. This is a thought. Please italicize. continue the italicizing from the start of the sentence. When the bus tour guide had announced for the passengers to reboard the bus, she opened her eyes and smiled, that she now had a unique memory; one acutely different from the ordeals witnessed in the many hours past. As they both boarded the bus, the last stop before Cattlewash and Bathsheba would be the Barbados Wildlife Reserve.

## 2.

In the harbour south of Bridgetown, the group of college-aged students who booked Ernie's private evening party catamaran cruise was loudly waiting at the dock to board. Some were awkwardly dancing TikTok vines, others looking over the side of the harbour wall at the colour of the water. All the guests had excessive intoxication already and were waiting on the dock for their chance to board. Nobody suspected that in a few hours, their partying cheers would turn to bone-chilling screams as they would be too drunk to comprehend the horrors of Captain's calculated attack. Ernie, the boat captain cheerfully joked with them that he had no more spirits on board, which created a drunken harmonious rant, but he brightened their mood as he held up a giant bottle of extra vintaged dark rum. As they hobbled across the gangplank, one fell, almost taking out the lot of them, but Ernie helped the group board, then quickly untethered the boat, and swiftly pushed out to the open harbour water. Within fifteen minutes, they would be sailing too far out to turn back to the safety of the busy harbour. Their route would slam directly into the *Assailant's* path within the next hour, as the sun was beginning to set in the western sky. With a nervous newcomer at the ship's wheel, taking a medium group of six drunk partiers, this would undoubtedly be a night to remember, but it would be Ernie's last voyage and the final adventure of his life.

## 3.

Wodan lifted one of the water bottles to his lips and took a generous drink as he was fighting the afternoon sun blinding him through the windshield. As he fitted the water bottle back in his drink holder, he heard glass splinter behind him. Swiftly looking up in the rear-view mirror, he slammed his foot on the gas pedal, briefly leading in the chase. *Who the hell was that? I gotta get out of here!* His mind exploded! Frantically looking for an escape route, he heard bullets whizz past him, hitting the windshield. Barely seeing the short opportunity of a side entrance to a young cane field, Wodan kept his head low and veered violently into the cane reeds to escape the chase. He turned his car's wheels to allow a more random trail as he strained to look through the shattered glass in front of him. He listened to determine if the gunfire was still a threat, figuring he had only a brief window of time. With his heart beating out of control, he quickly exited the car with a stale shirt snatched from the back seat, soiled from a previous job. He wrapped his hand in the shirt and smashed the remaining windshield glass panel sections to break them free from the front pillars of his Nissan. Wodan was perfect in his haste, and discarding the shirt to the back seat again, he reversed over the destroyed cane field tracks and nosed the car toward the highway. His heart was still pounding, thinking he was in a precarious situation should they return to shoot at him again. He knew the local police were not chasing him as most officers did not carry guns or would not draw them during chases, figuring bystanders or quaint houses on the roadside would receive the direct line of fire if they did. Realizing that the assassinating car had passed by and could be turning around, he floored the pedal again and raced out to the road.

Trotting along the road was a rental car filled with a large German family, sightseeing and photographing their scheduled activity. The mother in the passenger seat was leaning out of her open window, trying to focus on a distant classic lighthouse. She fitted the lens up to her eye as Wodan roared out from the area, barely missing their front bumper. The camera flew from her hands and smashed into the passenger door panel. The rental van's load of passengers began shouting and cursing louder over the screaming children, wailing from their rental car seats. His speed blew bits of sugarcane stems over their car, obstructing their view to get a clear look of who had cut them off. They swerved and blocked the oncoming traffic for a moment, allowing Wodan extra getaway time. The horns sounded behind him, suggesting the tourist's car move out of obstruction. Wodan craned his neck to witness the assassin's car beginning its pursuit once more. He assumed with freshly reloaded guns, and noticed they quickly equipped laser sightings to track with lethal accuracy.

# 4.

Klara had been trying to adjust her leg as it was tingling from the medication wearing off. She had overheard various tour guests remarking about a yacht in the water that looked like a military ship or an undercover police boat. Derk was looking out the window too and texting. She looked out the window and gasped. She remembered Kennedy's strained conversation yesterday from when she courageously escaped that dark-coloured boat. She ran through the conversation's thoughts and deduced that this mysterious boat on the sea in the late afternoon sunlight might very well be the same. Derk had looked at her strained face as he mentioned that Chandler thinks that boat might be the one to find Wade and his partner. Suddenly they both snapped their heads to the front of the bus when a woman started screaming.

"Look! Are they going to hit us?!" Shouted a man in the seat in front of her. Klara stretched up; her eyes widened as she saw a red Nissan and white Audi speeding towards her. More people were shouting, and several guests were shoving to get into safer seats on the opposite side of the bus. Derk was calming a hysterical teenager as parents were handing their children across to the adjacent seats, sandwiching their tiny frames into the middle of two towering bodies in case of a motor vehicle collision. Klara braced for impact as she heard gunshots coming from the Audi and saw the Nissan swerve directly away from a crash with the front of the bus as the driver slammed on the brakes. The Audi shot several times with the red laser sight shaking all over the road. Klara could see the Audi's masked shooter hanging out of the passenger window. In a flash, she saw the brief glint of gunmetal resembling a small machine gun and a gloved hand slam the magazine into the slide stop. The whole magazine change process was lightning fast and highly professional. The Nissan was hit by several bullets and drove right into the rear tires of the bus. Feeling the bus tilt, Klara saw that the bus began to shift between the two speeding vehicles. The Audi slammed into the front of the bus crumpling the passenger accordion doors. The impact shattered the front windshield glass as airbags deployed, obstructing their view.

Everyone grew loud, frantically screaming as they tried to escape from the bus, causing Klara to clamp her hands over her ears to reduce the echoing stridency. Derk covered her with his muscular arms. As she turned her head to peer out the window, she saw the driver of the Nissan tortuously scrape his wounded body through the partially opened driver's door. Klara gasped as she saw his body stained from the blood pouring from the bullet holes. He struggled to pull out further but awkwardly fell to his side and lay motionless on the hot pavement. Klara couldn't believe her eyes; on the roadway, a few feet from the bus, lay Wade Barnwell breathing his last shallow breath.

"Derk did you see what just happened? That's the fake lawyer Wade Barnwell" Klara wailed her voice lost in the shouting.

"I don't have any way to protect you. Stay as low as you can. I don't think they have anything to do with the bus tour. I'll call Chandler." Derk spoke directly to her ear.

She strained to look for who was in the Audi or if they had died, figuring the airbags may have saved them from the bus's impact, but people were getting in the way. There was chaos as passengers rushed to the back of the bus, navigating their exit through the rear emergency door.

Derk called out to the frantic passengers, "There is a deceased man by the red car. Don't take the children that way. Take them to the other side, far away from the bus," then he turned to the driver, "did you shut the engine off?"

He was trying to help an elderly woman to the back of the bus, "Can you? It's still running."

Klara exited with the children as Derk took a few careful steps towards the bus driver's seat, looking towards the Audi's smashed windshield. Fearing the worst that the driver or passenger were dead in their seats, he saw that the two doors were open, their bodies were not inside. Derk checked the side mirror to look back at Wade and saw that his body was gone. Glancing a second time, he felt a hard pull on his arm.

"We have to leave now! See the fire. Can't you smell the gas from the engine?"

"What?!" Derk looked back to the Nissan again, wondering what fooled his eyes. "Where's the body?"

"We're going to be bodies too if we don't get out of here! We have to go now!" The driver's grip was tugging him away.

With the children and elderly tour passengers safely away from the bus, the exit route became clear. The bus driver and Derk ran for the exit and heard the sizzle of the flames licking for them. The explosion soon ruptured through the bus coach, blowing out windows and bubbling the exterior painted mural. Derk flew forward and scraped his forearm on the scorching pavement. Klara retreated to the safety of the others and watched the steel frame of their tour bus expel thick, stinking black smoke.

Klara moved to Derk and poured some water over his scrape as they stared where Wade's body was. Klara puzzled *how did he get up with all that blood loss? Wait, were they hired to kill him?*

# Chapter 14

# *PLEASURE CRUISE*

## 1.

"Piper! Have you seen Chand?" Rakeef cried out frantically searching Nelson's office.

"No, Rakeef, Chand stepped out to look for a dark-colored yacht in the southern sea." She scanned Rakeef's pained face, "Did something happen? Another murder?"

"A tour bus is up in flames near the cane fields by the Wildlife Reserve. A helicopter with a searchlight is heading over to there now to add some light on the scene. Fire personnel are en route. I heard it was a mix of locals and tourists including Chandler's girl, Klara and Derk. Their bus just went up in flames. Gladys said to hold Chand's calls, and I tried his personal cell, but nothing."

"What? Okay, let's get Jones Towing to head out there to help. The media will be getting in the way, so we must move fast. You grab some rescue blankets and water. Get the most fuelled up Rover we have on the lot and meet me out front."

## 2.

The sun was permeating rich hues of golden oranges and deep indigos as it broke to an open starry sky. Captain was peering through binoculars at the partying catamaran with its private charter of college partygoers. He had slipped into a black wetsuit and fitted the waterproof spear case to his diving belt, loaded with ten tungsten diving spears. Captain had slightly sawed partway through the base rung to be snapped off with medium force if the situation warranted it. On other jobs, he worked quickly to remove the spears upon impaling his victims.

Captain also brought his waterproof case designed to secure his silenced pistol. He had drifted past them in the deeper water where the glowing sunlight would blind the view from their boat. They could take notice of his monstrous silhouette, but they were dancing to The Merrymen and Spice and Company music tracks from the catamaran's speakers. With drinks in hand, the atmosphere did not suggest murder by harpoon or drowning with nerve gas. They were utterly unaware of Captain's recent turn to now trail behind them.

Captain set the *Assailant*'s GPS unit to anchor at specific coordinates automatically. The numbers, 13.042; -59.515, were selected to anchor just southeast of the Silver Sands Reef Break digitally. Wodan had mentioned before that this tour would stop near the reef break for an informal look at the reef from their glass-bottom feature. Seeing that they were beginning to turn to the reef, Captain opened a cargo hold, lifted out a Sea-Doo RS Dive scooter, set the *Assailant* to auto, and jumped tank-first off the port side dive plank. He briefly surfaced to track his bearing, squeezed the scooter's trigger, and propelled towards the loud party where some were beginning to feel the effects of their bar service limit.

## 3.

One of the assassins dragged Wodan's body from his passenger car door across the road and into an overgrown cane field. In their quick departure, the Audi driver had grabbed the tarp from under his seat, and his partner, the shooter, had gone to work, emotionless and tactfully skilled with sharp accuracy. They had left their electric car running with the fuel cell set to disintegrate within a half hour to ensure a volatile explosion would incinerate the evidence. After dragging Wodan's body headfirst into the cane field, they kicked down cane reeds to make a more even area to take the termination photos to collect the remaining funds from the Shandwick Trust. Due to the sun reduced behind the Western sea horizon, the shadows cast were not sufficient to capture the face of Wodan against a sugar cane backdrop. The phone's camera had shown a blurred face but began taking intermittent shots, as it was challenging to focus on the current lighting condition. As the sun set deeper, it pained to resume taking burst shots when by happenchance the area was instantly brightened when a search and rescue helicopter traversed. If by luck, the camera took a clear picture the brief second the searchlight shone past. Satisfied that the image held enough clarity, they uploaded the shot to the Shandwick Trust to collect their reward. They disappeared into the cane reeds leaving Wodan Crandall facing up, staring up to the starry night. The tarp was arranged for the rappeler to hook his body up and be carried off the island.

## 4.

"Did you see that? In those cane fields?" The helicopter pilot asked over the radio to his co-pilot.

"It looked like a bloody body from one of the car wrecks. Should we call it in?"

"It seems weird how a driver could be ejected that far from their car. And it seems odd that there are so many canes down around him." They were shining the spotlight over Wodan's corpse, several feet away from the burning bus.

"Who the hell is in that chopper?" the co-pilot gasped seeing a stealth helicopter silently hovering a few metres from Woden.

"Can you patch the Hasting detachment in? They are not going to believe this." The pilot said over the radio.

The fire truck that arrived on the scene smothered any remnants of fiery destruction. The Nissan and Audi lay burnt to an unrecognizable state; their interior body mouldings had disintegrated, and the rising toxic smoke expelled into the clean open air could be seen for miles. The ambulance crew assisted the tour bus patrons and marvelled at the smooth bus evacuation. They beamed that there were no injuries. Detective Thomas and Officer Piper arrived with other officers to collect statements and provide water and fruit to the children and the elderly. Derk recognized Jones and made his way over to him as the tow truck arrived.

"Jones, this is heavy my man. Offshore assassins for sure. That Nissan is local, but I've never seen an Audi like that before. I think it's electric. The gas was pouring out of the bus, nothing from the Audi." Derk was glad to see his trusted friend.

"Crazy, Miss Klara on the bus with you? I hope she isn't hurt?" Jones motioned to the helicopter overhead, then thought for a moment, wondering why the spotlight was hovering on the cane field. "What's in the field?" Jones craned his neck to see.

"Not sure, you should load up the Audi first. I think the police want that one for sure. Check the VIN or see if there is a connection." Derk shot a glance back to Klara.

"I'm on it, you going to check out the field before the unit shows up" he smiled. "Want your vest for more protection than that mesh shirt? What were you thinking?" Jones kidded.

"Remember the lawyer, the one Chandler told me about? The fake one? He was in that Nissan over there." He heard Jones smirk. It was now unrecognizable as both cars were smouldering rubbles.

"Hi Derk, and er, hello Jones." Klara looked at the wreckage and noticed round bullet-sized holes. "Did he crash because he was shot?" she paused. "He had at least four gunshot wounds spilling blood down his back as he fell out of his car. He got out of the driver's side just barely, but when he hit the bus, his car swerved, and was closer to the bus then it is now. Any idea where he is?"

"Okay do you want to do me a favor? See that officer by the woman in the purple sundress? That is officer Thomas, can you get him to come over and check the field with me? I think his body must be in these cane reeds somewhere." Derk smirked.

"Sure thing, I can't get away from police work, even though I'm supposed to be on vacation. I keep getting drawn in for some reason."

Klara returned to the other bus patrons and spoke with officer Thomas to meet Derk by the cane field. He thanked her and handed her a bottle of water. He looked over to Derk, who was gesturing with violent arm waves, signalling that he found something of notice.

"What did you find?!" Rakeef demanded from afar.

"It's just a tarp with some blood on it. Where's the fake lawyer?" Derk yelled back.

"Are you sure? Check those canes, see they've been broken."

## 5.

Some of the quieter college students reaching their exhaustion limit on the dancefloor, found a more tranquil area on the edge of the sailing yacht to relax and share a joint. With the catamaran dropping anchor shortly began rocking gently on the dark sea. Ernie cut the engine and moved to the bow for the anchor and light.

"Well, Carl, when are you going to give me a kiss? This night has been amazing..." Joy watched for his reaction, but he looked confused. "Carl?"

"Let's hit this first. Did you see me drop my lighter? I guess mine is back at the hotel, no wait, I know I brought it…"

"I know where it is..." she leaned back to expose the lighter in her bikini top, tucked conveniently near her left bikini cup.

"That's not your lighter, that's mine from before..." he smirked, "wait a minute, I know what you are trying to do here..." He drunkenly leaned across her, his sweaty cheek tickling her slightly sunburned skin and bit the lighter with care, then retreated quickly, rubbing his rough goatee across her bikini top, making her giggle like a preteen. Producing the joint like a magic trick at a child's birthday party was Carl's final attempt at foreplay; then deliberately dropping at arm's length, the night's pleasure, for Joy to retrieve.

"I seem to have dropped my blunt, Joy." Carl half squinted with his eyes, hinting that he was too drunk to pick it up.

"Woah, like for real? I can get it for you, babe." She rose from her seated position with a hip dance, shaking her bikini bottom in a twerking style while tilting down and using her hand to scoop up the teetering joint. She noticed that the waves were interfering with her dance, but she rose to hold the joint in her left hand and performed an artistic dance wave with her right. When she spun around expecting to see Carl's lustful stare, she screamed, causing the other partying guests to notice. Carl was unable to speak as a scuba spear had impaled him, the tip dripping with blood and a moderate seep from the torn bone and skin in his chest.

"Joy?! What happened? Are you hurt?" One of the female partiers gasped as she caught the sight of Carl's injuries just before he fell backward into the water.

Captain had completed Wodan's task. Carl was sinking and he had to work fast to get the spear and loot out in the dark water.

Joy was shaking, pale and drained, swaying from the waves' gentle rock, clearly in shock. Diane went to the boat's edge to look for Carl, and leaning over the edge, could only make out a few small bubbles. "Does anyone have a light brighter than a cellphone?"

"What happened to her?" Ernie asked.

"I think she was with a guy named Carl and he's gone. Maybe he fell overboard."

"Is that her blood?"

"What? Blood!" Diane stepped back.

"I'll get a light. Make sure you two don't fall overboard. Or maybe move her to the front where the others are." Ernie went below.

Joy realized what was happening but couldn't make a sound. Diane moved to sit beside her but saw something move in the water.

Captain raised his gloved hand with the nerve agent canister and sprayed the nozzle at Diane's face. Diane staggered and violently swung her arms to try and catch her balance. Then teetered back towards Joy and fell into the water as well. The boat listed slightly, drawing the full attention to the guests. Ernie returned and cut the music and yelled to his guests, "Hey everyone! We have a situation."

"Diane? Diane?!" Meghan had begun her search for her friend, hoping to find her quickly as the men—she had noticed—we're getting dangerously close to her cleavage. "Diane?" She turned to look at the crowd, who were displeased that the music had stopped. Some of the men were taking off their shirts and deciding to take a dive.

"Everyone, please be careful not to touch anything on the boat. I think one of you fell in the sea." He took the key out of the ignition to be over-cautious if a drunken guest were to try something with the controls. He travelled over to Joy, who had sunken to an inner seat far away from the edge. Her eyes had grown dim, fixated in a hollow stare; as Ernie moved closer, she began to cry.

"What happened?" he whispered as he briefly checked to see if she was crying from the drinking or if she was seriously hurt. He then realized that when the boat listed to the side, men had performed a group dive overboard. When he moved to the bow and peered over the edge, he saw something that resembled a body in the water, but as the sun had set, the water grew dark. He lifted his hand and realized he had touched blood.

Captain had swum fully around the catamaran and had recovered the spear that pulled the first student into the water. He had watched the one he sprayed struggle then become lifelessly still as the air left her lungs.

He could hear the men swimming but decided they might do themselves in if they get too tired from being drunk. He surfaced and noticed a quiet couple sitting on the starboard side of the boat stargazing. The boy trying to move in close. The girl nervously laughing at the pleasant feeling of being drunk with a boy's attention glued to her for the first time in a long while. Captain found his opportunity and sprayed the gas canister as the boy leaned in whispering in her ear. The spray had lingered slightly but when she gasped at his musing, the two began to choke. They turned to the sea gasping for air as Captain sprang up and grabbed the back of their necks dragging them into the water. They tried grabbing one of the catamaran's ropes, but their arms wouldn't reach.

One of the investment brokers reached over the side and grabbed the girl's outstretched hand. He pulled her up, but the nerve gas had disfigured her face to a frozen scream, he got spooked and let her go. The broker fell back as Captain gripped the edge of the pontoon and pulled himself up. Moving fast in the water to flip onto the boat, he didn't notice that the broker was watching his every move.

Captain's diving bag laid at the broker's feet. It was full after he dug into the pockets to find wallets, phones and jewelry as the bodies were sinking. He had them all in his diving bag. The broker recognized the loot. He picked up Captain's spear gun.

"Why the hell are you stealing from us? You're finished!" he squeaked, aiming the speargun. The men swimming didn't notice when he announced, "Hey everybody! There is a guy here who is attack—" silencing his voice in mid-sentence as Captain sprayed. The broker dropped the gun and gasped for air as Captain pushed quickly, making him fall hard and land on his back. He landed on a half bottle of gin and smashed it. Shards of glass penetrating at his flesh from the back, nose bleeding from nerve agent to the front.

Captain had to act fast to take out the rest of the men in the water. If the crew spotted him, it would be all over.

He dove off the bow and swam quickly under the boat, crossing to the swimmers without notice from them.

With little nerve gas left, Captain had to resort to a new method to get the job completed. The two men in the sea were beginning to tire and made no attempt to aid the broker before the attack. Captain swam to the first man treading water and brushed his foot.

"Charlie, some fish just swam by me. I'm getting back to the boat." Just before he turned to swim, Captain looped a slip knot around his feet and tied them. Within minutes the man struggled thinking he was tangled in fishing line, and Captain pulled him under.

"Grant?" Charlie questioned. "Felt a fish? Grant? What the hell was that?"

The swimmer felt around in the dark and touched Captain's mask. "Grant where did you find a mas—!" the last bit of nerve gas made him gasp. His head fell forward and bubbled as he sunk.

Captain surfaced, reaching for the snorkelling deck, removing his mask as it began to fog, and tossed it aboard. Completely silent, he rose out of the water and quickly detached his flippers. Quietly unzipping the dive pouch, he brought out the handgun case. Watching for the crew, he opened the snap-tight lid and removed the silenced gun he brought to finish the job. He moved towards Joy as she was the last one alive clearly still in shock. The aim to end her misery. As he began to squeeze the trigger, he didn't notice the scuba tank swung towards his head. Ernie had a firm grip on the supply valve and struck Captain's head with such force; the empty tank immediately dented. He fell then lay unconscious as Ernie rushed to collect his gun and return to the captain's chair, fitting the key to the ignition. The boat started, and he began to steer back to the Bridgetown harbour. In turning the boat, he had aimed in the right direction of the harbour, but the voyage would be several minutes until he could get in range to radio for help. He failed to recoil the anchor which delayed his escape as he focused on his hostage in his black diving suit and saw that blood had begun to trickle from his forehead lightly. Not seeing the shore distantly in front of him, he reached for the spotlight.

In his blunder, he switched on the spotlight seconds before his boat's bow slammed directly into the *Assailant*, sending the motionless bodies and Captain forward with a high-paced thrust. Ernie had ejected forward and slammed headfirst into the hull of the *Assailant,* landing on the netting of his catamaran.

Captain began to awaken and gather the items of value. He would not tow this catamaran like he did with the *Dingolay*. He found his gun stuffed in the back of Ernie's shorts, who now lay with a twisted neck from the impact's force. As he retrieved the gun, Joy jumped into the water, and began swimming to shore.

Captain let her go as she would never make it to shore and collected the tech, rum, vacationer's money, bags of marijuana, and two small metal suitcases with American cash and the brokers' investment portfolios, cocaine, and fentanyl-laced heroin. He moved his new treasures to his diving gear and loaded everything in a plastic cooler conveniently located near the stern. He went to take the key out of the ignition but figured the police would suspect that.

With one last look over, he left the anchored party boat, grotesque from the attack, and returned to the *Assailant*. Out in the ocean lay his first victims, scattered several metres around the location making the rescue effort lengthy. Captain unlocked the GPS position and entered the coordinates for the *Assailant* to return to his private dock. He wanted to inspect the damage from the collision and fuel up before leaving Barbados.

# Chapter 15

# *CRISIS TEAM*

## 1.

"What did you find? Is he there?" Chandler tried to listen. Heavy traffic was actively passing him on the narrow roads. The partying atmosphere near the Gap was beginning to erupt. Taxis were dropping fares. Drunk tourists ready to join the party.

"There was a helicopter that was hovering over the cane field. The canes were trampled. There is no way to find a footprint, but we did find a latex glove. Also, Chand, his body is missing. There is no way that the explosion could have caused his body to be moved."

"Who do you think hunted him down? A local or do you think it was an offshore contract from the yacht owner?"

"That cute tourist of yours, Klara, said that she saw a professional guy load the gun with tact. She couldn't give a detailed description, but the guy had gloves and for sure the two suspects are male."

"Is Klara there? Wow, she never gets a break. I'm in heavy traffic near the *Gap*, but if you can contact the pilots to circle around again, they can see a bird's eye view path of their escape. How is Klara? She is a strong one, one of the calmest tourists I have ever seen."

"She only received a few bumps and bruises, nothing major. She should be a member down here. She has the right mind and demeanor for it." Rakeef passed his phone to Piper. Telling her to radio the helicopter to do a second pass. See if any perpetrators are in the area. While listening to his instructions, Piper checked for her torch. *I guess I'll use my phone.* With her police issued phone glued to her ear, she walked back to the cane field. Her cell as a torchlight. Puzzled from how the suspects moved haphazardly. In their haste to escape the blast. While she was crouching down and extensively studying the bloodstain, she heard a faint crackle. The cane reeds behind her. She put her finger over her light. As the darkness returned she felt the warm sting of a gun barrel pressed to her neck. *Damn it! Rakeef come back!* "Chand…" she whispered.

"Call off the helicopter," the voice pained, trying to disguise his European accent.

"I don't want any trouble; I was just investigating. If you let me go, I won't press—"

"Shut up! You have no idea who I am. Listen close. By this time tomorrow, you could be going about your night, alive. But if you don't call off that helicopter, you won't be seeing another sunrise. Our contract is finished. You are not a target. If you waste our time, your life is over."

"Piper? You still there?!" Chandler worried. *Piper had never stopped speaking during a call.* "Are you on an S?" demoting his voice to a whisper.

Piper had the police phone tucked closely. Hiding the fact that her lifeline was talking. The helicopter searchlight was off in the distance. Rescue crews nearly finishing the remaining injured passengers. *I'm going to die here.* She tried to regulate her trembling voice.

"Please call off the helicopter Gladys. The S-two that is investigating the car wrecks. I have found nothing more in figuring out where the suspects went. They may still be in the area. Or near Springfield."

"I'll call it in. How many are on you? Two?" Chandler whispered while he parked the car. Typing into the detachment that an officer was in a crisis. Digicel could triangulate her location exactly, and with any luck, take a picture of the situation.

"Just the one helicopter, right? You didn't send the second chopper?"

"One on you, but maybe two?"

"That's correct to cancel the chopper, it is not needed."

Piper felt a hand grab the police phone but sensed that her attacker had not removed the gun. Its strong presence irritating her skin.

"Don't worry Piper, it has been radioed in, I told them the crisis team would be needed." Waiting for her response. The phone chirped ending the call.

"Piper is it? You want to die, don't you?

"She made us. She was talking to another cop?" a new voice asked.

"They mentioned their crisis team, and that they were sending a unit. The job's done. Target chopper is safely out of range."

"What was that for Piper? Oren, should we dispose of her here. Do you have a silencer on you?"

"Don't use my alias!" he snapped.

"Relax guys," started Piper, frantically thinking of a plan to escape. "It won't matt…"

Piper felt the butt of the gun bludgeon the back of her head. One swift movement. She fell forward, unconscious. Oren's accomplice carefully stripped Piper of her uniform top.

"Go," mouthed Oren's partner. He tossed his shirt to him, fitting Piper's uniform perfectly. Moving next to collect her service issue handcuffs and gear belt. He pulled off the keys and joined Oren over by the parked SUV. Piper lay vulnerable.

Waiting for the tour bus passengers and rescue personnel to become distracted with final questions. They watched Rakeef move to the cane field to check on Piper. Escape would be easy. Slipping through the dusky darkness. Professional stealth as they entered the police car door. With lights still oscillating, they exited the crime scene to their safe house. Where they could hide out until their pickup later that evening.

Oren crouched in the back. The driver was undetectable. Once away from the bus passengers and rescue units, Oren sat up. Ordering his partner to shut off the overhead lightbar. Headlights would have to be broken. Standard to cloak them in darkness. The driver pulled over. Using the butt of the weapon, he busted every lit exterior light. They would dump the vehicle after a wipe down. Take care not to leave unnecessary prints. With night vision goggles on, the driver sped into the countryside. Fearless and fast.

# 2.

Klara tried to relax as she sat sandwiched between two bus passengers. She was part of the last minor injury load back to Bridgetown. Klara had requested a drop-off close to Hastings. She figured she could board an out-of-city bus to get her back to her hotel. Both hips were stiff. A large man and woman with her child on her lap cramped the EMS vehicle's foot quarters. Derk had already left. His injury put him on the first unit. He figured his truck would be fine until morning. The woman's daughter was holding onto a plush monkey from the Wildlife Reserve. Playfully flicking its curled tail. She mumbled about Chefette to her mother. Mom greeted with a nod. Klara thought for a moment. In Canada if a comparable situation would have occurred. The children would be remarkably different. Their composure following a huge disaster would be filled with a mixture of chaos and shrieking. Klara shifted minutely in her seat. *Chefette's barbecue chicken sounds good.* She had fish for lunch with Derk. Barbeque chicken would be familiar comfort food. Chandler will want to complete his investigation. Derk gave a detailed explanation to Officer Thomas. Klara figured her priority was Flo. She felt the vehicle enter a roundabout. Looking up to the ripe scent from a local fruit stand. She shifted again in the tight space for her hips.

"You should go to the sea tomorrow to let the water heal your leg. You keep shifting it," the woman spoke, motioning to her cramp.

"I wish. I have to pick up a friend of my sister's at the airport. So, no beach for me, sadly."

"When you do, the local men harass you on Accra beach, or Sandy Lane's beach all day. The boys' job to get to the tourass as soon as they please. They come find you as soon the sun rises up from the sea. "

Klara chuckled to herself. The woman sucked her teeth and shook her head, witnessing the surprised look on Klara's face.

## 3.

Captain returned to his boat launch, and GPS auto-locked the *Assailant* to the location. He shuffled down the stairs to the captain's quarters and spread his treasures out on the desk. He badly bruised his left shoulder. Feeling the back of his head where the scuba tank had knocked him unconscious. Finding his hair was still slightly matted from the blow. *Focus.* Tally the gear collected. Weigh the drugs. Captain smiled a menacing grin at his spread. Upwards of twenty-eight million from the investment portfolios he could hack. The drugs would be a quick sale. Phones would need a reset before his buyers could unlock them. He heard someone walking on the top deck. *Police?* He quietly crept towards the wall gripping a pistol.

"Sir?" Hector Gubbs voice familiar and non-threatening. "What happened to your ship? Looks like you got hit by a white catamaran... Sir? You down there?" Hector tried the handle. It opened. He peered into the dark cabin.

## 4.

Chandler arrived at the crash site. Rakeef sat beside Piper on the grassy roadside tossing rocks in a cup. Chandler exited his vehicle shaking his head.

"They stole my shirt, keys, cuffs, and ID."

"And number eight SUV," Rakeef added.

Chandler smiled, "They won't get far. There is a GPS chip in the front headlight unit. You ready to go?"

"You got any painkillers in your car? They smacked me upside the head with a gun. Back of my head is really tender." Piper gingerly felt to see if the swelling was improving.

"We'll get you some. Rakeef ride upfront so Piper can lay in the back. Use my jacket to get comfortable." Chandler sat the keys in the ignition. He punched in an alert for an APB lookout for Unit 8. He started the vehicle. The air was cool now. He lowered the windows and began heading back to Hastings. Rakeef watched the screen for movement of Unit 8. Nothing for that last half hour.

## 5.

Derk texted Jones.

**Derk:** How is the wreckage going?

**Jones:** Still slow.

**Derk:** I'm done at the hospital. Can you pick me up?

**Jones:** Sure, then we can go back and get your truck before the Audi.

**Derk:** You haven't moved that yet?

**Jones:** The bus took most of my time. I'll see you in a few minutes.

**Derk:** Kk.

Chandler grabbed his detachment phone. Speed-dialled Gladys. "Where is Unit 8, Gladys? Where?! That is a residential area! We're on it. Set a tracker to this detachment phone and send a couple of units to us. They stole Piper's handcuffs and have her uniform shirt. Nobody has any idea what they look like, but they are professional. Thanks Gladys. Oh, and have one of the units get Piper some pain tablets. She's resting in my back seat."

"Chand take the next left. It will save some time." Rakeef pointed.

They took the turn. Slowed to a creep. Scanning at a languid pace. Rakeef squinted to find the SUV.

"I don't see it Rakeef. You sure it's here?"

"Maybe it's in that garage?"

"You think so?"

"That's where it points. Stop the car Chand!"

"What did you see?!" Chandler stopped the car. Rakeef took off towards the signal. "Rakeef! Wait for backup!" He opened the glove compartment. Collecting his torch, he left Piper half-sleeping in the car.

"Rakeef?" Chandler used a hoarse whisper.

Rakeef clicked on his flashlight. He hovered it in a tight circle to show his location.

"Find anything?"

"They knew about the sensor. Look."

"Are they cops? What the hell? Nobody knows about those." Chandler was puzzled.

"Well, they stashed it by this garage, so they're gone by now. You were lucky I had a few evidence bags in my pocket..." Rakeef trailed off. He walked back to the car.

Chandler shone his flashlight around the area. He noticed a unique shoe print in some residents' garden's fresh mud. He took a picture with his cellphone. Heading back to the car pondering. *Whoever did this is not an officer, but how did they know about the sensor?*

He called Gladys, "Cancel the backup. The suspects dumped the GPS locator. Have there been any vehicles that have headlight damage?"

"Chand, this sensor is missing a chunk out of it, so the guy who took this out did it in desperation, probably with a tyre iron." Rakeef was holding the evidence bag. Scrupulously inspecting it.

"Rakeef just told me it looked like it was damaged and hit with an iron... What's that, Gladys?" Chandler listened intently. Thanks, Gladys." He turned to Rakeef, "They found Unit 8."

## 6.

"Hector, just stay there, the floor is wet." Captain reached around the bar to grab a towel.

"Why the lights off Sir? Tis night." Hector's eyes were beginning to adjust to the darkness.

"I had to use the bathroom. Just getting a towel. It's late, you need something. You, okay?"

"There was some policeman looking for your boat earlier..." He winced when the lights came on. He was still holding the cabin door, with an immediate plan to escape if there was a confrontation. His trust in Captain was gone.

"What did the policeman say he was looking for?" Captain tossed the towel on the floor. He offered a bottle of Banks to Hector. An invitation to divulge information. *Could they have found out about Wodan's hit?* "Want to sit?" Captain moved behind the bar. He pulled out a barstool.

Nervously, "No Sir, I've got to go, but I just wanted to warn you in case they come searching your yacht in the morning. I don't want any trouble, no trouble." Hector exited the door, leaving Captain by the bar gripping a silenced handgun.

"Thanks Hector, have a good night." Captain removed his finger from the trigger and picked up his cell phone. A system notification: battery saving mode just activated. "Operator please. It's me. Has the job been fully completed? I expect perfection for the price I've paid."

"The job has been confirmed. Do you require more work before my client leaves the safehouse?"

"They are at the safehouse? No. I heard that a cop came to check out my yacht."

"Are the police still there?"

"No."

"Then this concludes our business."

"Make absolutely sure that they are not followed to the airport. I'm planning to get off the Island later tonight once I refuel."

"Bon voyage sir." Captain ended the call. He took a long slow drink of his Port Ellen #13 single malt. Sighing after a long day of plunder and requisition. *So long Wodan.*

# Chapter 16

# *CINNAMON SCENT-BOMB*

## 1.

Klara slowly walked up the stairs to her room. She saw that the door was left open a crack. It slowly swung from the light breeze. Her kitchenette was quiet. *I know I closed that door tight before I left.* Feeling uneasy, she lowered her purse and slowly exhaled. She positioned her back beside the restless door. Looking around to see if she was alone she swung her bag. The hotel room door opened. She listened as it turned inward—nothing, not even a whisper. The only sounds were the far-off waves crashing on the beach. She stood listening. A moment more. Thirty seconds for any other intrusive sounds. Klara's heart pounded. She figured the room was empty. She took a calming breath. Just a quick peek inside. The light switch was a few paces into the room. *I hope the light is not broken.* She stepped into the darkened room. Her foot almost squished a tiny lizard who was hurrying out. The moonlit porch was the safe zone. Klara realized that the lizard must have been the culprit. A simple scurry into her room; after the cleaning staff had changed the bedding. She let her heart rate return to normal. Calm, Klara flicked on the light.

Nothing had been molested. Satisfied that she was alone. She freshened herself in the bathroom. She returned to the entrance door and firmly shoved it into its jamb. Slid the deadbolt across. Secure. Klara returned to her bed. Quickly stretched her hip. Relaxed and remembered *Flo is arriving in the mid afternoon.* The last thought before she slept.

"You see that car up there?" Oren pointed.

"Yeah, should we ditch this cruiser and pinch that?"

"It would be less conspicuous, and not draw us into the news for tonight. Let's do the wipe down and then take that car."

"I'll drive you back, you get out and get the keys or wire it. I'll ditch this cruiser over by that pile of coconuts. I'll do a complete wipe-down. Where's your black light? In your case?"

"Here. Take the alcohol pads, rag, and gloves." Oren also held his silenced revolver up and asked Jed if he wanted to take it. "If the dump gets spotted, you can handle yourself. Don't get into the unexpected."

"No, you take it, might need it to break a window." Jed pulled over. He cranked the steering wheel, just barely making the complete U-turn. He dropped Oren off at their new ride. At the approach, Oren quietly opened the door. Silently disappearing into the darkness. Jed reversed to the pile of coconut rinds. The SUV would sit abandoned. The movement ceased when he felt the rinds. In the stillness a faint crunch was heard.

"Hello?" a voice called out from the house.

Oren, approaching the new getaway car, saw that the back driver's door had been left unlocked. A backseat backpack lay unzipped. Inspecting it found a metallic glint that suggested a key fob. He paused in the darkness. A car drove past. He listened for intruders. Oren saw a figure running towards him. His partner was finished. He opened the door, entered, and raised his hand to cover the interior dome light. Its light muted from pouring out and flooding the interior with incriminating light. Oren took no time. He started the car.

"Who's here? Maxine. Did your car just start?" The house light turned on.

Oren took no time and quickly reversed. He sped over to Jed before Maxine was out in her yard. A girl unmistakably owned this car. The smell: a scent-bomb of her cinnamon air freshener, ashtray remnants, and overripe fruit. The look: hibiscus seat covers, garbage everywhere but not in the garbage pail and a broken muffler. Oren lowered the window. He gasped for fresh evening air and zoomed over to his partner.

"Who the hell stole my car?" Maxine stood outside watching her baby stolen in the night.

Jed completed the detailing and wiped the keys. He left them on the driver's seat. With a hip check to the door, he was free to join Oren. A short trip to their safe house. Their helicopter pickup in a few hours.

"Nice choice. Cinnamon."

"Shut up."

"I wonder how the police handled the Audi."

Oren checked his watch, "it should be going off soon."

They drove away, undetected. They had one stop to fuel up then relax. They'd share a few rum punches until their scheduled pick up. They had another job lined up, back over international waters.

## 2.

Derk rode with Jones to collect his truck. He followed the towing rig to finish collecting the Audi. He parked off to the side. Jones hooked up the chain. He switched the lever to hoist. He watched the Audi's charred body start to slide.

Derk approached. "Why is that light blinking?"

"On my truck?"

"No, the blue one on the... its getting faster." Derk's voice became alarmed. "It's going to blow! Jo—!"

The force scattered both men like autumn leaves. A fire started. Jones slowly rose to his knee. His jaw hung open. Watching his truck burn.

"Can you walk?" Derk's voice didn't register. "C'mon in case there are more explosions."

"My truck..."

"I know. At least you're still here. We had someone watching over us."

Jones crumpled in Derk's passenger seat. Tears fell. Derk drove south to his house. He promptly reported the fire. Then put a supportive hand on his friend's shoulder. We'll get things straight in the morning. You're staying at my place tonight."

"Everything was in my truck. Why?"

"This may be hard to hear, but…" Derk paused for Jones to look. "At least you'll get a new truck. That one was getting ripe."

"I always wanted a sky blue one. Black gets too hot." Jones leaned back, pondering the next stressful chapter in his life.

## 3.

Chandler turned into the station, "Piper you better get your shoulder and head checked out before you rest tonight. How stiff is it now?"

"I was working it in the back seat here. My girl friends back home watch this YouTube channel that shows yoga poses. Don't laugh when you hear this but one stretch that is working is called a Child's Pose. It might help relieve it tonight after a shot of rum."

Rakeef glanced over to Chandler. He checked to see if it was appropriate to crack a joke. Chandler's face was solemn, obviously with something on his mind.

"Hopefully that Child's pose might do the trick. You're not shaken up too much from those guys roughening you up?"

"No Rakeef, they wouldn't have shot me, they said their contract was completed and they didn't have a silenced weapon. They were looking to escape undetected as fast as they could to get out of there. Hey, watch the bumps Chand. You know this driveway is full of potholes."

"Sorry. I want to get you dropped off so I can get back out there with Rakeef and find Unit 8."

They came to a short halt. Rakeef jumped out and ran into the detachment. He returned after "Piper gingerly ebbed out of the backseat. Fingered a half salute to Chandler, she looked at Rakeef. He had brought out a wheelchair. Piper smirked and stalked into the detachment. She turned back to Rakeef, "I'm not a cripple!"

Rakeef looked at Chandler, peering at the situation. He motioned for Rakeef to leave the wheelchair and get into the SUV. Chandler rolled down the window.

"Thomas, leave it and get in here! I want to go check out the location of Unit 8 before the other officers mess it up." Rakeef jumped into the seat, "buckle up! And get your body cam ready for some footage, this may be a rough investigation." They were ready. Even for the unexpected. Their route would eventually take them on a long chase. Their location was on one side of the Island. Unit 8 on the other. The night wasn't over. A botched rescue attempt, and a runover body would keep them busy for a few hours.


"Piper!" Jarvis gasped as she stumbled into the waiting area near the reception desk. Gladys ended her phone call and went to the hall, calling for Alessio's assistance.

"Jar, I'm fine. I just needed to rest a little. The lights are giving me a slight headache."

"You might have a concussion! Chand said you were hit on the head. Lemme have a look…" Jarvis placed his soft hand to the back of her head. He checked her scalp for swelling with a pen light.

"Jar, you're wearing that cologne—deep reef. Feeling anything back there? What do you say we take a little trip to the hospital…together."

"Piper!" He snapped in a furious whisper, "keep it down; nobody knows we're seeing each other, right? Isn't that what you said last week at the harbour front?

"Jarvis, is Piper, okay? Will she need an ice pack or a shot of rum...?" Alessio jeered. He arrived just in time.

"I'm heading to the *Gap*. I'm on till eleven tonight. You should take her to the hospital if you're not too busy. Heard there were four fake liquor permits that were confiscated this afternoon. That alcohol will get sold somehow."

"Jarvis, we should go. My head is fine, but the lights here are terrible. The flickering is getting to me. You should drive though, just to be sure." She saw that Alessio was checking his pocket for his keys then realized that they were on his desk. As he retreated to his office, Piper leaned into Jarvis and silently gave him a quick peck on his cheek.

"You two aren't getting any younger;" Gladys announced with a wink as Piper sank back in her chair. Jarvis stood in shock that their secret was out, then left the room. Piper stood and smiled to Gladys that she didn't mind her knowing. Gladys placed her coffee cup down as the desk phone rang. She shot a wink over to Piper's bashful grin. Resuming her composure she answered a domestic assault call.

Piper met up with Jarvis and took a uniform coat off the hook.

"You cold?"

"A little, but these jackets are padded, and will help if any drunk tourists bump into me."

"Good call, you sure you are up to it?"

"You betcha!"

# 4.

Rakeef stared through the front windshield when he decided to ask Chandler the questions on his mind. "What is happening here, Chand? I didn't think we would be having such a mess from overseas European assassins coming to our Island. Have you ever seen this happen before?"

"It is highly unusual, and for the seven years I've been working as a detective, I've never seen this kind of destruction."

"Is this going to be the new trend? Terrorism?"

"I certainly hope not. And we will be working hard to get whoever these guys are. I don't want them on our soil or even flying overhead from now on." Chandler reached for the scanner. "Gladys? Where was the road you said the SUV was located?"

Jones reached into the glove box. He removed a pad, fishing around for a pen. He found one that wasn't leaking from the sun's heat, baking it for months.

"We're on H2, approaching the Wildlife Reserve marker. By the Argo products place? By the Cricket club? No, that's south on H6. We're more north. Thanks, Gladys. We'll call in what we find." Chandler looked over at Rakeef, who was drawing out getaway lanes and thinking of the quick routes to the Island's quieter areas. "You've got a tourist map drawn there Rakeef. You think you know where they could be?"

Out of the corner of Chandler's eye, he saw a little black car. It had no lights on. It exited the intersection in front of them much more expediently than what was safe. Chandler slammed on the breaks and reached for the lightbar to signal that a traffic violation had occurred.

"What is it, Chand?" Rakeef looked up.

"That car looks suspicious. Almost like the car is stolen."

The car zoomed past them. The driver stared straight. Chandler knew that he was not a local man. "Hold on, Rakeef!" He swerved the SUV taking off after the car. Rakeef reached for the receiver. He dropped it. Chandler took his eye off the road. Looking down at where the receiver went. Checking if it was under his pedal. At that second, a gunshot sent a bullet toward their windshield. Splintering Rakeef's half of their view.

"That was a gun shot. I thought it was a rock that hit us." Rakeef ducked. *They're shooting at unarmed cops!* He watched through the cracks. Listening if there was any other threat. He opened the window as Chandler pulled over for a moment. He was still looking to get the radio receiver. Rakeef lifted the body cam to collect the getaway. The car was clearly out of range. With the receiver now in hand, Chandler resumed their pursuit. "Gladys! We are under fire, a little black car with no headlights went speeding by Thomas and me, and now we are travelling northbound on H2 looking for this car. They shot at us and splintered the windshield. The bullet didn't pass through; it ricocheted off the windshield somehow."

"Chand!" Rakeef shouted, "Isn't that them? In that car?"

Chandler looked up and saw that the car faced toward them. Another shot went off. A front tire blew, causing the SUV to dip and swerve to the ditch.

Both officers heard static with a faint sound of shouting from across the radio. A local in a yellow roadster pulled out of the adjacent lane. He stopped by the SUV. Chandler looked through the windshield. The black car headed north again and out of sight.

"Freeze! Step away from our vehicle! Stand down!" Rakeef was motioning to the man.

"I got no gun man! I want to know if you two are all right?" The man had his hands up and was backing away.

Chandler opened the door and told Rakeef to relax. He stepped out of the vehicle and looked at the man who offered help. "I know this is a big ask, can we borrow your vehicle? I can't promise that it will be in the same condition in a few hours, but we need a fast car to catch these guys! They are our prime suspects."

Without hesitation, he tossed the keys to Chandler. "I'll stay by your unit here, and wait until they pick it up, officer..."

"Nelson. Detective Chandler Nelson. Thanks a lot, sir. Rakeef, do you have your cell? Call it in."

"Sorry about jumping all over you, we had no idea that you weren't part of their team, out to flank us." Rakeef quickly grabbed the first aid kit from the SUV. They entered the roadster and remotely locked the police unit.

"It's fine officers. I saw you were in a chase."

Chandler started the roadster. He let a rev pierce the evening silence.

"I did the only logical thing I could. Since I'm retired, you need it more than I do. I have another one in better condition." The man seemed calm and smiled at them. "Go catch those bastards!"

Chandler gave the man a nod. He took off down the highway, slightly spinning the rear tires. Where the perpetrators fled was their new objective.

# Chapter 17

# *HECTOR'S HEART*

## 1.

"Hello. This is Hector Gubbs. I called in earlier that a man at the pier has been up to some trouble on the Island. Yes, ma'am his boat is in the harbor." Hector glanced through the little plate glass window to see if Captain had returned. "He's approaching. My heart can't take this!"

"Did you want to speak with an officer, or do you feel that you're in danger?" Gladys calmly inquired but rose from her desk chair as her eye fixated on troubled youth, back in the waiting area with what looked to be a school principal designate. She placed her hand around the phone mouthpiece, channelling her voice over the waiting area chatter. "Sir, are you in danger?"

"I know this man, and he seems to me like a dangerous bloke. I think it might be a clever idea for you to send an officer because it looks like this man might be a little bit brash; he usually has a fishing knife tucked in his khakis."

"I'm going to try and send a couple of officers to you, they just stepped out around the *Gap* to break up some rowdy tourists, but they should be right over. Please be careful, always be careful."

"Should I go out to greet him if he asks for fuel?" Hector whispered, crouching beneath the little window. He tried to remain hidden in the rising moon's evening light.

"Sir, I would highly advise you that that is very dangerous, and you should not do that at all—can you hold a moment?" She put the receiver on her desk. Dramatically stomping over to the youth inches from his face. "Excuse me young man but around here we do not tolerate any foul language. I know you have some good language in there somewhere, so think hard about where you put those words and use them. Otherwise, child, I'll call in the guard and you'll be in a jail cell faster than you can apologize." She returned to her seat and went back to the call, "In fact, why don't you just sit tight, and we will send a couple of officers over to you. Please do not attempt anything or offer him fuel, if you feel that you are threatened at all or you feel that you are in danger."

"Okay thank you. Can I hang up now? Thank you ma'am." Hector quietly placed the phone back on the wall socket and froze. In glancing again through the window, he saw Captain was opening the gate and lowering the gangplank. Hoping to remain hidden, Hector quickly left the place and waited behind a nearby palm tree. He watched, relieved no one noticed him as he made his escape.

Captain was thick with tasks and moved cautiously. He stepped onto the dock heading towards the potable water valve. With deliberate steps, he made his way to the fuel hoses, handling them with ease. Pulling the coiled fuel hose towards the gangplank where the fue doors awaited, he worked efficiently to connect it. He maintained a nonchalant demeanor to avoid arousing suspicion, even though hundreds of gallons of premixed petrol were being siphoned off for a smooth getaway. He began looking around casually and listened to see if any dock workers were still on their shifts. At this time in the night, workers were rare—the sun had set an hour ago. Glancing around in the moonlit darkness, he dialed his cell phone, pretending to be engrossed in a business call to maintain his cover. He was keenly aware of the need to appear legitimate, especially with limited time.

Captain turned to the cruise ship on the sea. Hector's heart was beating heavy. Seizing the opportunity to reach up with his right hand he firmly clamped the fuel tank shut. He removed the key and held it. Watching from a distance as Captain switched on his cell phone light when he felt the flow stop. *Maybe he thought the hose might have kinked or slipped off the dock.*

Starting his retreat, Hector left his spot near the hut. Captain's phone faintly illuminated the pier and stopped directly at the tank. "What the hell? Where's the key?" He looked towards the palm tree near the hut and paused. *The fronds moved without a breeze.* Squinting through the dim moonlight towards the shore, he called out, "Hector?!" but failed to notice as Hector remained hidden. Frozen and watching with fright. His heart about to explode.

Hector realized that his angina pectoris condition must have risen from its dormancy. As Captain moved his gaze, Hector clutched his chest in pain—still with silence. *Oh no. Father I'm not ready.* His heart sent searing pain through his chest. The agony made him stumbled briefly.

He rose to a knee just enough to observe Captain's moves. If he were lucky enough to speak with the police when they came, he would have a detailed report of the fuel theft. Hopefully alive to report any attack Captain would strike, would be a bonus. Placing his wrinkled hand up to his chest Hector drew deep, slow breaths. He released them silently, trying to suppress his racing heart.

As Captain walked to the hut, Hector stared. *He has his gun tucked in his slacks. Why didn't I warn the police he carries guns.* Captain moved silently then shut out the cell phone light. The low battery warning notified when Hector intruded an hour before. Placing it back in his pocket he inspected the pump.

Hector might make it through the night to catch fish after tomorrow's sunrise. With an unwavering attitude to stop Captain's evilness, he grabbed the shovel from behind the palm tree that he had placed there earlier that day. Gripping the handle like a sword, waiting, and trying to calm his heartbeat. He watched like a docile animal trembling before its hunter in silence for Captain to go inside the hut entirely. His pulse was thrashing in his chest. Rhythmic flicks that he could feel in his cataract-filled eyes. He tried to focus. Beads of sweat were beginning to drip. They stung as he waited. *Go in. Go in!*

Captain gripped the hut's hand carved handle and swung it open. He listened. He watched. The dim antique lamp didn't shine much, and he needed the key. Scanning the shelves for any clue. His gaze disappearing into the shadow of the fishing net crates. No key, only mounting frustration. He snapped back and watched if Hector was approaching. His hand brushing against his concealed gun for reassurance. In the hut, there were shark hooks he could use to kill Hector. He pictured the others he killed. He figured he'd make it look like a fishing accident. *Gun or hook? Either method would suffice.* Captain's rage could gut Hector like a fish if he did anything to surprise him. Seeing no movement, he returned to his mission.

Hector had a racing heart rate before—once in high waves over a treacherous coral reef— nothing since had made his heart thump this unbearable. He slowly began to turn his head. Thoughts of getting caught or passing out from his heart haunted him. He knew he would only have a few seconds. Hector listened for the steel door to lightly latch shut. He carefully shuffled his bare feet across the dock. The shovel in his hand. Sweat dripping from his brow. He slowly, with purpose, expertly placed the shovel. Undetected he worked and succeeded; both handles were secured. He waited for a split-second, scanning the shovel to see if it was level, and then retreated. Hector took giant silent steps back to the beach. Adrenaline activating his old body, he took off as fast as he could. His heart raced to pound even louder in his chest. Hector ran for his life. He scaled the embankment, making it to the edge of the road. Still undetected but feeling immeasurable pressure. He wanted to cry out but winced. Hector grabbed his chest one last time, He awkwardly collapsed with his body lying at the roadside.

# Chapter 18

# *SNACKS AND ALCOHOL*

## 1.

"How's your head Piper?" Jarvis asked as he turned on to the St. Lawrence Gap Lane.

"Pain is gone. Gladys gave me some tablets. There seems to be a break just up by that blue car. We can park over there.

"We're looking for *The Honest Gambler* and the *Scotchman's Traditional Irish Pub*, to start with."

Fake permits were not the only problems these bars had. First, back alley sales. Offshore accounts in the Caymans, second. Third, the connections to the grand theft of autos ring.

"What do you know of BB's Steakhouse? Is that one on your list?"

"Yes, that's one of them."

"And there's the Honest Gambler over there." Two crazy bars with the heftiest violations. Ripe for fines.

They exited the SUV. A horde of obnoxious drunken bridesmaids singing White Wedding horribly loud and off-key echoed everywhere. Barely dressed tourists to the left of them, others making out and awkwardly trying to learn dance moves from a TikToc video by the water. Both Piper and Jarvis navigated to the first suspected bar. They talked to the bar owner. He was distracted over the pumped-up volume of their hired DJ. He had the club jumping. Spinning a live stream to the street nightclub scene. Piper's headache returned promptly. An underaged girl in a thong and a spaghetti-strap bikini leaned up against Jarvis's shoulder. She began to sway. She looked at him and puckered her lips like a supermodel posing for the camera.

"Miss, you need some water, a lime to suck on and a taxi. Piper, hail a taxi or see if there is some bouncer who can take this girl. She's about to pass out."

"Rodney, I like your beard." she said, then started regurgitating as Piper twisted her body. She splattered the contents of her last three hours of snacks and alcohol. The nearby palm tree planter was chunky. Piper tried to keep her composure and carry on the questioning.

"Pina Coladas and Strawberry Daiquiris were on her menu this evening." Jarvis softened, "no doubt from the three-for-one happy hour special."

The bar owner grabbed hold of the ice bucket and tossed cubes and water over her deposit.

"Here's a bouncer that can get her to a taxi. Becky!"

"Woah, did she just throw up?"

"Get her out of here."

Jarvis's cell phone began to vibrate. Gladys was calling. He answered the call. "Hello, Gladys…What? Over at the fuel docks? Right now? Alright, we're on it."

"The owner handed me an envelope of fake bills and his card. I don't think there is anything we can do tonight. What did Gladys want?"

"There is a frightened dock worker that says the dark colored yacht, that Chandler has been looking for has resurfaced and the captain is in port to fuel up and run. The worker might try and stop him, so we must go."

The furious Captain fumbled in the fuel hut for twenty minutes. Each bump and scrape made him worse. Useless gear scattered around the floor would grab at his feet. The hut's handles wouldn't budge. Built tough in the August of 80 after Hurricane Allen. Hector's cheaply maintained structure was solid. Cedar hewn timber beams from Miami were strong enough to withstand hurricane-force winds. Captain tried the knob and peered through the slit between both doors. He saw the tool handle or pipe that him locked inside. He exploded in rage. "Hector?! When I get out of here, you are a deadman! You hear me!" Captain reached for his gun and, as he brought it around to shoot through the slit, he banged his hand on the side of the pump. He nearly broke his fingers, dropping the weapon. He tried to find it in the dark. It was lost. Frustration piqued and Captain's mind snapped. Forceful kicking was his prime option. The hut withstood his siege like a parent with a frenzied toddler.

Hector slowly rose to his feet, feeling light-headed and dizzy. He heard Captain trying to escape. He slowly rose and paused for a moment. *I gotta hurry.* Regaining his posture, he walked along the roadway back to the dock house. Bursting through the door to the power circuit panel. He opened the fuse box. Hector watched the dim light in the fuel hut go out as he flicked off breakers four and five. He heard the roar of Captain screaming his name. Hector quickly retreated. He feared another heart attack. His eyes locked to the tool wedged through the handle. A set of lights appeared far down the road. Hector climbed again. Moving branches and coconut husks scraping against his shins and bloodied feet. No current pain was worse than if Captain escaped. Hector reached the lane. He bowed his head. Heart spasming. Hector caught his breath.

Deciding to sit by the road's edge, he watched the headlights come closer. *That's them.* Familiar Police SUV headlights nearing the harbour parking lane. He stood up. Waving his arms in the air; his watch band twinkling.

Jarvis turned onto the lane and switched on the oscillating lightbar. Piper saw a man rise to his feet and wave his arms for them to pull over in the flicker of the lights.

Jarvis rolled down his window. "Mr. Gubbs? Are you all right?"

"Thank you for coming. I locked him in the fuel hut, and he has a gun. He kills people. I put a shovel shaft through the handle about thirty minutes ago, and he was kicking it wildly to break free. Father help us. Please. My heart is feeling tired, can I wait in the backseat?"

"What happened to your face? Your feet? Sir, I assure you that we will handle this quickly. I'm sorry. If you wait-" Jarvis stopped mid-sentence looking at Piper. "That was a gunshot, wasn't it?"

"Mr. Gubbs, please make a quick decision. It is getting dangerous out here. Piper, did you bring the pepper spray bag?"

"In my hand. I have the cuffs and the old taser is charged up in case he does get out. If this guy is lethal, I'll suffer the risk of using the taser to protect ourselves. I don't care if it is banned. I'll pay the fine from my paycheque or they can send me back to Australia."

"Alright, let's go. Mr. Gubbs stay here if you want. Do not come down from the lane for any circumstances. Piper, lock the SUV."

Jarvis listened for more gunshots but only heard banging. Carefully with a penlight, he could scale down the embankment, occasionally slipping on coconut husks till he reached the bottom. He shone the light towards Piper and moved his hand in front of the lens to provide a code between the two officers that the route was slippery. Once both were together they began their forward investigative assault on taking in the trapped shooter.

## 2.

Captain's anger and force in kicking the door panels' gap could not bust the shaft free. Each time he would kick, beams of light would illuminate the hut for a brief second, enough for him to see the shovel shaft shake but not break away or fall through. The banging continued for a few more tries; then, he tried the gun again in his rage.

"Sir, this is the police. I will ask you to cease your attempts to escape and allow us to place you in protective custody and transport you to the detachment for questioning. Do we have your cooperation?"

The banging stopped.

"Sir, I will ask you again. Do we have your cooperation? We do not want to use force."

Captain listened to the direction of her voice and scoured around the hut to find an area to have a clear shot. Above, there was a small broken window from a tropical storm several years ago. Palm fronds were above the opening. Captain knew he had few options, and he had five bullets left. Two to break the shaft, two for the police officer and her partner. One bullet for Hector, if he didn't die from the fear. He aimed directly at the gap in the door and squeezed the trigger.

"Move back!" Jarvis grabbed Piper, retreating to a safe distance. Realizing that the shot was not for him, Jarvis began to question the situation.

"I can throw this spray canister to try and choke him out."

"That is a pretty small shot. That open window up there?" He flashed his penlight to the roof of the hut.

"Easy. Cover me in case he gets free." Piper began to move towards her target, spray canister in hand. She froze when another shot went off. Then continued the pursuit to get into position. Just as Jarvis aimed the penlight to the window, Captain fired a third shot that splintered a chunk of the shovel shaft as Piper tossed the squealing canister through the window. Yellowed smoke began to seep through the rickety walls. Captain reeled in, gasping for clean air while trying to kick the shaft hard enough to release its grasp. As his eyes began to tear up, he collapsed and put his shirt over his face. Jarvis removed the shovel and flung open the doors. The yellow fog was everywhere, but he navigated with his penlight and found his target. Taking the cuffs in his hand, he kicked the gun away from Captain and cuffed his left arm. Seconds later, Captain was fully restrained and hauled away to the clean open air.

"Sir, since you were firing a weapon from inside a fueling station, which is highly dangerous, you will be detained and questioned at our detachment. Do you understand? Some of your charges might include, resisting arrest, and endangering the life of a police officer, to name a few."

"I retrieved his gun," Piper beamed. "C'mon mister, let's go."

Captain first moved along the docks to the fisherman's gravel path and small boat launch, then climbed the embankment and was placed in the back of the SUV. Hector was nowhere in sight, and as Piper grabbed the radio to call in the capture, she realized that the man in the picture from the evidence box left on Chandler's hood earlier that day was the man they had sitting in the backseat. "Gladys. Call Chandler and Rakeef. Yes. Tell them, we got him. We got the Captain!"

# Chapter 19

# *THE CHASE*

## 1.

Couples of drunk tourists were walking haphazardly along the road's narrow shoulder as the getaway car quickly approached. Headlights began to illuminate the walking tourists as they tried to shoot selfies and drunkenly dance to the music that was still ringing in their ears. They were not aware of the approaching bright lights or heard the engine of the little black car zoom around a tight bend and slam right into one of the drunkards. The body was launched lifelessly through the air and landed in a crippled state as three girls had broken their selfie pose and let out a blood-curdling scream. Oren had hardly blinked an eye at this setback and had wished that the distraction would buy them some time. The engine hummed as he recovered the lost acceleration just as Chandler and Rakeef rounded the corner.

"Hey, Chand, there are his lights!" Rakeef glanced a second time, "what is that though, ah you've got to be joking, damn tourists." he pained to see through the windshield.

"No, look! I think someone's been hit. Rakeef I'm going to let you out and call for an ambulance with your cell. You've still got it right? Call Gladys and have all units that are available get on this chase. We've got to stop these guys before they take out any more people."

"You sure you want to chase them alone?"

"We've got so much going on in this investigation that I can't lose any time. If these tourists are drunk, hopefully, the accident will be just bumps and bruises. Take the first aid kit, just take the whole bag. Check their head and see if you can find any person who is willing to be a witness. Not that I wish anyone to die, but if the cards fall right, it will be vehicular manslaughter and grand theft auto, two counts!" Chandler stopped the roadster, and Rakeef had just barely put his foot on the ground before the engine roared. He floored the pedal and took off again in the only direction that the assassins could have gone.

Racing up the hill, wiping the sweat from his eyes, Chandler strained to see if there were potholes and debris on the road scattered by the getaway car. He could barely see the taillights in the distance but was glad that the suspects were still in pursuit and the road was all theirs. Most locals and tourists were either still out partying or off the road at their houses. Chandler rounded the next corner and had made up a little bit of time. The power of this yellow roadster, he thought, was an excellent aid to catch criminals. For a split second, he imagined the police service having a couple of these for the tight turning on these old roads. As the warm smell of a Bajan fish fry wafted through the air, Chandler could make out the taillights of Oren's stolen car just ahead. They were brighter. He was about six car lengths away. Further seeing in the distance, the lights of the cement factory. *Nice spot for an escape. Factory workers are all gone.* He knew where they would be hiding. The factory had lots of open space for a large drone or helicopter to whisk them out to safety. As Chandler approached the O'Neal Highway roundabout in Church Hill, he saw that the getaway car's passenger had hung outside the open window and heard his handgun release a shot, penetrating the roadster's grill. Steam began to hiss as Chandler was able to make the roundabout and pass St. Lucy's Parish.

## 2.

Farther westbound down the highway, Jed resumed his seated position and reloaded his magazine. "These cops are pissing me off. I missed a headshot, but at least he won't be able to get far. He started hissing right after the shot, so we'll have no problems. How much longer? Any word from the chopper?"

"Just a little bit farther. I radioed in the pickup when we shot their police unit, so the chopper should be already there in the quarry. I hope this little goat of a car can handle the loose gravel and off-roading." Oren gripped the steering wheel tighter with his leather gloves and scanned the soccer field to the right. "There's the sports field. It's just up this road." Oren looked back to see if the officer was still tailing them. They were in the clear for now. The black getaway car drove down the wrong way on the Arawak Cement Company Road. Turned quietly into the back alley connected to Maycocks Road. Thinking about the next steps, Oren turned the car off and waited in the dark, reaching down to his leg pocket, quickly checking his phone to confirm the pickup's arrival time. He flipped to the messaging app and saw the text. "We're just over twenty minutes till pick up."

"We're dropping the car here?" With the window still down, Jed positioned his pistol at the highway, waiting for the target. As Oren pulled the key out of the ignition, his partner opened the door to begin to wait outside, still scanning the highway. Seeing nothing, he habitually took to the task of wiping off the fingerprints all over the car. He wiped for a solid minute, then gave up, as they would be off Barbados before the police would be able to tow the vehicle. "Good, we got time. Want to wait here?" he said, raising his pistol, "and stop whoever is following us in that yellow car, or head over to the landing strip? That man sure wants this bullet." His eyes not losing the highway, gun comfortably in his hand.

Oren opened the door and tossed the key into the brush. He stood and grabbed the black bag from the backseat before closing the door and answered, "Let's move."

With the roadster hissing and Chandler coaxing the car to make it go just a little farther, he rocked the acceleration but noticed that all the gauges were flashing at the red line. In the distance, still on route, was the cement factory; he turned towards the sports soccer field as the car finally inched its last and rolled quietly as the engine died. Derk got out and looked towards the sky, sighed, and contemplated which location should help start the pursuit on foot. He hadn't had to chase after any of his suspects for a long while. Running on the beach would be a breeze, but on foot in pursuit is a different scene. *I'm so tired.* Closing the car door and giving his neck a short stretch, his gaze focused on the two figures walking along the back alley about two hundred feet away from him. Smiling in the darkness of the night, looking to the sky, he whispered, "Father, help me, and keep me safe. May my skills be sharp, the wind be at my back, my feet steady and give me some smart thinking." He made sure his vest was strapped on tight, then began a light jog towards the men.

## 3.

Rakeef was neck-deep with tourist trouble. Drunk, dehydrated, overheated, whiny, noisy, and all getting in the way of the crime scene.

"You've got to help him, mister. Please help, help him," her voice whiny and high-pitched as she ran off to vomit by a sugar cane field. The tourists were college-aged with tan lines, thong bikini briefs wedged up their cracks, and mesh shirts barely hiding their overripe sunburns. Everyone was upset, including Rakeef, as he tried to call Gladys.

"Gladys, oh my, what a night. Chand is currently in a yellow open-topped sports car roadster chasing after two guys who shot at us and wrecked the police unit. That noise? Yeah, I'm in what looks to be the field just north of Gilkes Road. The assailants were driving a little black getaway car and struck a pedestrian who was drunk and walking with a group along the C highway. Please send an ambulance out to pick the whole group up. There are five of them in total, including the guy on the road who was hit. He is fine, but his face is torn up a bit from the landing. He's still got all his parts, eyes, ears, but he might need a new lip, his face jewelry sliced his lip in half. He has nice teeth though." Rakeef looked at the group and saw them huddling together and figured he should treat them for shock. "Oh, Gladys! Another thing. Chand told me to let you know that these idiots driving the black car are not locals, but he thinks they are hired assassins. He's chasing them now, so you should send all units that are available to the north end of the Island around St. Lucy's Parish or to the cement plant. Thanks, Gladys, I'll wait here with these tourists but if Piper or Jarvis come, I'll make my way to the roundabout and meet them." He looked over as a group member found an accessible area of grass by the road to deposit his stomach contents. "They are lighting up their social media with pictures and videos. Thanks Gladys." Rakeef ended the call and then reached for the shock blankets. Three of them were already asleep like school children coming home from a day in the sun, the others quiet and respectful. He approached the one looking after the guy on the ground.

"His lip is pretty bad; do you have any butterfly bandages in your Medi bag? Tape even?" She looked at Rakeef, "I'm on spring break with my roommates and their boyfriends in the best tourist vacation spot, and I still can't get away from what I'm learning in school. I'm in agricultural sciences, but I want to be a veterinarian." She held out her hand and received the bandages from him. "Blair, this may hurt a bit and when we get you to the hospital, they are going to have to stitch your lip closed. I have your lip ring though." She held it up so he could see it, the flesh of his lip still wrapped around the ring with a bloody smiley face stopper in her grip. Rakeef gave her an evidence bag and asked her, "Did you see what happened clearly? I understand that you are on vacation, but you seem to be the most responsible one of your friends here, and I would like it, if it is okay, to ask you to provide a statement, or be a witness for our investigation."

"Sure, I got a good look at the guy that was driving. He looked European, white skin, but that was about it. Didn't make out the hair colour, or any distinguishing facial features. Typical dark eyes."

"That's great." Jones started writing some notes as he heard the ambulance siren off in the distance. "Try and remember everything as it happened. The ambulance will be here soon, and all of you will go to the hospital to get checked out."

## 4.

Chandler had heard the ambulance rush by the roundabout and then faded into the southern winds but heard the distant murmur of a helicopter echoing through the evening air. He had to act fast and intelligent. These were two trained killers against an Island police detective. He had managed to cut across the edge of the soccer field by the basketball court without being detected as he saw the two men disappear into the brush outskirts of the cement factory land. Figuring that the helicopter was to pick them up, he moved quickly along the back alley road and then turned left on the northern alley gravel road. Enough auxiliary lights illuminated the grounds, and these two guys would have to make a run for it when the helicopter landed. He knew that it would be an all-out gunfight in a matter of minutes if he wasn't careful. Staying motionless and holding his breath, he waited for a brief minute listening for any sign of the assailants. His eyes were scanning the treeline and looking at the quarry excavation pit, gravel mounds, and factory buildings. Nothing seemed out of the ordinary until he saw a shadow. He found them. He moved towards the trees and almost missed hearing the stealth helicopter fly overhead.

The pilot began the descent on an open mixed field of overgrown grass, making the first attempt at landing but had to rise again attempting another spot with less uneven terrain and large rocks. Jed waved to the pilot as he landed the aircraft in whisper mode. Chandler was amazed that these helicopters existed. The expense probably miniscule for the funds that flowed like a waterfall in the crime world. The engine stayed on, and Chandler had to move fast. He looked around and found a rock the size of a large lemon and figured if he could hit the rudder blades in the tail, or something mechanical it might slow their escape. Chandler hesitated. *What am I thinking? There's no way it'll work.* He moved out towards the helicopter's back as he saw a police unit's lights reflecting in the cement factory buildings' windows. Jed began to move. *No gun?* Chandler ran towards the helicopter too, crouching and watching for the fugitives' reaction if the perpetrators saw him.

He rotated his arm back and threw the rock towards the rudder's blades. Nothing stopped or gave away his position. He had missed. Jed hoisted himself on board, as Chandler took one chance to grab for his legs. The police in the area were many and began running with torchlights and batons drawn. The second fugitive made a run towards the encouraging hand of his partner as Chandler crouched in the grass. With calm stillness, Chandler switched on his body cam and aimed to catch one of them in their escape.

As Oren sprinted, three officers closed in on him, while the helicopter's skids lifted off the ground. Chandler abandoned his cover, rising from his knee, poised to apprehend in any direction. Seeing the police cornering his partner, Jed commanded the pilot to ascend. Oren spotted the dangling rope just as the helicopter hovered a few feet above. He grabbed hold and began scaling it, but Chandler lunged and struck him. With minutes dwindling for his escape, Oren swiftly tripped Chandler with a jujitsu takedown. As the rope slid beside him, he seized it, securing a foothold and lay on his back, ready for liftoff. Frantically searching, Chandler spotted Oren on the ground, not in the helicopter. Oren grinned as he felt the loop around his foot lift him to freedom. In haste, Chandler drew his knife, slicing at the rope binding Oren. He weakened it enough that Oren looked down at the fraying fibers, faced with the choice to hold on or let go.

## 5.

"On your stomach, turn face down! Hands outstretched. You know the drill!"

With a curt grin, Chandler leaned towards his face and whispered, "You're under arrest, and I'll be using that rope if you don't mind." Oren's eyes stared out across the grassy horizon watching the helicopter's lights fade

in the distance. Watching it disappear into the star-filled
atmosphere, he continued plotting his escape from the
holding cell they would be taking him to. It would be
near textbook perfect, as he had vanished without a trace
several times before, and the Barbados police would have
to follow protocol with a tourist in apprehension. He had
a plan and hardly heard what Chandler was saying, "The
helicopter's gone, and you're in such a heap of trouble right
now. Let's go. On your feet." Chandler hoisted Oren to his
feet and marched him conveniently to the other officers
that had now joined him to help take this perpetrator
into custody. Walking towards the row of police SUVs
with lights illuminating the Arawak Cement Plant stacks,
Chandler acutely listened for the helicopter's distance. In
concluding that the other fugitive was gone, he placed the
man in custody into the back of the SUV. Oren's head
bowed, and he sat handcuffed in the backseat. An assassin
being arrested and escaping while in the Shandwick Trust
was usually as stress-free as ordering an ordinary cup of
coffee. He fumbled with his hands to press the mute
tracing button on his wrist tracker, and with the internal
GPS linkage, had started the location trace app on Jed's
phone, minutes away.

The helicopter Chandler thought was gone returned
to the eastern side of the Island. "Are you clear to fly over
them, so I can drop down and blow out the back window
of my partner's SUV? I'll use this rappelling rope and take
out the two accompanying vehicles too."

"We are on our approach," the pilot had said, cold
and heartless. "You may now open the door and ready
yourself for your drop." Jed reached for the handle and

released the door; a gust of warm Caribbean air filled the air-conditioned cabin. He hooked his carabiner to his harness, grabbed his silenced semi-automatic rifle, and leaned out over the landing supports. Taking steady aim with his night-scope, he placed his finger on the trigger.

# Chapter 20

# *RESCUE CHALLENGES*

## 1.

"You have some nerve, coming to our Island and plundering innocent tourists that just want to find some relaxation." Chandler glanced at the rear-view mirror, hoping to gain a detailed response. Oren failed to return eye contact. "Hey! Did you hear anything I said?!" Chandler rounded a corner, trying to think of some incriminating questions that might get information from his captive. Oren, cold and motionless, remained silent, enjoying the brief travel in air conditioning before the driving would change to erratic, with a cataclysmic finish. Chandler tried again, "we did a background check on the body found in the cane field." A brief pause: more silence. "Do you remember the bus crash? If you get matched against that accident and homicide, you are finished, and I don't care what European group you are part of—" stopping abruptly then, "Oh my dear Lord!" Chandler floored the gas and reached for the dispatch radio. He heard and saw the helicopter that was just over him minutes ago. It returned and was in relentless pursuit. Oren, feeling the increased horsepower, positioned his feet in the manner of bracing for a roll-over. His GPS tracker was vibrating that the tracking may not be as accurate due to the drive's high speed. Using his fingers, Oren calmly pushed the dual-function side button to end the distraction. He thoroughly enjoyed the panic that his driver was under, knowing that within a short while, his useless questioning would turn into pleads for his life.

## 2.

Next-generation stability control technology equipped the helicopter, so hovering turns of the uneven landscape or rising to tower over the occasional palm tree wouldn't make Jed's safari rough and uncomfortable. He squeezed the trigger and sent a bullet piercing through the air shattering the driver's side mirror of Chandler's SUV. He ejected the used casing and popped the next round into the chamber, fitting his eye to the sight and taking aim to fire through the driver's window. With his skill and sniper training, this execution would be a textbook maneuver, and Oren would be clear to extract. Without warning, the pilot told him, "It looks like there are a few more joining the parade. Hold your fire for a second. I've got to climb." Jed looked down at the two other Police SUVs that had joined Chandler in trying to get the perpetrator in custody into detainment at the station. Jed changed weapons and gripped an M201-Z riot gas gun illegally stolen from a few Israeli border guards in a botched arms seizure. Aiming to fire at the back of Chandler's SUV would cause the other two in pursuit to fail. Steadying his aim, letting the canister discharge, Jed watched the action unfold.

## 3.

"Who are the other units with me?!" Chandler's voice slightly squeaking from his adrenaline. "Can they be split up? This helicopter has a group of snipers or something on board, and they have already shot my side mirror. Gladys, call them to dissipate. I don't want them to get hurt. I'm at the—" Chandler heard the explosion and felt propulsion forward. Witnessing the horror behind him, he drove on a back-alley road into a residential district and parked under a galvanized tin roof. Reaching for the fire extinguisher, Detective Nelson quickly ran to the back of the SUV to extinguish the bubbling plastic bumper cover before it melted or spread the fire to hit any fuel lines. Working as fast as he could, he ran back to the driver's seat, threw the extinguisher over to the passenger foot cavity, reversed back out of the driveway to the main road and continued south to deliver his cargo. Chandler pained to see if any of his fellow officers were downed in the blast while keeping his vigilant, attentive surveillance on the whereabouts of the helicopter overhead. Looking briefly in the rear seat that his passenger was still there, he noticed Oren slightly smiling at him. "You like the show, do you. Just wait until I get you to the station. You are going to bleed, not only information but from all the crime you and your partner put us through. Smile now, as I'll be smiling later. You can count on it!"

## 4.

When the riot gun's shell exploded, the SUVs had just received the alerting message from Chandler, as Gladys had pushed the all-call button so all units could hear his distress. Realizing the team against them, he aimed and fired. Jed's expertly placed shot was destructive but unfortunately not lethal. As Chandler went to extinguish the fire, the other two SUVs could barely keep on scene. The first unit slammed into a palm tree, exploding both airbags from the collision. The driver, Nathan Wilson, was on a police exchange program from Aruba. Having no official driving training on Barbados' unique road system, he was not prepared for such defensive driving with such little training. The rear SUV suffered the most damage. The SUV driver was the rookie Tyson Mahonie, who joined the Barbados Police Force two months prior. He started as an intern, helping the cases with drug deals and weapons possession. He was tired of seeing his friends being caught up in gun violence and wanted to clean the neighbourhoods' streets needing restructuring. Here he was now, turned upside down, with the seat belt digging into his chest. Tyson realizing his left arm appeared broken, tried to reach for the ignition button to cut the engine, severely fighting the flooding rush of pain. He had already put the 4-way hazard flashers on before the crash, but now the task at hand for the young 22-year-old was to divert the possible explosion as he began to smell a fuel leak. Tyson began to weep after straining against the agony to reach the engine stop button. He closed his eyes as the sounds around him died out. To him, it sounded like being underwater after a scuba dive from a boat, gurgling, then a peaceful dead silence.

## 5.

Rakeef, who had helped the paramedics with the group of tourists that were now beginning to sober up, began to run north to the roundabout when the paramedic called out to him, "Where are you going, sir?"

"I have to meet up with my partner, who was chasing after the two motorists that hit the guy you have in the ambulance. I've called into the station to send a nearby unit to pick me up."

"We can give you a ride up front, in the passenger seat, as Bradley needs to be in the back checking on vitals and easing that man's emotional pain. I have to go up that way anyway, so you might as well hop in."

Rakeef turned and jogged back to the ambulance. The usual coffee and fried foods around the office had put on the freshman-fifteen he heard about from his training days, and having no partners that liked jogging, he tried to sneak in some extra steps as the time allowed. Helping to get the tourists' remaining articles to them, Rakeef smiled at the veterinarian student, who the detective got to know as they were working on her tourist friend. When he rounded the rear corner by the taillight, his foot hit a stone out of the way and clear of the rear tires. He worried about Chandler as he sat in the passenger seat and neglected to hear the first words the driver said to him. "Sorry, I didn't catch that; I was thinking about my partner and how he is doing with these two perps."

"I said thank you for what you did to help those people. I don't get a lot of thank-yous from the people in crashes, and I can tell you have been through a lot. You look tired. Do you want some coconut water? My wife packs me these, saying that they are essential to a healthy lifestyle. I laugh and tell her to come for a ride-along and start drinking rum, as, for some of the people in the back who have good health, bad timing can take it all away in an instant."

"Thanks, I'll pass on the coconut water for now, but when you drop me off, I'll take it to have while I'm waiting." Rakeef smiled, then spoke warmly, "it has been a rough week. My partner and I think that we can finally solve multiple cases from the two guys we were chasing. They are not Bajan by any means. European assassins or hired killers. What made you want to be a paramedic?" Rakeef asked, trying to change the subject.

"It's in the family. My mother met my father from a drunk driving crash as he worked the scene. He's got icy-blue eyes and lighter skin with a charming accent—which was a huge turn-on—then they got married, had two kids. My sister hesitated, mind you and did not want to do the wet-work as she calls it: she's in education helping the 11-year-olds with their entrance exams. She loves it, saying education is the foundation of everything. She is so proud of Bajan literacy benchmarks, saying that everyone can read in Barbados, which is a wonderful achievement. We're at the roundabout, but I don't see your pickup; oh, wait, is it that black truck over there?"

"I think so; it might be the undercover private investigator's vehicle. Oops, I guess I shouldn't have told you that. Try and keep it on the down-low."

"No worries, my man. Here's the water. Good luck." Rakeef took the water and waved to the paramedic as it sped down the route to the Bayview Hospital Road. First shaking his beverage, then walking over to the undercover unit, he opened the coconut water, took a few swigs, and joined the new coach. The driver was fiddling with the radio. Rakeef asked, "Have you heard from anyone about a chase?"

"No way?! Don't tell me that you haven't heard anything?" Derk had said, placing the truck into all-wheel drive and took off towards the carnage. "We've got a helicopter which is chasing some SUV units that Chandler called were in a life and death situation. Keep working on the radio Jones," Derk rounded a corner. "It may be a long night."

"Hi, Jones. I didn't see you back there." Rakeef sipped his water.

It's been a hell of a night. My truck blew up from these guys' Audi from the bus crash! I'm still coming to terms, but Derk and I couldn't just sit at home with the full police force out here training to be in an action movie! I don't know how we are going to catch these guys!"

"Sorry to hear about your truck Jones. Chandler is the one who called it in? Is he still on the route? What happened?! We were on a chase, and now this little black car has turned into a helicopter chase?!" Rakeef activated the radio.

"I know it's a little crazy, but you don't have to bring out the boxed beer Rakeef. What is that? Coconut flavoured beer?"

"Just coconut water from the ambulance that dropped me off. It's good for victims in roadside shock, the paramedic told me. Some sort of brain function, that when you drink water or anything, it helps the brain reset so it can keep the person from going into shock."

"Yeah, it's called executive functioning; did you connect to dispatch?"

The all-call was broadcasting Chandler's voice just before the explosion.

"Did you just see that?" Derk remarked. Over there is where they are. That seemed like a bomb went off."

"Step on it Derk, Chandler may be in trouble!" Rakeef downed his water and tossed it behind his seat in the vehicle-sized garbage pail.

# Chapter 21

# *TUCKING THE DUPPY*

## 1.

When Derk, Jones, and Rakeef's truck arrived at the scene, they were unsure where to start. Onlookers snapped pictures while a unit was rammed into a palm tree. Mothers scolded their children to stay back, and nearby teens watched the action from their bikes.

Jones tried to calm the crowd with a quick speech about safety and preserving the crime scene. Meanwhile, Derk rushed to help Tyson out of the overturned wreckage. Tyson, visibly in shock, attempted to walk towards another unit where Officer Wilson stood with the rear truck door open.

Rakeef heard the helicopter, initially thinking it was south of their location. As its blades grew louder, it seemed like it might be attempting a flyover to wrap up the situation. Derk swiftly settled Tyson into the back seat, calling back to Jones that he would take Tyson to the hospital and report in. "Fire trucks might already be on their way," he added.

Jones also heard the helicopter and, after conferring with Rakeef, reiterated to the crowd that they should disperse, assuring them there was nothing more to see. As one child screamed and was led away by their mother, Rakeef spotted a man rappelling down from the helicopter directly over the last SUV.

"Jones, we're ready! Come on, hop in," Derk called out, motioning for Jones to join them. Rakeef thanked Jones for managing the crowd.

Nathan, clearly shaken, approached Rakeef. "I think twenty people are still trying to get home. What should we do?"

Rakeef waved to Derk as he drove south and turned to Nathan. "We're going to have a mountain of paperwork at the station after tonight. Let's not add to it. See that helicopter? I hope no one else gets hurt."

Jed had told the pilot that he would repel down and get a better look for Oren. He may have had the SUVs crossed and could have accidentally killed his business partner. Chandler was almost to the highway when the helicopter dipped for the repel maneuver.

"Keep an eye open. Oren will get a good grip then pull us out of there." He wanted no mistakes. Jed had performed hundreds of drops but few with motion. He leaned out and jumped off. He was lowered behind the SUV's smashed window and Oren's outstretched hands. He grabbed on the window frame as his carabiner snapped open.

"You ready?" he whispered to Oren, and they gripped hands.

The road was straight, and the extraction would be simple if Chandler had not checked on his vital cargo. The SUV swerved sharply to shake Jed's grasp free. Chandler knew the helicopter would have to ascend as the hotels were coming up. Looking back at the hanging partner's next attempt, he floored the pedal and took off. Jed's arms were bleeding as he tried to get Oren out of captivity.

Feeling the rope begin to pull, he tried for Oren's hand one final time. He couldn't reach as the rope began to lift him out. As he looked in his partner's eyes, he smirked, "hang tight, we'll get you out tonight." Oren nodded as he watched his partner float out the rear window. The helicopter rose in the air over the jagged roadside. Jed watched the SUV speed away as he felt the pilot recoil the rope. The pilot had him dangling twenty feet in the air when his carabiner broke.

Rakeef could hear but not see the helicopter, but he heard a man scream. "Nathan you stay here and wait for the detachment's crew to pick you up. I'm going to check out who screamed. It may have been another victim. I've got my cell phone. Tell them I'm in the area." He took off with a moderate jog. *Chandler must have things under control, or maybe they got away. I'm not cut out for this.* The night was still. A few frogs were croaking in the distance. The helicopter was gone. Rakeef brought out his penlight and shone it towards the chase. *I didn't hear the chopper crash. I don't know maybe it was a domestic or a spooked scream I heard.*

"Oh, what have you got for a snack? A bone? Oh…" he looked with his flashlight as the dog started growling. "Drop it!" he ordered, pulling out an evidence bag. "Hopefully, I can get another one. I don't know whose finger this is, but you're not chewing it anymore."

He pulled on the back of the dog's neck to release the evidence. The dog went running in a determined path to fetch another snack. "I guess you'll know who screamed." *I hope he's not too shaken up. This finger is pretty mangled.* Rakeef put his evidence packet in his pocket, then pulled out his cell phone.

"Gladys, wake the coroner up. Yes Rayna. I found a body that she will want to take a picture of for her wall of fame. Is Chandler back yet? When he comes in, tell him I think the assassin's partner that shot at us earlier is here at my feet." He scoped Jed's body and turned to vomit.

# 2.

Jed looked like he was uncomfortably deceased, not slumped in an armchair from a heart attack or peacefully in a sleeping position dying from natural causes. He would make the coroner's greatest list for him being a mess.

Rakeef looked down at the body before him and wondered what to do next. He saw an older man approach out of the corner of his eye. "Sir, please back away," he said to the man who was shuffling towards him with a bedsheet.

"Is it okay with you, that I help you keep the duppy quiet? My Mama says when a body dies, you put a sheet over to comfor the soul. Dis man's soul gots to be tormented, so the sheet is all to help the soul. You not wan' any man's duppy haunting' round here scaring the lil' ones."

Rakeef watched in amazement, the man doing the work of flipping the sheet over the carcass and tucking it in like a child sick from too much sun. He went about the area making sure the entire body was covered. He let no air escape from beneath the sheet. His work suggesting that the soul was still lingering in the body. Rakeef watched the sheet soaking the wet blood—creating an ink-blot drawing. Looking at the fabric he thought he saw an image similar to Wodan's face. The man's voice interrupted his trance.

"There, all done. You did good. Only sick once. You're partner sure aim'd with sight like a sea bird gettin its fish." He shuffled over to Rakeef, who grew alarmed that there was blood on the man's hands.

"Thank you, sir; I think you should go home and wash your hands. This man did many dreadful things, but you have helped him and taught me that we have good in the world still. Thank you for teaching me today; I'll take it from here."

In the distance, fire service vehicles approached, illuminating the sky slightly as Rakeef watched the man slowly make his way back to his chattel house shack. He reached for his cell phone and called the dispatch again. "Gladys, yeah it's me again. Have you heard from Chandler yet? Is he okay?"

"He's here, Rakeef. We've got two high-profile customers in the station tonight. Piper and Jarvis brought in the man who owns the yacht in question, Brett is his name, and Chand brought in a ruined SUV—you should see it, burned to all hell—and a cold-looking fellow. No word yet from the coroner for the other guy you found. Chand said somethin' about the helicopter chasing him for a bit, then moving on to another area as they neared the coast. He tried to grab his partner through the back window while Chandler was driving. They are crazy. I'm glad they are in here now.

"His partner is right here, at my feet, under a bedsheet now in a soggy mess. You'll never imagine what old man Basil did to trap his spirit. I'm certainly having a Banks when this night's over. Can you send a unit like Alessio's traffic truck to get me? I'm fine, exhausted, but my feet hurt, and I've got a headache..."

"Alright, Rakeef, I get it. I'll send someone over." Gladys changed lines and spoke with the coroner. Rayna spoke frantically to Gladys on the phone, saying how eager she was to recover a killer's body.

## 3.

"Get this murderer out of my back seat and set him up in exam room A," Chandler told the auxiliary police officers who would remove Oren from his seat. "I need to get a drink! Something ice-cold, from the rum hut down the street after tonight is over. Just get him in there soon. And as fast as you can!" Chandler was livid. He watched for a moment, then let the Auxiliary officers do the processing.

"Do you see this shield? If you spit at us or do anything crazy, you're wearing it. Got it?!"

Oren complied with another curt smile. He had no idea he was now alone on the Island. No jail break rescue attempt scheduled and no way to contact the Shandwick Trust for another pickup. That didn't bother him. They would send a rescue attempt after 24 hours. He began surveying the station's hallways, checking the cameras briefly without turning his head. Exit doors were conveniently fire-route marked, so getting out of the hallways with ease would be possible once free from all the law enforcement personnel watching him.

Oren was led past Brett; for only a moment, the two men made eye contact. The officer led Brett to the jail cells, was nearing retirement, no longer on the scene in the bar fights or gang arrests. He was a desk job officer now, and both Oren and Brett could see that.

As Brett rounded the corner, it occurred to him that the man in custody must have been one of the hired guns that took out Wodan; a long-time friend back in the early days when he helped form the Shandwick Trust. As he was led and placed in the cell, he leaned against the wall and plotted his escape.

Oren figured by Brett's look that he was happy to reunite with his old business partner and optimistic that he might be placed near him while held for court with a bit of luck. The Auxiliary officer opened the exam room door and led Oren to the chair. "Sit here, arms on the table, by the hook." Oren cooperated. The officer locked his handcuff chain to the hook, which closed with a keyed lock. Another officer opened the door and held it open for Chandler as he sauntered in.

"No coffee, no lawyer, just us. Recognize him?" Chandler showed Oren the picture of Wodan obtained from blood records off the tarp in the sugar cane field.

"No"

"Well, that's good you speak my language. I wasn't sure if you are Russian, German, or some other European hitman. You're going down for this guy's murder. And when we get your partner in here who was chasing after us on our little joyride back to the station, I'll charge him too."

"When are you sending in a lawyer? I want a white one, not one of your locals."

"I'll just add hate crimes and racism to the list of charges racking up on you. Do you have a code name I can call you? Something I can tell the lawyer?" Chandler leaned back in his chair across from Oren.

"Or so you can track and begin your investigation. I wouldn't waste your time. I have immunity, and my name is not on any database. I don't exist on any system your little Island can search up."

"We'll see about what we can search and what doesn't come up."

"Can I have some water? Paper cup is fine, but plastic is preferred."

Chandler laughed, "Basic rights, I guess. No refills." He rose and knocked on the door. While he waited, he turned around and watched Oren; *This guy's too calm; he's going to be a handful; maybe if I have him in with the other guy, they'll kill each other.* The door opened, and Chandler exited. Out in the hallway, he spoke with the Auxiliary officer, "The guy wants water in a paper cup. I told him no refills. Oh, I got this," Detective Nelson reached into his pocket and stopped the recording on his cell phone. "I've got his voice. Save the cup, and we'll have his DNA." He gave the officer a nod and went around the corner towards Gladys's desk.

"Chand, have you heard the good news? Rakeef caught the other guy you say left in the helicopter."

"What?!" Chandler boasted, "is Rakeef all right? That guy was packing pretty heavy, and Rakeef wasn't wearing any protection when he left me to help those tourists earlier."

"He's fine. He told me the story, and some guardian angel saved you. The coroner is picking Rakeef and the body up, and they are bringing them back here. Traffic should be light; it's almost 2 am," Gladys muttered to herself, "no wonder I'm tired."

Chandler's mind raced. *We've got the perp and the yacht owner here in custody. We can't put the two partners in the same cell, so we'll have to move some drunk to a shared enclosure, so the other two don't talk.*

"Great news Gladys. I'm exhausted and can't wait to go home. Tyson and Nathan get back yet? Wait?! You said body! Is he dead?"

"Rakeef said it was the worst he's seen yet. In the morning, we must look for the guy's arm. Tyson is in with the counsellor and Nathan stepped out for some fresh air."

"I need a paper cup of water for the guy in Exam A, some gloves, and a coffee for myself. You want anything?"

"No coffee right now; I've got a water bottle here." She held it up, highlighting it was half full. "I usually finish it, but it has been busy; Lord help us!"

# Chapter 22

# *RAYNA'S NOTES*

## 1.

The coroner approached Rakeef, who rose to his feet.

"Hey, where is my mango bubble tea? Just kidding detective. You told Gladys it's a good one for me," the coroner beamed.

"It was crazy. The guy is under this sheet, as you can tell," Rakeef pointed toward the body with his foot.

"I'll get the stretcher."

"Maybe a tray would be better."

"Oh?!" The coroner inquired, almost excited that it may be a more significant crime scene as a hide-and-seek event. "Is the body missing any parts?"

"This guy's sure mangled, and yes, his arm is gone. So is his nose, and an eyeball is hanging on with some fleshy muscular stuff."

"Excellent. A juicy one. Are you okay with helping? Not too scared of the look? I need to take some notes before the body is moved."

"I'll have a nightmare tonight or tomorrow. I don't think I'll be dreaming much tonight by the time I get home. How can I help, shovel?"

"I've got some tongs, forceps, I guess, and we should glove-up before we begin. Here." Rakeef received the gloves, watched the coroner peel back the sheet, and collected small evidence pieces. "Wow, the wound where his arm exploded is severely fractured. This male slammed into the rock unbearably on his shoulder. Here look Rakeef, it's crushed."

"Disgusting. You like this stuff, I see."

"It's fascinating. I love accident victims, so real. The body is tough, but not when it gets launched towards a rock wall. Oh, he's missing fingers! Did you find any?" She looked up at Rakeef. He held the baggie from the run in with the chihuahua.

"A dog was chewing this one, I didn't look around for more. I have a headache, as you can imagine."

"Well, either the birds or the kids will find them tomorrow, but we should get a crew out here in a few hours to clean the scene." Rayna took out her headset and plugged it into her tape recorder to orally record the discovery examination. Placing the recorder in her pocket she began, "His face looks torn. The inertia popped his left eye out of his socket. His nose is missing, and his jaw is fractured, no, broken from impact. It's clearly shattered. Moving to the skull, it appears fractured as well. His scalp wet with cranium fluid. He wears a trimmed beard, but bits of his chin are lacerated and full of sandy, maroon-coloured gravel. The subject's neck, back and both legs appeared twisted and broken. One arm is missing three fingers—shaved jaggedly, the other arm is missing entirely—clean socket ejection. At the point of impact, the subject must have swung with such force that the result would have killed him instantly. His body smashed into a jagged rock face at the side of the road." She looked up and continued, "bits of flesh and near-dried bloodstains have painted this ragged wall as if the site would be an execution backdrop for a firing squad." She removed her gloves, hand in hand and stopped the recording.

Rakeef had turned away from the sight of his body and shuddered when Rayna tapped him on the shoulder.

"Ready to lift?" Rayna fitted a medical mask over her face. She looked at Rakeef who hesitated.

"Lift or flip?" he replied.

"Your call." The coroner slid a thin stainless-steel tray under the body and told Rakeef to help position the body on the bedsheet, "let's flip. He's pretty soggy underneath."

Rakeef and Rayna worked in unison and collected Jed's main body and juicy bits. His arm would be recovered later in the morning light and retrieving two of his fingers wouldn't be too challenging for the team, with the help from the locals. With only service vehicles on the road, their trip to the lab was quick. Rakeef looked at the countryside in the moon-lit sky. *Two days ago, it was nice and peaceful, but as I look now, I feel numb. Chand and I should get a medal from the president or prime minister for what we did today.* He felt his eyes close.

"We're here. I'll get my crew to help from here Rakeef. Get some sleep." Rayna lightly punched him in the shoulder.

## 2.

Chandler took the paper cup back to the Auxiliary officer and reminded him to collect the DNA. Moving towards the medical bay, he was joined by Rakeef who greeted his partner with a solid two minute embrace.

"Why don't you go home? I just had a coffee so I'll be here for a bit. You said your headache is getting severe, why don't you catch a ride with Piper or Jarvis if they are still here. Or you can crash at my place. Here take my keys to the D Max. I'll be right out too, Rakeef. I just want to do a quick check."

"Thanks, Chand. We've had one helluva night."

"I, like you, deserve an ice-cold Banks. It won't be long, I promise."

Chandler went through the medical bay doors and saw the tray containing Jed's sanguinary carcass. "Is there anything on him that we can use?" he asked the coroner's assistant.

"We're about to rinse him off. He was wearing an expensive Apple Watch kind of health tracker, but it's all smashed up and doesn't have its button left. Oh, we did find a unique ring. I don't know how that stayed on his finger... Over here, sir." Chandler moved to the assistant's side.

"Can I have it after you rinse it off, and take some pictures? I'll put it over with the other valuables by the sink, but I wonder if there is any engraving on the inside that might help to identify him."

"Sure, sir." After a quick rinse, the assistant slid the ring off the bleached finger and handed it to Chandler's gloved hand. "Anything engraved on it?"

"No, it's smooth. Oh well, worth a try, I guess." Chandler walked over to the sink and took a few pictures with his cell phone of the ring and the health tracker. Then placed both on the drying mat on the counter. Looking at his reflection in the mirror above the sink, he stared. His face was dirty, sweaty, and drained. He bent down and drew some warm water, splashing the water on his face. After a couple of rinses, he grabbed a paper towelette and wiped, pausing on his cheeks for a moment, before pulling the paper down over his chin—*what a night! I have to get Rakeef back to the house and share a Banks. Tomorrow will be another busy day.* Chandler thanked the medical team and made his way to the door, depositing the paper towelette in the trash bin. Walking out of the detachment and into the warm, slightly moist morning air, he joined Rakeef in his Isuzu D Max, eased the seat slightly back, buckled, and drove.

"We should skip the Banks tonight; I'm tired, Chand. My headache is getting better since I'm off my feet, and there was silence for a little while."

Chandler laughed, "I agree; let's skip the Banks, take a rain check." He rounded the roundabout and took the north exit. "I hope that is all the excitement for this week—or month, for that matter."

"I agree; hopefully, the murders stop. And we've got the right guys."

They both watched the road, which had barely any traffic, as they made their way to Chandler's Heywood's home. He entered his driveway and under his garage overhang. He paused then turned to Rakeef, "I know you are tired, but I need you to help me with something."

"Sure, what do you need?"

"Are you wanting to stay in policing?"

"I do love helping the tourists and some simple crime, but to be honest, Chand, I am scared to death of Crab Hill—even if the crime rate is lower than last year."

"I know. The gun violence scares me too. These two guys that we chased today were ruthless. Unlike our gang members on the Island, these killers are professional, and it was a little too close for comfort today for me. I don't want this to leave this car, but I'm considering retiring from the Police Force."

"You have my word Chand, you always do. Something happened to me tonight too. When I saw old man Basil tonight, I felt alive. I remember standing there watching an old man tuck the ruthless killer's body up so his duppy wouldn't haunt the area. I haven't been to mass in a little while and feel a little bad about that, but I prayed today."

Chandler stared at his partner, relaxed with the conversation. "You were through a lot today. How did the guy die from the helicopter? The medical crew said that there was a lot of damage to his body."

"I guess fell or something. The helicopter must have took off, probably to get fuel somewhere off the Island. He was on a rope, but he fell off, or the line snapped, and he had no chance. His body looked like a shark got him and spat him back out because he was bitter."

"Crazy, well, I'm glad you were safe. Let's go to sleep. It's almost three."

They exited the D Max, and Rakeef used the bathroom as Chandler found him a pillow and sheet, placing it on the pull-out chesterfield, tufted with luxuriously rich white leather. He went to the kitchen, drew a glass of water for Rakeef to take his medication, set it on the side table, and quietly knocked on the bathroom door. "You okay, Rakeef?" hearing the toilet flush.

"All good. I need to be eating more fibre, I guess," he announced through the door.

"Too much info man, honestly," Chandler shook his head. "Good night, my man. Thanks for your help today."

"It was my pleasure, Chand. Thanks for the bed; I love your chesterfield. Good night too. Oh, Chand!" Rakeef opened the door, "you interested in grabbing breakfast at the Fish Pot in a few hours I think that is where Derk and Jones are headed. Jones lost his tow truck today. I think we all need a cheer-up!"

"Sure. Set your alarm; I'll do the same. 7:30 should give us enough time to leave. You can shower in the second bathroom."

"Sounds good."

Chandler entered his room and closed the door. He undressed and ran the shower water to get pleasantly hot. Standing under the massaging waterfall, Chandler rested against the tiled wall, letting the steamy water wash the day's adventure down the drain. *I came close today. I don't know what to do. Finish out the year; be like Piper and Nathan and do an exchange?* Chandler washed, lathering the velvety cleanser, and rinsing not only the day's sweat but the ache for the victims that these criminals killed. The water screeched shut. He dried himself with his favourite towel. His body felt tense, sore, and exhausted, which interrupted his usual evening stretching routine.

Dropping the towel on the hook, he flopped into bed and slept nude, passing out within minutes.

# WEDNESDAY

# Chapter 23

# *CLOUDLESS SKY*

## 1.

"Hey, Derk! Here's your breakfast on the kitchen island. I took the Jimny back to my place this morning to change, then ordered the breakfast fish cakes and garden omelette for us to split. You were pretty low, so I filled her up too, and now I'm ready when you are." Jones took a swig from his black coffee. "Oh, there's coffee too."

"What time did you get up?" Derk said through the door, getting into his beige pants.

"Around 6:15. No alarm needed I guess, natural time clock. You sleep, okay?"

"Fine. And thanks for filling the Suzuki up, I was going to wait until the weekend. You should grab my investigation bag; we should get going. I think the detachment will need both of us today." Derk made his way to the kitchen, picked up his meal, and headed towards Jones, who held the front door open. He followed Jones through the door. "Thanks for getting breakfast. I didn't really want to get up."

The morning was already looking pleasant, soft southern winds, cloudless sky, slightly sweltering heat, nothing like the angry action and injustice that occurred last evening.

The drive included the usual honks for motorists to proceed into traffic, men on the side of the highway roasting corn, and setting up fresh coconuts with their machete wedged in their wagon cutting board. Tourists in their hired cars would innocently become their victims, paying US currency for their tourism commodities. Traffic flow was good, as most drivers this early were locals. The courageous tourists with newly rented cars usually cause traffic to come to a halt as they navigate the lanes of a right-hand turn slightly before the lunch rush. Arriving at the station, Rakeef joined them in the parking lot.

"Good breakfast today eh Jones? You two sleep, okay I crashed at Chand's last night. His couch is amazing!" Rakeef was running on three hours of sleep and would crash in a few hours. "In other news, a crew went out early this morning around 6 am to try and clean up the crime scene a bit. The guy's arm and two fingers were located, blood was rinsed, and besides that things look pretty normal." Rakeef waved his hand for the automatic doors to open.

"Only two fingers? Hopefully, you can get a match for his prints. Jones and I figured we'd be of service since you are down to just a few officers." Derk looked at Rakeef and lowered his voice, "it was crazy last night!"

"Good morning Derk. Jones, I heard about your truck. I guess you're a tag-along today. I know it will take a while, but you'll get a new one that I'll want to definitely take a ride in." Chand smiled and handed Rakeef the preliminary report. "This is what I have started. The lawyer was a no-show but called. The detainee was getting irritable when he forced him to talk on the phone. One bathroom break, a frozen dinner, and back to the exam room. The cup you had asked Leroy to collect went to the lab though."

"Anything come back on it?"

"We had to connect with Interpol to see any wanted perps that had criminal charges with DNA records." Piper announced as her usual cheerful self. "Two potential matches were found, but they are a little loose. No birth name, but his two aliases are Claudio or Oren. Hi Derk." Piper motioned for Derk to check out the next page of the file as Chandler logged on to his computer.

"Blood type is Rh A+ for the perpetrator's body brought in last night. Any leads to him being associated with any of the open investigations?"

"We took some fingerprints, checked the DNA and it might take a while. I'll keep at it though. In Australia, these kinds of victims come from boating accidents, or scuba trips gone horribly wrong."

"I love how you say your words with a w-sound. Your accent sounds so chipper."

"Hey, watch it, Derk. I know what you're doing, saying words like, chipper, so you can hear my scratchy voice."

"Just being friendly, Piper. Nothing sinister. I know you're only here on exchange."

"I've got a boyfriend back home Derk, you'll find someone." She held up her left fingers. "He popped the question at the airport. I should text him a beach sunset, it's the rainy season over there."

"I bet the guy's Oren. He doesn't look like a Claudio." Derk checked his phone.

"Have you heard from that Canadian girl from the bus crash, Klara?"

"Nothing since yesterday. I imagine she's trying to soak up some sun on some beach. The sky's perfect for sunnin' on a beach towel. I think she said something about a friend coming in today." Derk's cell phone chirped. "It's Gladys. She has some information about one of my cases." He stood by the door. "Thanks Piper; and excellent work. I don't think we hear that enough around here."

Gladys had sorrow in her voice, "I've got some more sad news, and we just started the day. I just got a call from your Canadian friend, that a boat angler found bodies. You might want to help check it out. Don't ruin the morning for Chand and Rakeef."

## 2.

Klara woke up just after 7:20. Having only two days left on the Island, she wanted to get to the beach today, enjoy a quick dip, and then lay on the hot sand to catch some glow. Having medium skin that would tan easily, Klara figured a little sun exposure in the morning wouldn't be too harsh for her skin, as it was dry from the heat. She worried Flo would send a text, but she could reply from the beach with a picture to lighten the conversation. She packed up her beach bag, sunglasses, Derk's sunscreen, Kindle, and a chilled water bottle from the refrigerator. In her waist-pouch, she had around $28 US with a handful of Bajan change, her room key, passport, and her cell phone, still on airplane mode over the night so no updates

would install. Klara was ready to treat herself to the whole
tourist experience. She figured a crowded taxi would be
a memorable addition to the public transportation choice
over walking, figuring the men on board would be silent
in their conversations as a cute tourist was in their midst.

Grabbing a healthy serving of fruit at the continental
breakfast bar, she padded out to the road and hailed a
taxi. Within minutes, she saw the front passenger seat
empty when a muscular Bajan man hopped off, opened
the door for her and then held onto the top rack rail with
his feet resting on the door trim. Klara turned to him
and thanked him, sat, and spoke to the driver. She hardly
had time to close the door before the taxi was jutting into
traffic and on the move.

"Hello, miss, $4 Beewee, or $2 US take you to Accra
Beach, near the chattel village."

"Hi, here you go," Klara quickly counted out the
local change; realizing she didn't have enough time to
sort through the collection of coins, she handed the driver
a US $5 bill. "I need some sun today! I was touring around
yesterday on a bus, and I remember hearing about Dover
Beach. Is it a good recommendation? A woman with her
baby told be about it."

"You gave me too much girly. I don't have any coin."
The driver put the $5 in the farebox. "I can take you to the
access lane for a shor' walk to the beach. When you wan'
to catch another taxi, head to the Sandals pickup. There is
other tourass there, you might make a friend." The driver
was efficiently chatting with Klara while jabbing through
breaks in traffic to drop off his fares. Some men would
hardly wait for the taxi to stop before jumping off.

Klara loved the local people, so vibrant and playful, always helping tourists feel welcome. She was glad that Flo could see the fun side of Barbados when she touched down this afternoon. Also, glad that Flo didn't come with her on Monday constantly complaining as the crime outweighed the comfort on this trip. She also enjoyed the company of Derk, lighting up every time their eyes met.

"Dover Beach!" the driver announced in rich calypso dialect, turning south on Dover Road. "The sand not be too hot on your feet yet. You'd be all right but come midday the sand is hot-hot just be careful."

"Thank you, I will. That was a quick trip. I'd get so lost if I rented a car to tour around, but that is my plan for tomorrow, my last day. Your roads are very nestled, like spaghetti." Klara waited for the taxi to stop and exited, waving to a few men on the taxi watching her. The cab took off with a short honk to re-enter traffic, and Klara could hear the ocean. Feeling incredibly excited, she found the beach access path, took her sandals off, and let the soft sand envelop her toes. Klara walked in the sand, alone aside from a fisher out more profound in the water trolling with his sports boat. She smoothed the sand with her foot and unrolled her towel. Placing her beach bag on the surface, Klara did a quick second glance for any beachcombers that may rifle through her belongings. Seeing that she was still alone, she took off her shirt and shorts, revealing a teal stylish bikini set, and walked out towards the surf. The water was perfect. The push from the crashing waves and the draw from the recoil massaged her ankles with grains of sand. Her feet would find the occasional shell or seaweed, but Klara wandered unaware.

She felt free and at peace—finally, hugged by the ocean's heat. Her eyes blinded by the glare from the sea water's surface, but a genuine tourist grin on her face. Free from all the troubles life had recently thrown at her.

## 3.

The angler in the boat could see that Klara was not out too deep. He had been out since just after five in the morning, collecting his traps and cages, hoping to find some prized lobster, jumbo-sized shrimp, or king crabs. Most fishing cages were empty, but one held a valueless piece of barnacle-encrusted technology. Trolling in towards shore, he kept an occasional eye on Klara to see if she was swimming or just relaxing as most tourists did with one or two days at the beach.

Something else that caught his eye was the sea birds swooping towards a thick patch of kelp at the water's surface. The angler paid no attention to the gathering birds, but when two of them began to squawk and dig at the kelp, the angler couldn't take his eyes off the scene. He began increasing the speed while turning to get to the port side of the weeds. He gasped as he rose and cut the engine. It wasn't kelp; it was a body. Shooing the birds, he began yelling. Klara awkwardly turned to face the boat and wondered if the man was intoxicated. Deciding to move in closer to the shore, he shouted to her, "Hey, Hey! Can you go to the hotel bar, and have them call the police?"

Klara walked out over the surf and wrapped her towel around her chest and trunk. Spilling her bag and getting sand over her shirt and shorts, she put her sandals on and walked closer to the shore, "The police?! Are you okay? Boat trouble?"

"There is a man in the water, dead, and he wasn't here this morning. The tide must have brought him in." He looked over at Klara, then hysterically exclaimed, "there's another one. Oh no, no! Call the police!" The man went to the bin under his seat and pulled out his most extensive weighted cargo net. Holding the weights, he tossed the net out over the first two bodies and tightened the top loops webbing the net into a scoop, working like the bodies were a fast-moving school of flying fish. The angler recovered four college-aged and two middle aged tourists and used an oar positioned under the armpit of another. *They're all dead.* Tears began to stream down his face. In shock, he wondered how this tragedy unfolded.

Klara ran up to the Sapphire Beach patio bar, "Hello?!" she turned and pointed when the bartender came to her, "That boat out there, has found at least two bodies, drowned, and surfacing in the water. He said that when he went out this morning against the tide, he saw nothing, so I'm asking you if you could call the police, or investigator Derk Warrows to come to Dover Beach, because Klara, that's me, was trying to have a beach day, but crime keeps interrupting my vacation." She paused, "Did you get all that?"

"One moment please. Here, have a seat. I'll get the manager."

"Wait! Just call the police, ask for Chandler Nelson or Derk Warrows!"

# Chapter 24

## *MALIBU RUM*

**1.**

Jones brought around the last police SUV that was in fully tuned condition. "Derk, I'll drive. Do you think this is the fall-out of the yacht owner we have in jail, or another suspect? The jail is only big enough for the crew they have in there now." Jones looked at his friend.

"They just need one linkable piece of evidence, and we'll have no more issues from any of them. It's starting to make sense to me now that Piper had gotten some preliminary speculation underway." Derk entered the SUV and set the air conditioning to high. "In the report, she found that the Wade Barnwell lawyer was Wodan Crendall, murdered by the sugar cane field on the bus trip Klara and I were on. The guy that Rakeef found is the partner to the Oren assassin; the yacht owner, Brett, must be the leader. He's got the wealth, the time, and the motive. See I should be a cop, but it's more fun being a detective."

"Any of the ladies call the station and ask for you on a first name basis."

"You think so? After this call we should go to the dealership and take some brochures of a new rig for you. Ladies always love a guy who has a nice set of wheels." He winked.

"I have weeks with the insurance first. It's ok. I might head to the beach myself. Try to show Klara that I'm a little rough around the edges. Hold up, why is Piper running out to us? Maybe we can't use this unit."

"We have a warrant for his boat, and Wodan Crendall's address. I judge by the street he lives on, it is a dead end, but the yacht might be our goldmine. Officially Derk you are on the case. I guess you too Jones." She ran back to the detachment door as if her sandals were melting on the pavement.

"She'll make a great police officer back in Australia. Alright, let's head to the beach!"

## 2.

Klara grew impatient. She waited for the bartender to return and explain that she was free to go back to the beach, as the staff made the call to the police. She finally saw a server approach. "Please accept my apologies for the wait, we had an elderly guest fall asleep in the whirlpool jacuzzi. We have called the police, and two are coming, Mr. Edgehill and Mr. Warrows. You can have this too," She handed Klara a voucher for a complimentary neck massage, "the bartender is making a pineapple-mango infusion icee for your trouble."

"You don't have to do that; I just wanted some confirmation that I could go back to the beach and collect my bag."

"Here's the bartender," she turned and grabbed the decorative beverage intended to draw bar patrons to order a few for their table. Klara reached under the souvenir glass and flicked the little black switch, shutting the tri-coloured LED lights off.

"Thanks for the hospitality, I'll see what I can do later today about that massage." Klara rose and headed back to the beach, feeling a little pampered, sipping the colourful frozen beverage, and making her way back to her bag, e-reader, and the crime scene.

## 3.

Jones and Derk pulled up to the Sapphire Beach Condos parking lot and made their way to the water's edge. Klara waved them over. "Well, hello, gentlemen. I swear I didn't do it," sipping a loud slurp from the bottom of the cup. "I think there's Malibu rum in here."

"Good morning, Miss Hockley," Jones gave Klara a brief wave and then went over to the fisher who had now docked the boat and did the heavy lifting of recovering the bodies. College aged victims lay face up on the beach, also the captain and some shirtless men. "You brought in all of them sir?"

"I went out in the morning to collect my traps, and when she came to the beach," he pointed at Klara. "The fish swam in, so I started coming in shallower. I saw some birds gather, and then," he paused as he saw Jones's hand raise. Jones brought out his cell phone and a notepad.

"I'd like to record your statement; in case I miss writing it down. Please continue."

"The birds were pecking at a body. I flipped him over and saw the look on his face. He may have been shot in the chest, you can see here," he pointed to the first victim's chest. Under his wet shirt, you could see the torn hole, matching the puncture wound, terribly bloated and fleshy.

The angler explained as vividly as he could the experience of recovering the students lost at sea with the apparent boat captain. At times, Jones looked back at Derk to see if he had any insight but figured he was taking Klara's statement as they had now moved back to one of the beach gazebo-style tables.

"I don't know why, wherever I go, there seems to be crime with me. I live a normal, calm life you know. Nothing like this happens in my town in Alberta, Canada."

"Barbados is not like this either, Klara. We try hard to make it a safe, friendly, enjoyable stay here, so people come back, year after year. We depend on tourism, we are busy in the winter season, and a little slower in the summer, but you have made my week this week. Seeing your face, hearing your troubles, how strong you are through all the rough patches as well. We owe you a debt of gratitude, I see you got a little sun today, or tried to. Did you go for a dip in the sea?" Derk gazed into her eyes.

"Thanks, Derk; I know that Barbados is comfortable for tourists, this being my first trip and certainly not my last; that's for sure. I hoped to get a bit of sun today but only managed to slip into the water," she looked around for a garbage can for her glass. "What am I gonna do with this?" she said, holding the glass while picking the shiny plastic film accessories away from the rim. "Is there recycling in Barbados?"

"There is but not for a piece like that."

"My sister would keep it, as a souvenir of her trip. She has several cups from Las Vegas. I'll take it with me, it might be fun to have back home. The men on the taxi might strike up a conversation instead of just watching me too."

Jones began walking over to Derk, "Eight bodies, four of them college aged; all of them were attacked in some way like a harpoon but it might be something else. I called it in, the medical examiner at the hospital will take them; we must get them out of the sun soon. Did you take Klara's statement?"

"In the process. Are we done here then?" Derk turned back to Klara, "do you want to finish up at the station?"

"I think my suit's dry, so I'll just put on my shorts; it's funny. These shorts were my last day shorts, the only ones that don't have blood stains on them."

Derk smiled. "Let's keep it that way."

## 4.

Gladys was loudly slurping her oversized water bottle when a frustrated caller interrupted her morning. "Good morning, Royal Barbados Police Force, Southern Division, how may I be of service?"

"I woke up this morning, and my car was stolen. I know it was locked and I didn't see or hear anyone messin' with it last night. If Roddy's taken it again, I'm pressin' charges."

"We did have an altercation with a black Suzuki Swift in a chase last night. We recovered it near the cement factory, and it is currently in the impound. Can I get some particulars from you to help identify if we are talking about the same vehicle?" Gladys spoke gently, looking over the delicate details of her hair stylist's latest brochure.

"It was stolen?! And used in a car chase?! Is there any damage to it? My boyfriend will kill me if we must buy a new one. I'm due in about 2 months, Lord have mercy, and we must save for the baby. It will be our first—if he sticks around—we can be a family." The girl began to choke up.

"Oh, deary, you'll work out fine. My sister had horrible times with her boyfriends, then the right one just blew in on the wind, and they're tight. I hope the little one will be a bundle of joy. But you might want to get started on your insurance claim. Your car will be drivable, but there is a cracked front bumper cover, and the passenger side mirror frame is missing a few parts. You can still drive it, don't worry. We have little stickers that say the damage is noted with the police and the insurance won't find you at fault since it was stolen. If you are okay with the look, your right as rain, nothing will stop you this week. Do you have someone who can drive you here to fill out some paperwork later this afternoon?"

"Oh, I think my baby brother can find me a ride. He's eighteen, and has his license, so we'll try and decide. Thank you, Miss. I was struggling to find an answer to figure all this mess out. My name's Jackie."

"We have a match then Jackie, it's your car, we've got in the lock-up. We'll keep it safe for you, not to worry."

Chandler approached the desk, leaning over and surprising Gladys with a long stem bird of paradise, with a card saying that she made this office paradise—Happy secretary-dispatcher day! She ended the call and accepted the bouquet, whispered a genuine thank-you and set it down, then ran a few fingers through her hair and flattened the creases in her uniform. Various police force personnel arrived for their shift, including the lawyer for Oren, holding a tray of espresso coffee, which leaked gourmet aroma about the front office, a pleasant change to the bleach sanitizer spray, the prevalent fragrance. Gladys watched him sign in and ask for his client to meet him in the conference room. She picked up the phone and called the guards to bring out Oren, as Derk and Jones walked in, followed by Klara, who waved at Gladys.

"Derk, the European detainee's lawyer is here. If you want to speak with him, he's in the conference room. Hello, Miss Klara, so nice to see you, but why are you not on some beach, or enjoying a rum punch and a fish cutter?"

"It's a little bit of a long story, but I've been to the beach, found some dead people, got a coupon for a neck massage and a very fun drink," she turned to Derk, saying she left the glass in the back of the SUV. Jones assured her they would retrieve it in a few minutes, not to worry. Klara turned back to Gladys "then I figured I'd give my statement, and of course see your smiling cheerful face, Oh my, It's beautiful!" Klara saw her bouquet. "You deserve a raise too for all the things that have been happening. I swear I didn't bring a curse to Barbados."

Jones joined Derk in leaving to the conference room, as Gladys told her about wedding locations, in a heart-to-heart confession as if they were soul sisters. Klara's comfort with the locals grew to a family connection while briefly on the Island. Having been on vacations to tropical destinations, Klara did not feel the same as when she spoke with the Bajan people. She listened and thought about Marcy, picturing her wedding, their walks on the beach, tourist shopping, dancing at nightclubs, and saying goodbye to Barbados sitting on the beach watching the sunset. She looked up from Gladys as the guard brought Oren to the conference room, then sharply turned back, and stared, "That's the guy from the bus crash! He was the one who was driving, I saw him get out of the car, and drag Wade out of his Nissan, just before I had to evacuate. There were two of them. The shooter and the driver both should be charged for the crime. Did you find the other guy?"

Gladys held her index finger up as she was going to answer another call. Klara saw Derk head toward Piper's office. "Derk!"

"Just getting the file on this guy."

"He pulled Wade out of the Nissan after they shot him. He was the driver of the Audi when we were in the bus crash." Klara began to tremble.

"What time do you have before you are picking up your friend from the airport? I have an idea, you go back to the Sapphire and have your massage, when you are relaxed after, take some time to jot a few items down. I'll meet you on the beach, pick you up in my truck and we get your friend with some snacks, juice, and we try to have some relaxation. Ease the shop-talk, just have a nice evening by the sea."

"That sound's perfect. I would like them to give my hip a massage."

"Don't worry, with all the evidence they have in this file, this guy, Oren they call him, is going down. I have to work with Chandler and Rakeef for a bit. Go, try, and soak up some more of beautiful Barbados before you leave tomorrow, right?"

"Right, I'll take the bus, or walk, it's not that far."

"Be careful; I'll see you in a few hours Klara." Derk smiled and turned to take his turn with Oren.

Klara walked out to the street and waited for the bus. Fishing for the massage coupon, she pulled out her cell phone, took it off airplane mode and saw that Flo had sent a message. She took a selfie with the Police station as the backdrop. Knowing that when posting to social media, her followers would have a remarkable story to read. She would tell anyone when she was back home, this picture was the before the massage selfie, and she would take one after the massage showing how her day would have ended. Klara boarded the bus and headed out of the city. She read the message and smiled that everything was on schedule. Flo was in the air.

# Chapter 25

# *MANY ALIASES*

## 1.

The medical examiner had called Jones's cell, asking that he and his partner come to the hospital. Upon arrival he began telling the tragic tales of the latest victims. He had concluded that the wounds were from a highly specialized harpoon. Some individuals were shot from behind, leaving significant tissue damage in a recognizable pattern, but must have had a smooth narrow end, as the bruises were not visible. Confirming that the wounds were from at least 18 hours ago, Jones thanked the medical examiner and turned to Derk. "Before you go in there, I think I know. He says the killer used a harpoon. It must be Brett, because Oren could not have enough time to be hiding out, the car chase, the helicopter pickup, and now be locked up. Brett was brought in by Piper and Jarvis after they visited the *Gap*, so I'll check with them and get back to you. When you're done with Oren, we'll switch him out for Brett for questioning."

Clearly seeing the medical examiner was busy they quietly left and headed back to the detachment. Derk collected Klara's souvenir tumbler from the back seat.

Jones went in to Piper for report generation and photo printing. Derk hung out in the break room planning what snacks he'd get for the afternoon with Klara and her guest.

"Derk, can you help with questioning Oren? He won't crack for Chandler maybe you can do something." Rakeef leaned in the door frame, as Derk put his shopping list away.

"Here's the report from the hospital. Jones had the pictures from the beach." Rakeef said. "He filled me in with his theory."

"Thanks, this won't be long." Derk stood by Leroy at the door and waited for the lawyer to finish. He said to Leroy, "this lawyer is wasting his time. You see how thick this file is. He'll be an expensive one when a police jet comes over from Europe to collect him. Might even be a Concord."

Derk took a step back so Leroy could unlock the door and let the lawyer out. They met eyes, and Investigator Warrows held the file up, emphasizing the thickness and paperwork volume. The lawyer exchanged the usual banter of innocence until proven guilty, and though in a confident Diplomatic Immunity phrase, Derk ignored all of it. *I just need to get the charges wired over to Interpol, and they can pay the tab to get this guy off our rock.* With the door still open from Leroy's hold, Derk breezed to his seat and slapped the file on the stainless-steel table.

"Have I got a story to tell you," Derk leaned in, "Oren." He watched for a reaction.

"I have many aliases, go on with your story," Oren leaned back, sipping his espresso.

"Some die, some live. Let's check the cast of your little production. One bad guy, your partner, dead." Derk flipped to Jed's examination photos. "We found his arm, and two of his missing fingers as he exploded when that helicopter last night was chasing after you. I guess he doesn't mean anything to you, by your heartless expression, but I'll continue. Officer Piper, one of the good ones, was hit over the back of her head, and when she recovered, gave this statement." Derk read that Piper heard the name Oren right before she got assaulted. "Oren, funny name to remember when you are in a life-or-death situation, but I know the Oren, that she remembers hearing, is you."

"Your point?" Oren appeared calm, bored of the plot so far.

"Then we have this guy, Wade Barnwell the lawyer, or Wodan Crendall the accomplice. I have an eyewitness that makes you at the scene of the crime, where his body was riddled with bullets, dragged through broken door glass, left in a cane field, so you could end your job and time here on the Island, and go back to wherever it is you go, to murder and pillage innocent lives. Funny thing, his body was whisked away by a helicopter that is not from around here."

"You're saying his body is missing? You can't lay those charges against me."

"I wouldn't get too comfortable here, and if you, Oren, would like, I'll arrange for an enjoyable stay in solitary to help you relax. Try getting out of this one."

Derk rose and walked over to the door. As Leroy was working the lock, he turned back to Oren. "Your partner got off easy. Too bad all the evidence now falls on your side of the partnership. I hear the case could take weeks. Anything you want to say?"

Oren stared at him coldly, his voice hoarse and dry. "Watch yourself detective!"

Leroy opened the door, and Derk saw Brett on his route, transferred to the additional conference room, without a lawyer, but in the company of Detective Nelson and Jones.

Derk went to refresh his coffee after smelling the aroma of Oren's espresso. He placed the new report containing bodies recovered and processed from the ME on top of the thick file on Oren and headed for his second round of questioning. Chandler had already had Brett placed in the room and ordered Oren to return to the cell. In confusion, Jones cross-communicated that Oren returns to Brett's cell, a fatigued blunder, which would cause more tension and life-threatening situations within hours.

## 2.

Around 10 am, the *Assailant* harboured at the docks where Brett's arrest took place, had two teams of investigators rifle through the contents, collecting pictures, fingerprints, bags of evidence. Piper took the lead on filing the warrant and enjoyed investigating the yacht's luxurious interior layout, instructing her team to check bottles of alcohol, glasses, pillows, bathroom articles and device cords. The teams split into a general living area and the below-deck mechanical location, where the crucial discovery appeared. In a cramped room that Wodan used for storing ammunition, flares, and unregistered firearms, a team member found a key in a magnetic case behind the door.

Within 20 minutes, the key proved extremely useful and unlocked the holding chamber that Kennedy Glenning and other kidnapped victims were held. The rope, IDs, jewelry, and possessions were confiscated and tagged in a forensic hypoallergenic bin. Any DNA evidence that the police could salvage would help link the unsolved murders to the sole man in custody. Upon returning to Piper, the below-deck team concluded that they had sufficient evidence to prosecute, holding up several IDs of tourists that were missing or deceased. Piper scanned through the names and called Jones when she discovered an Australian girl's ID.

"Hi Piper, Derk, Chandler and I are in with a detainee! Can you call back?"

"Are you with Brett too?"

"Yes, He's here, why?"

"Put it on speakerphone!"

## 3.

Brett was conversing with Derk over not having legal representation when Jones's cell phone went off. The next time Brett spoke was after Piper had called out his name.

"Brett Vorek!"

"Yes."

Derk reached for his phone and set the voice memo to record. Jones looked at Derk as he watched Brett for any sign of guilt.

"I have been working on your case for the past week, with a dozen murders, and weapons charges. We had a warrant to search your yacht the *Assailant* and we found IDs, jewelry, guns, and forensic evidence that you used to tie your victims, including Mrs. Kennedy Glenning."

"That wasn't me. You can check my DNA against the rope's fibres; you won't find a match."

"It's on its way to the forensic lab now. Moving on. I'm holding in my hand the ID of a girl I went to school with, who was reported lost when I was back home in Australia, and I chose to transfer to the Royal Barbados Police Force to look for her. If you had anything to do with her disappearance, I will make it my personal mission to find all the possible charges against you and have her family seek millions of dollars in damages. You have my word. Thank you, Detectives. That is all for now. Jones I'll finish with the teams here onboard and then head back to the station to finish my report." Jones took the phone in his hand. Everyone in the room heard the audible click that the speakerphone call had ended.

After thinking for a moment, Jones texted Piper to have someone deliver a slip of paper with all the possible people linking Brett to the crimes from the IDs on board. He asked that this be swift; this new evidence to add to the file Derk had in front of him. Derk flipped through the pictures of the latest victims and stopped at the image of the man known as Carl collected off the digital passenger manifest from the boat charter transaction. He made it visible to Brett. "These were innocent tourists, having some fun, trying to escape the troubles of further education studies. What they can't escape are harpoon wounds; what was going through your head? Were you fishing for human victims, you murderer? You have a multi-million-dollar vessel, the ability to hunt sharks, or deep-sea kingfish, but you go after college students?! What is wrong with you?! Explain yourself!"

"I'm not sure what you mean by harpoon-fishing tourists. I had a touring partner, yes, but I did not do anything to hurt or kill these tourists. You have the wrong guy." Brett was sure to watch his wording as Derk had not stopped the voice recording, clearly visible on the table, uploading every split-second of testimony to an online cloud.

Chandler opened the file on Oren and flipped to the page on Wodan's particulars. "This travelling partner? Do you know what else we have in your file here Brett? Wodan's statement, he was running for his life, after your last phone call making abundantly clear that you were ordering a hit to take him out." Derk placed a copy of the statement in front of Brett. "We searched through his phone records and heard that conversation. He also wrote this."

Jones rose to stretch his legs and saw that Leroy was moving to open the door, allowing entry to the interrogation. He went to the door and received a note from Gladys. He put it down on the table in front of Derk.

"Twelve murders. A dirty dozen. And since your partner is one step ahead, you have nothing to get you out of this." Derk showed the note, freshly produced for the room's case.

## 4.

Brett was stuck. He read Wodan's confession outlining the comprehensive list of jobs, including those scribbled on the little note beside the file. *Hell, no! What am I going to do now to get the hell out of this? They have that assassin from the Shandwick Trust here, too; he's got to get out too. I have to get off the Island, but how?* Brett leaned back, trying to display confident behaviour. "You might as well put me back in lock-up, I'm done here."

Derk picked up the file again and rose, briefly pausing over Brett, "Enjoy your stay."

Leroy opened the door and let the detectives out, leaving Brett in the hands of Leroy's shift partner, who would lead him back to his cell. He sat in silence, contemplating the conversation he would have if he could speak with his hired killer. Brett still had plenty of money on hand in offshore accounts that he could quickly liquidate for his release payment. He heard the conference room door open and saw the guard enter with the table lock keys. Brett was released and taken back to the cells without difficulty, but upon arriving saw his opportunity. There was Oren in the corner of his cell, placed by mistake by the earlier order. The cell door opened, and Brett joined his cellmate. They made eye contact and exchanged a greeting. Their bonding over the next hour would get them out of incarceration before nightfall.

# Chapter 26

## *SAPPHIRE BEACH*

### 1.

Klara rode the bus to the Sandals resort bus stop, where a group of middle-aged American vacationers impatiently were tired from waiting. She was already approaching the beach access path by the time they found their seats, and she could overhear their complaints well past the bougainvillea plants, showering from their planters by the roadside. Klara closed her eyes and felt the sun's rays tickle her cheeks. She watched a romantic couple sitting together, one suntanning and reading a book, the other surfing his phone for the latest headlines of useless gossip. No aroma of the crime scene from earlier, was going to ruin this perfect afternoon. Seeing the ocean's water had erased the early morning's gore from the crest of the shore, the look now was picturesque. She made her way to the Sapphire Beach Condos. Her massage voucher in hand.

"Can I help you, Miss?"

"The spa, I'd like to book a massage or see if they can fit me in, if there's a cancellation."

"Certainly, I'll show you to the spa. Do you have your room key?"

"I'm staying elsewhere, but I do have this coupon presented by your management earlier today when the incident with the jacuzzi happened. Also did you hear about what happened at Dover Beach this morning, my gosh!" Klara acted like some of her students, overly dramatic.

"My apologies, I hope you enjoy your massage, and come visit us again sometime."

The spa's waiting area immediately held guests' attention, with rich glam style, gold hues, fan-coral accents, and the pleasant aromas of hibiscus and honeysuckle. Expensive porcelain tile floor with terrazzo accents, luxurious seating, and the feeling of a 5-star resort welcomed any traveller, begging their credit card. Klara sat down and heard footsteps approach.

"Hello, and welcome to the Sapphire Beach Spa. We are still under a few renovations as we just opened about 10 days ago. Please excuse our mess. Can I have your condominium number?"

"Hello, I have this, and I am just looking to see if you have any open massage time slots. I love the look; your spa is gorgeous! As my colleagues back home would say, 'it reeks in taste'!"

"Oh, let me have a quick look. Can I have your name?"

"Klara Hockley."

"Thank you, Ms. Hockley. We do have an opening, let me take your massage card, and I will see to it that your room is ready. One moment please." The attendant left the front desk swaying in her step as if exiting a dance floor.

*Oh, Marcy, you're going to love this! The view of the shore, the pampered service. A new bride's paradise.*

"Ms. Hockley, right this way please."

## 2.

"You hired the hit, right? For the Woden guy that is missing?" Oren looked at Brett, still leaning in the corner of the cell. He had already plotted his escape in studying the guard's rounds and mentally timed their whereabouts. He was currently relaxing his heart rate, taking long slow breaths.

"I don't know how the Shandwick Trust works these days, but you should remember my name, and yes I ordered the job. I got stuck in a fueling hut when I was taking the last load of fuel and planning to sail over the night to leave here for good. I guess now that the yacht will be impounded or beached, I don't know, I'm stuck in here with you. Do you have a plan to get us out of here?"

"Relax. See that guard." Oren nodded in the direction. "I plan to fake a fainting, then attack and knock him out in about 25 minutes from now. I assume that he is off shift at 3 pm, so if he comes to check right before his shift ends, we can surprise him. Don't make it obvious, just follow my lead."

"If you get us out of here, I'll pay you whatever I can. I've got millions of Euros in an offshore account."

"We'll square up later. When he comes back," Oren pointed towards the door with his index finger, "and unlocks the gate. Tell him to get over here because I'm dead, after having difficulty breathing. You were trying to get help, but no one was around. Escaping from here will be easy, compared to Dodds."

"What are you going to do? Strangle yourself?"

"They do something to your head, strangle your...? No, just follow my lead." Oren went to lay down on the bed, resuming his long deep breaths. Brett was confused over the next steps but trusted him circumspectly watching for the guard to return.

# 3.

"Hey Rakeef!" Chandler poked his head within sight of his open door as Rakeef passed in the corridor.

"What's up? More info or clues?" he sounded eager.

"I was thinking about our conversation last night, the one about feeling tired. What do you think about taking tomorrow off?"

"I'm not overly tired, but I'll support you in taking a breather. The other night still rolls around in my mind, and I don't think we are up to a point of sharing the load with the northern division. They have sent down a couple of SUVs and some officers. We could take the day off. You've done eight days on this week, right?"

"Piper and Jarvis are tired too, I mean Jarvis should have the most energy, but Piper, you and I have all felt the stress of death-threats. I need some beach time to unwind. Are we going to get that Banks, we were supposed to have last night?"

Rakeef thought for a moment. "I think I'll skip the Banks. You should go out though. Didn't you say you wanted to meet up with the Canadian to thank her before she left?"

Chandler checked the clock. "It's 2:48. We should head over to Wodan Crendall's address before the traffic gets packed. Tourists are going to be out tonight, all over the *Gap*."

Jarvis had already packed up his desk, itching to get out early too. When he saw the two detectives leave, he went over to Piper's desk, "Did you have lunch yet? Let's get out of here before they get back. Oh, how's your search through the yacht evidence going? Never mind, tell me on the way." Rakeef left, beckoning Piper to follow, who had a yard sale's worth of evidence piled on her desk.

"It's 2:53. Rakeef, Chand and Jarvis wants to grab an extended lunch. Did you want anything while we're out?" Piper called to Gladys.

"Maybe some Pepto, something didn't agree with me last night. I've been to the bathroom far too many times today. Not again! Piper watch the desk." Gladys ran to the breakroom bathroom. Piper already had her attention on a reel that she received and didn't hear Gladys leave. The front desk was empty as Piper went with Jarvis. By 2:55, the station was empty, with no office personnel around.

The front doors would slide open for only five more minutes. Oren's breathing was so shallow, his heartbeat was near-impossible to trace, and Leroy was approaching the cells on his last shift check. With 4 minutes left in his shift, Brett saw Leroy open the door and yelled out, "Officer, help, help me! He stopped breathing. I'll wait over at the back of the cell, but you need to check on this guy, he was starting to choke and then wanted to lay down. He hasn't moved and is unresponsive." Brett was convincing.

"Stay back, I have to check vital signs, and if you make a move, I'll beat you. There are cameras recording everything you know." Leroy's chubby fingers fitted the key into the lock. He slid the cell door open and kept an eye on Brett, one hand on his baton. The clock read 4:57.

## 4.

"How much do I owe you for a tip? My hip feels amazing." Klara rotated her shoulders, twisted at her waist, and tried a quick squat, marvelling at how fresh her muscles felt.

"You can just give your room number at the front desk, oh, that's right, you had a complimentary massage. Um, I would say it is up to you if you want to leave a tip." The massage therapist announced softly in a welcoming voice.

Klara pulled out a US $10 bill and set it on the massage table. "Thank you again, I really feel relaxed. Oh, it's almost 3 pm, I need to get to the airport!"

"It was my pleasure. Do you need a taxi?

"I think a friend of mine is coming to pick me up. *I have to get back to my room too.* Oh, do you mind if I take a selfie of this beautiful spa in the background? I took a before picture, and now I'd like to take an after-shot." Klara took out her phone and noticed that she had four notifications. She took the selfie, with the spa's atmosphere as a backdrop, and instantly noticed her relaxed and youthful appearance. She flicked back to the earlier picture in her camera roll and confirmed her suspicion. The before shot of the Royal Barbados Police Force Southern Division Station with her floppy beach hat, sunglasses, and slight sunburn was the typical tourist look. Flicking to the new spa picture, she looked like a celebrity. Feeling like today was ending on a great note, she wandered out of the spa, her foot hitting fresh soft Dover Beach sand, as Leroy was about to be laying on a cold jail cell floor, within an inch of his life.

## 5.

Derk had dropped Jones off at his home and headed to the Massy Supermarket in Worthing to pick up some supplies, drinks, and Canadian-Caribbean-friendly foods. Derk had only a few minutes to speak with and get to know Klara aside from the usual police questioning at the edge of the crime scene. Derk had gathered no food allergies of note, okay with most fruits and vegetables, loved fish cutters, and was fond of coconut rum. Purchasing chocolate drink mix syrup, a fruit tray, a carton of fruit juice, a 4-pack of disposable party cups and a small Malibu rum bottle, he walked out to his Suzuki and glanced at his cellphone. Seeing no messages, he put his phone in the glovebox and headed for Dover Beach with the hopes that Klara would be still there.

Leroy had no chance. As soon as he took his eyes off Brett and leaned in to check Oren's vitals, he was overpowered and fell to his side. His only available self-defence tool was the standard-issue baton—since Leroy wasn't carrying a sidearm—which now lay just out of reach. Oren sprang off the bed and elbowed Leroy in the face, breaking his nose. Brett stayed clear of the violence, knowing full well that the cameras were recording and remembering that Oren had said for him to follow his lead, he reached onto Leroy's belt and removed the keys.

Oren extended his arm around his neck and, in one expertly trained move, began a chokehold, suffocating the air travel to Leroy's lungs.

"Hey, just knock him out! Don't kill him, okay?! We've got enough evidence stacked against both of us." Brett sounded anxious, imagining that other police would catch them at any moment.

Seeing that Leroy was not putting up much of a fight, his hands desisted their struggle to try and remove Oren's grip; Leroy choked out a weak, "Stop." then his head drooped back. Oren released his grip, and Leroy slumped to the floor. Brett, careful not to step in Leroy's spilled blood, helped drag the police officer's unconscious body over to the far edge of the cell. Brett rolled him on his side. *Standard recovery position so he would not choke on his blood.* Leroy's heartbeat was low, but within moments began strengthening.

Oren had no time left; with only one minute before the front doors would automatically shut, he raced to the front door but failed to open his escape route. Doubling back, leaving a few bloody footprints in his wake, he rejoined Brett and headed through the corridor to the police parking lot. Gladys exited the bathroom noticing the bloody footprints and heard the escapees exit through the back door. She sounded the alarm.

"Quick over the barricade by those palm trees." Oren ran along the hot pavement in his bare feet. They left with a burst of energy, alarm bells echoing making witnesses a plenty. Their speed looked like they were in hot pursuit. Oren scaled the cement wall first, running straight for the vertical barrier like an American Gladiator contestant.

Making the work look easy, he ran up the wall, grabbed the top and housed himself up beside the palm tree for cover.

Brett had never done a vertical climb before and was certainly not as skilled or flexible as Oren's maneuvering. He decided to run straight for one of the small SUVs that traffic enforcement had towed to the parking lot from a crash and use the smashed wreckage as a step stool and leap towards Oren's hand. Oren had no time to tell him that his careless planning would give them away, so he helped his escape partner by grabbing his outstretched hand and pulling him over the wall to safety. In the getaway, hundreds heard the alarm, few saw anything substantial, and in Oren's strength at pulling Brett over the wall, a nearby painting crew only could make out that he wasn't a local man. They were now on the run to watch for a large plane to take them out of the Caribbean. Flights to Europe were scarce until tomorrow afternoon when the major airlines would land. They would have to lay low for a few hours.

## 6.

Just after Brett had joined Oren by jumping down from the wall, disappearing in hopes to steal a car, Leroy's replacement turned into the parking lot and began running for the door. Once inside, Gladys screamed at her, "Go check Leroy, they've escaped!"

Eloise Davis was not usually late. A blond American tourist and her group of girls swerved to the side to avoid a bus. She watched the tourist drive the passenger side wheels off the curb to the shoulder a half-metre below, bottoming out the rental and unable to lift the car back to the road. Three local men assisted in raising the vehicle back, placing all four wheels touching the pavement, and comforted the frenzied tourists.

That flustered her afternoon but seeing Leroy in his condition would send her into a panic. In the 19 years of working with the Royal Barbados Police Force, she had never had a situation of this magnitude, even being on pregnancy leave during the Glendairy riot and fire of 2005. She opened the door to the Southern Division station and gasped in horror. A few bloody footprints on the floor, smeared and spaced as if the perpetrators had attempted an escape. She dropped her purse on a nearby desk and headed for the holding cells. Peering through the safety glass, she saw that the two detainees were not in either cell, then screamed when she saw Leroy's uniform and the unhealthy spillage of blood.

Eloise ran through the door and frantically searched through her keys for the holding cell lock, "Leroy! Leroy can you here me?! Oh, Leroy I'm coming! Hold on. Oh Jesus!" She fitted the key and unlocked the cell; using newly found strength, she slid open the cell door and knelt behind Leroy, expecting the worst. She touched his shoulder and checked his breathing, seeing dried, cracked blood covering his nose. Eloise felt his warmth and found his pulse. Realizing he was still alive, she reached for her cell phone, "Leroy, I'm going to get a cloth for your face and get help. The men are gone, but that's not your fault. Oh, Leroy, I'm so sorry this happened to you. I'll be right back."

Seeing that the bleeding had stopped, and flakes of dried blood were creating a scattered pattern across his chin; she left the holding cell and returned to her purse. She grabbed her cell phone and dialled Piper. She ran to the laundry cupboard and grabbed two hand towels, making one soaked with warm water for Leroy's face. The call connected.

"Hello? Eloise?"

"Piper, we have a problem. Leroy was assaulted and is in the holding cell that those two men were in earlier. I don't know who had both of those men in the same cell, when the other cell was empty, but they beat up poor Leroy, and he's still here sleeping with a busted-up nose, and he's lost some blood."

"Oh, my god! That's terrible. Are the men still there? The one with the whitish hair, is an assassin, and I would take extreme caution Eloise. I'm on my way, I'll try and get a hold of the others. It's after 3 pm, so they have all gone out. I'll be right there. Help Leroy. I'll call the ambulance."

## 7.

Derk had parked the Jimny in the shade of a palm tree and called Klara over when his cell phone began to vibrate with Piper's message.

"I've got a few snacks, and I can take you to pick up your friend at the airport. She's still coming right?"

"Her plane is arriving shortly. I don't have time to head back to my hotel to charge my phone can I use your charger." Klara hopped into his truck.

"Sure. Just unplug my phone and toss it in the glove box with mine. The traffic is starting to plug so we better get moving." Derk placed his sunglasses on and shifted into gear.

Klara checked the flight status. She also read the headlines. "More attacks around the world. Maybe I should be an investigator instead of an officer."

Derk softened, "You've been to the spa, right? Don't carry the worries of the world on those newly massaged shoulders."

You're right. I'll just send a quick message to Flo and watch the shore. Phones suck you in. I wonder if it will every go back to just calls. I guess that is a personal choice."

**Klara:** Hi Flo. When you get this message I have a friend driving me to pick you up. No need for a taxi. See you soon.

# Chapter 27

## *EVENING FESTIVITIES*

### 1.

"Keep trying his number Jones, where can he be?!" Piper had the phone cocked by her ear as she was massaging Leroy's shoulder, trying to wake him.

"Nobody else is answering either!" Jarvis shouted.

"Where is everybody? Did they all turn their phones off? We have the two highest profile fugitives on the loose!"

"Okay, I'll try his line one last time, then I'll go over to his house. I think he's taking Klara to the airport, but he may have left his phone in the car."

"When you get a hold of Derk, tell him we need him. We have to try and find these guys before it gets too dark." Jones ended the call and gave Piper a flashlight to check Leroy's eyes by lifting his eyelids.

Eloise had cleaned his face and taken great care to photograph the process before putting ice on his nose to slow the swelling. He had a steady heartbeat now, and they were trying to wake him up before the ambulance would arrive to get some information. The surveillance tapes recorded the attack and some escape areas, but since they fled through the parking lot, the officers did not know their destination. Piper had sent Eloise to check for the ambulance and to notify Leroy's wife to meet them at the hospital.

The ambulance pulled in as Eloise checked the door for the second time, and she held the door open for them to bring a stretcher through the front sliding doors. It was common for the paramedics to get stretchers into the detachment. Bar assaults and drunk driving motor vehicle collisions were sometimes common. The craziest instances were over lost cricket matches or televised horse racing if the Garrison wasn't hosting a racecourse event. They were able to revive Leroy with some spirits of hartshorn, which helped Leroy gain consciousness with slight disorientation. He was in no mood to talk and needed assistance to walk. He kept trying to touch his nose as the paramedics were applying a brace. With his effort they slowly got him to the stretcher.

Piper, seeing that the paramedics had complete control of the operation, told Eloise to lock up until more officers came back and start the file using the pictures she had taken of Leroy. The chase would begin soon, and she would stake out the grey-coloured yacht the *Assailant*. Piper saw the ambulance leave imagining the fight, *Brett thinks he'll get away. He's going to have to deceive each one of us!*

## 2.

Trying to leave another message Jones sighed, "He's not answering." Figuring, his assumption that he was still out with Klara, he decided to pack up his loaner and head over to Dover Beach. With any luck, he would see if the black Jimny was still there, and he could inform Derk of the situation. Traffic was light, as most locals were eating, and the tourists were seated at restaurants or patios. He arrived at Dover Road but saw no sign of Derk, Klara or his Jimny.

Doubling back, he headed towards the *Gap* and checked the usual eateries for Derk's vehicle. Getting increasingly frustrated, he tried to remember the Hotel that Klara was staying in but figured that Derk would be home by the time he got there. Jones turned back to the detachment because he knew that helping the police catch these two was top priority. He would wait for Derk there, hoping that it wouldn't take all night.

## 3.

Derk's cell phone, still comfortably in isolation for most of the late afternoon, had now transferred to battery-saver mode since the phone was at 10%.

"There she is. She must have breezed through customs." Klara rolled down here window. "Flo!" She turned to Derk. "Maybe her ears are still plugged. I'll get out here and you can pick us up by that spot."

"Sounds good."

Klara moved through the tourists and cabbies exchanging bags. She remembered the feelings she had when she first arrived before all the crazy crimes occurred. Flo approached her with a tired facial expression.

"Klara, nice to meet you finally. I know you may have heard I travel with a full cargo, but my flight got shortened due to some mechanical issue and I'm here for just under forty-eight hours."

"Oh, that's horrible, the beaches are not too busy right now and once Derk gets us to the hotel I can fill you in after we sit on the beach for a while."

Flo grinned, "That sounds majestic! This girl's toes need some sand to wriggle in." She walked with Klara to Derk's Jimny and sat in the front seat so she could get excited seeing the beach right by the highway.

"Hello Miss. I'm Derk. Klara said you had a direct flight. Those are great; no lost luggage, no layover."

"Thanks, Derk. You have a nice little unit here. Lots of leg room." She turned the conversation back to Klara. "So, what have you done these past three days in this tropical getaway?"

Klara and Derk smiled simultaneously. Derk honked the horn as he waited for Klara's response.

"Let's just say I have found a few areas that Marcy can have for the reception. If she wants to do a spa day or some touring, I've done a little leg work." Klara thought hard about what details she would disclose. She didn't want to ruin the gentle bonding that was going on in the truck.

Derk had worn the badge of chauffeur with pride and enjoyed the calmness on his drive to the Sandy Wharf Hotel, totally oblivious that his phone battery was critical at 3%.

## 4.

Piper remembered Lena as she drove out to the docks. One of the popular girls in school, perfect skin, intelligence, diesel truck on her 16th birthday. She could eat anything and not gain a pound, had good teeth and was model material. Her only flaw was her makeup to cover up the bruises from her abusive boyfriends and stepfather. She and Piper would often sit together and reminisce on simple gossip and small talk when they were young. They both shed a tear when Lena noted some of her darkest secrets, and for the remainder of that year, both girls would form a tight bond.

If Brett would try and come back to the yacht, she would be ready for him. Piper exited her car and switched on her flashlight; she listened to the ocean waves playfully lap against the pier, and checking with her flashlight beam, she noticed no attempt to cut the police tape negating entry. She sat back in her car and checked for any messages from Jones. She hoped that they had found the two runaways. Feeling the sadness lingering for Lena, she was sure to look Brett in the eye one last time; the killer who ended her friend's young life.

## 5.

Brett and Oren had made their way to the St. Lawrence Gap tourist area, as it was beginning to erupt with the usual evening festivities. They would blend in and sneak into a cab with some drunk tourists who would love to offer them a lift back to their hotels. Oren had taken the lead in keeping them undercover since Brett was ill-prepared to be on the run and evade police. Although he did not like the tag-along shadow of Brett, he had no choice. Oren was trying to make his way to the airport as well and off the Island. He did not plan on being tried and sent to HMP Dodds for years since his business associate would not be aiding him on any new jobs or breaking him out of incarceration. Brett mentioned he had cash on hand in the Caymans, but he would have to get there first. Brett asked if IDs would be a problem since a compartment hid his passport on the *Assailant* but was now under police guard. Oren had assured him that with the right strings in place, Brett might be able to re-join the Shandwick Trust and join the ranks with his impressive kill count and relaxed demeanour.

The bar scene was alive, with many tourists bumping into one another and spilling drinks, loud cackling, and the occasional early hangover. One couple caught sight of Brett in the crowd and initiated a conversation as if they were old friends, only realizing that he was mistaken for their friend who returned from the bathrooms. Oren blended in more quickly from his training and watched for a moment to steal a cab if a cabbie went into a bar to use the washroom. He would have to be quick, keeping Brett at his side if such an opportunity arose.

## 6.

Rakeef followed Chandler and parked at the detachment. He left his Swift and joined Chandler on route to meet with Piper and watch for Brett. Jarvis had teamed up with Nathan to start the search for the two fugitives.

"Get Piper on the line and switch it to speakerphone." Chandler ordered as he made his way to the docks.

Rakeef called, "Can you meet us at the docks… oh, you are already there, okay. Any sign of Brett or Oren? Chand and I are coming to you."

"Speakerphone Rakeef!" Chandler sounded impatient.

"Oh right!" He switched to the speaker, Piper's voice mumbling as she walked.

"Piper, it's Chand."

"Hi Chand, everything is clear, with no sign of any movement out here."

"Great. We are coming to you, and I have a strong suspicion that Brett is going to try and get back to the yacht for ID or money, something to get him connected to a way off the Island. A tracker or something like what was on the body of the guy they called Jed in the lab. This guy is a millionaire so he may have a gadget that we've never seen."

"Okay Chand, I've got my flashlight, and I can enter his yacht to look through his stuff. How far are you out?"

"We just passed Oistins."

"Are you in the main cabin? Anything yet Piper?" Rakeef asked.

"His passport case is here with a wad of cash, but his passport is missing."

"And you're 100% certain you are alone?" Chand spoke carefully, not to cause alarm.

"Wait, I found his passport, the active one, it's not expired. He's from Belgium!"

"Good, hold on to it. We're pulling up now. Meet us by your car; let's start a quick check of the area." Chandler had Rakeef end the call then pulled into the marina parking lot.

Piper had reached the port door and made her way back to the gangplank. They would search the grounds with a three-person sweep for a short while. Finding dead ends and wasting time, they decided to head back to the station where Alessio switched to sit at the marina. With the *Assailant* docked and Alessio's trained eyes on his usual night shift, the stakeout would be a comforting change to looking for reckless driving infractions.

"Piper let's head back to the detachment. We'll get the team together and formulate a plan of action. These guys are not leaving tonight!" Once Rakeef, Piper and Chandler left, the pier sat quiet. For little over an hour while they travelled back to base, Alessio would arrive to be a sentry on duty. If the fugitives had a set of wheels, their time window would have allowed them to get the supplies that they need and some cash for a hideout.

# THURSDAY

# Chapter 28

# *TOURIST ATTRACTIONS*

Klara woke to the gentle sound of waves lapping against the shore as her phone alarm. She recorded the sound piece so that in the blistering cold of a Canadian winter, she could wake up to the sound of a Barbados beach. The morning sun filtered through the curtains of her hotel room, casting a warm glow over the elegant coastal decor. She stretched luxuriously after her spa massage, feeling the excitement of the day ahead with Flo. The two girls hit it off well despite the background Klara had heard about her. Today was all about wedding planning for her sister Marcy, and she couldn't wait to share the experience with her travelling partner, Flo Wickworth.

She glanced at the clock. It was just past seven in the morning. Perfect timing for a beachside breakfast before diving into the day's activities. Klara quickly freshened up and slipped into a breezy sundress, ready to start the day.

Downstairs at the hotel's pastel painted café, she found Flo already sipping on a freshly brewed coffee and enjoying a fruit platter. Flo looked effortlessly chic in a floral blouse and white linen pants, her blonde hair cascading over her shoulders.

"Good morning, Klara!" Flo greeted with a bright smile. "Ready for a productive day of wedding planning?"

Klara nodded enthusiastically as she settled into a chair opposite Flo. "Absolutely! I can't wait to see your take on what Barbados has in store for Marcy's big day."

Just after breakfast, they pored over mini pamphlets of wedding venues and discussed floral arrangements while soaking in the serene ocean view at Dover Beach. Klara shared Marcy's vision of a beachfront ceremony at sunset, with tropical blooms adorning every corner of the altar.

Near noon, they hailed a cab to Oistins Fish Fry, a local hotspot known for its vibrant atmosphere and fresh seafood. The cab driver, a jovial Barbadian man named Winston, regaled them with tales of island life as they cruised along the coastal road. Klara smiled as Flo was beginning to realize how friendly everyone is down in Barbados.

At Oistins, they savored grilled mahi-mahi and spicy Bajan fish cakes, sipping on cold Banks beer to cool off from the midday sun. Amidst the lively chatter and music playing in the background, Klara and Flo brainstormed ideas for Marcy's bridal shower and bachelorette party, drawing inspiration from the vibrant culture around them.

After lunch, they strolled through downtown Bridgetown, exploring boutiques and artisan shops. They picked up handmade souvenirs and sampled local delicacies like rum cake and coconut water straight from the husk.

As the afternoon waned, they ventured to the upscale shops near Sandy Lane, where Klara indulged in trying on bridal gowns fit for a princess. Flo offered her expert opinion, marveling at the intricate lace and silk designs that Klara modeled with grace.

## 2.

"Listen up, everyone," Chandler stood in the conference room in front of Piper, Rakeef, Nathan and Jarvis. "I contacted the Northern Division and asked for their help. They had told me that they are a few officers short over an ongoing investigation in the Crab Hill area. We have Alessio down by the docks, watching for Brett to attempt to regain his passport. Piper collected it yesterday, and there has been no sign of him or Oren so far." Chandler took a quick sip of water.

"I must apologize for not arranging this briefing yesterday. My excuse won't be creative; I took a long hot shower and passed out from fifty straight working hours. That is why I take full responsibility if the hunt is long. There that's the story. However, let's do this before anyone else gets burnt-out. Piper and Jarvis will head out to the airport; Rakeef and I will head out to the *Gap* while it's still busy, and we'll all head back if they return. Nathan you can supervise Jones for our dispatch. You can help with reviewing the security footage and such. Please everyone, take precaution, these guys are murderers, and even though they haven't killed any of us, Piper and Leroy came close. Life is too precious to be wasted from their selfish deeds!"

The officers stood and conversed as Nathan came towards Chandler. "I can help out there you know. Just because I am on exchange, and a rookie here, I can do more besides being stuck behind a desk."

Chandler softened, "I know you want to get in on the action for what he did to cause Tyson to get all shook up, but believe me, we'll find them. They are bound to surface somewhere." Chandler motioned to Rakeef to meet him by the D Max.

"Hey, Chand. If he dies, I want to know." Piper gave Chandler a nod before she joined Jarvis on their patrol.

## 3.

Klara and Flo were getting exhausted. Since they would be both leaving the Island tomorrow they rendezvoused with Derk at St. Lawrence Gap. Flo wanted to experience the bustling strip known for its nightlife and lively bars. Derk, offered to be the attentive host, and secured a prime spot at a beachfront bar where they could watch the sunset while sipping on cocktails.

"Over here! Check out this great spot!" Derk greeted them with a warm smile. "You two look like you've had quite the day already. How's the wedding planning going Klara? Flo are you enjoying your first day so far?"

Flo beamed. "It's going magnificently, Derk. Barbados is hitting all the checkboxes today. You should have seen Klara and the dresses they tried on."

Klara blushed as Derk faced her. *I should kiss her, but maybe after when we are alone.*

As the evening progressed, they danced to Caribbean rhythms under the starlit sky, surrounded by tourists and locals alike. Derk kept a watchful eye on their surroundings, scanning the crowd discreetly as they enjoyed the festivities. He wondered if Klara was beginning to have feelings for him, but he didn't want to ruin the evening if she was having a fun time. *She's been through enough this trip. If she comes back, I'll do what I can to be with her.*

As the night wore on, Flo decided to head to a bar offering karaoke and Klara suggested they should text back and forth in case anything goes strange. She thought leaving Klara and Derk together might allow for her to find out what the nightlife would be without Derk's protection.

## 4.

Rakeef and Chandler headed to the Grantley Adams International Airport and toured through the terminal for a few hours, interviewing security, custodial crew, and gift boutique staff. Their search did not find any clues but created an awareness for the suspects. In speaking with the on-duty security captain, it was clear that the threat to tourists and airport staff was a present danger until further notice. Having completed the first walk-about, they returned to the SUV and stood to watch at the entrance lane.

## 5.

Jarvis had waited by the SUV until Piper came out of the detachment. He had thought about the possible escape route they could have taken as he looked around the parking lot. "Didn't Eloise say that the painting crew heard someone run on top of that wrecked car when she collected statements?"

"They said something like that. Do you think that was their starting point?" Piper paused at the edge of the driver's door.

"Five hours from here. They could easily make it to the airport, getting lost in the *Gap*." She got in.

"You're right, Piper, let's go." Jarvis shifted into gear, taking off in the direction of the hottest tourist area along the southern coast.

The *Gap* was packed still with tourists and street dancers. Music was blaring; tables crowded with guests, drinks were flowing freely. Piper and Jarvis both were not in uniforms, so they blended in with ease. They took turns checking with cabbies and bartenders, describing the persons of interest. One bartender thought the description of Oren was familiar and pointed out a shady-looking man near the back of the bar, but upon seeing him, Jarvis made no effort to ask any additional questions.

Piper was beginning to tire from the ear-piercing sound volume and smell of cheap drinks. She met back with Jarvis in front of a closed restaurant. "Anything?"

"No, I checked with taxis, but they didn't have any weird people who wanted to get home fast, if you know what I mean. One cab driver was looking for his friend, who took a group of younger tourists home, and never returned, but besides that there were no other instances of our guys."

"They're gone. The *Gap* was a good cover for them to find a way to slip away. I wonder if they are sleeping somewhere in an old chattel house. We'll never find them tonight, might as well call it and start fresh in the morning."

"We should call Alessio too. If he hasn't seen them by now, he should go back to traffic."

The two detectives walked from the *Gap* to the SUV and sat. With windows down, viewing their cell phones that took a few minutes to recharge. Their search had not proven any success, and feeling deflated, they started the SUV and headed back to the station. They paused when they saw a lone tourist crossing at a cross walk to a waiting taxi.

Flo had crossed in front of the two spent detectives and got into the cab, hoping to return to Sandy Wharf swiftly. She settled into the backseat, exchanging pleasantries with the driver, a middle-aged man named Curtis.

Suddenly, the atmosphere in the cab shifted. Two shadowy figures materialized from the darkness, forcing their way into the backseat. Flo's heart raced as moments before she saw two capable officers that could have prevented this hijacking.

"Keep driving, old man," one man growled, pressing a sharp object against Curtis's side. "Keep things causal, or you're dead. Ask her where she's going."

Curtis, visibly shaken, complied, fear etched across his face as he drove with trembling hands. Flo kept her composure, trying to memorize details that could help the police. She wanted to text Klara but figured they might suspect she is trying for the police.

They drove past Flo's hotel before Brett barked at Curtis to stop. They shoved Curtis out of the cab. Tied lengths of rope around his neck, and limbs. One swift kick knocked him out. They got back in the cab. "I thought you wanted to go to your hotel. Isn't it right back there?" the man said with no remorse for his past actions.

"Please don't hurt me. I just want to get out." Flo's hands trembled as she fumbled for the door handle. She opened the door and stepped out to the hot evening air. The cab took off before she could close the door and immediately dialed her phone. Seeing the in-case-of-emergency number on the back of the cab she connected with the police.

Nathan's late evening was dull. No calls, surveillance footage reviewed, and no coffee. Just after 1:15 am, the phone rang, startling him as he was nodding off to sleep. "Hello, Southern Division of the Barbados Police Force, how can I help you?" He placed the call on speaker while he fished around on Gladys's desk for a sheet of paper and a pen.

"Oh my god, it was so freakin' scary!" The woman's voice not local, hard to tell if she was from North America or England. I was in this cab, heading back to my hotel, and this guy went up to the driver and asked him for directions or something. Another guy opened the door, got into the cab, and told us if we said anything, we'd all be dead. They only wanted the cab, and our lives meant nothing to them. It's crazy, what they did to that cabbie," The girl's voice drew tight, "They tied a rope around his neck, his arms, and the other end around his feet. He was then kicked in the head and knocked out. I don't know if anyone has found him, or if he's okay."

"Miss where are you now?" Nathan wrote notes as he acutely listened to the girl's statement.

"I'm back at my hotel. I would have called sooner, but 911 doesn't work over here, and when I saw the cab speed away I called you."

"Are you okay? Any injuries? Did the car thieves do anything to put you in danger besides threaten you?"

"It was weird, the two guys didn't speak much, besides ask the driver to proceed as normal and ask where I was staying so they could drop me off."

"Where are you staying?"

"What's this place called? Stingray Cove? No, sorry, It's the Sandy Wharf; a 2-star place if you ask me." The caller trailed off as she took a sip of water.

Okay, I'll send over someone to check on you, unless you'd like to file a statement in the latter part of this morning." Nathan checked his smartwatch.

"Yeah, sorry for calling this late, but I feel bad for that cab driver. Weirdest car theft I've ever seen. Can I go now?"

"I just need your name for the report."

"It's Florence, Flo Wickworth." She ended the call.

Nathan noted the location and called Chandler, "I think we have finally got a lead." He explained the attack and the car theft, to which Chandler and Rakeef listened on speakerphone while Rakeef ran routes in his head.

"So, they might be in a taxi? Wait, did you say Sandy Wharf?!" Rakeef sharply looked over at Chandler.

"Isn't that where Klara is staying? The other hotel complex from where the murders happened?"

"Have a unit go check on the cab driver, on the route from the *Gap* to their hotel. Jones and I are beat, Alessio can go check on Sandy Wharf. I can hardly keep my eyes open here."

"Okay. Drive safe, we'll figure this out."

## 6.

Derk returned Klara home, exhausted but exhilarated from the night's festivities. They bid each other goodnight, Derk promising to call Klara in the morning to check on Flo and the karaoke experience.

As the clock ticked past two, the nightclubs began settling over Barbados, leaving Flo shaken but safe, Curtis recovering from his ordeal, and Derk and Klara drifting off to sleep, unaware of the danger that had lurked so close to them that night.

Chandler drove Rakeef back to the station to pick up his car, then took the highway and scarcely made it back to his driveway with barely enough energy to make it to his bed.

# FRIDAY

# Chapter 29

# *GIRL FIGHT*

## 1.

Klara overslept, and in partying with Flo and Derk last night, it was an ambulance siren whirring by that woke her up. Feeling both stressed and a little unhappy that Flo missed seeing the few last touristy destinations. She decided to see the night life along the *Gap* instead. To Klara the drinks were heavy and around midnight she preferred the quiet place Derk found to unwind. She never reconnected with Flo, but she remembered telling her the taxis were friendly and the Sandy Wharf was just up the road.

Klara packed her final toiletries in her suitcase, transferring necessary items for her flight back to Edmonton, Canada. Feeling her phone vibrate produced one new message from Flo.

**Florence:** The cab ride was hell, I had to call the police.
**Klara:** Really? I'm sorry. What happened?
**Florence:** Two guys roughed up the cab driver and I was almost hijacked.
**Klara:** Oh my God! Are you ok? Where are you?

**Florence:** I'm checking out then waiting by the lobby. See
          you in a minute.

She figured by the hour of the morning, Derk was
working with files but remembered him saying he wanted
the day off to drive us to the airport. Klara quickly grabbed
her belongings and closed the door. As she turned, she saw
a black pickup truck parked in the parking lot poised to
catch speeding motorists. She checked in her key and
collected her receipt, shoving it into the side pocket of
her carry-on bag and grabbed an apple at the continental
breakfast bar.

Flo came from the pool area. "What the hell happened
last night? You and your boyfriend left me, and I had to
fend for myself. I'm glad I'm only here for another few
hours!"

"You wanted to split up and do karaoke so Der—"

"Don't bother! You're just like your sister."

"Hold it right there! We had an enjoyable day yesterday
and just because you wanted to break away to find a juicy
bar experience, don't blame me for leaving you when you
took off from us!" Klara was livid.

"I'll find my own way to the airport. I'll take the
bus or a shuttle. I'm glad we are not on the same flights.
Yesterday may have been fun, until the disaster in the
cab. Those two guys kicked a tied up man in the head!
This place may be beautiful, but I wouldn't get married
anywhere near here!" Flo stormed off.

Klara sat with her luggage, feeling horrible that her
vacation was always full of crime and stress. She also
thought she may not have time to see Derk for their

goodbye, and soon she would be back to Alberta and its oil and gas pipeline partnership problems.

She rose from her seat and wheeled her bags over to the front desk. "Hello, can I call a cab to take me to the airport?"

"Certainly, what time is your flight leaving?"

"I think 2:30 pm, and I need to be at least 4 hours ahead of the flight, so that gives me about 45 minutes to get to the airport."

"Thank you, can I have your name again so the cabbie can call you when he is here?" Sang the desk attendant, cheerfully ignoring the girl fight that happened moments before.

"Klara Hockley."

"I'll get on that call right away Ms. Hockley. You can leave your bags here and sit by the pool if you'd like, I'll watch over them for you, and call your name on the speaker when your cab is here."

Klara thanked the girl and walked out to the grotto, realizing that Flo was on the way to the airport, she wanted to try and get her mind off the stress she was under. Stretching her legs on a white vinyl pool lounger brought her a bit of calm. A family with small children splashed in the shallow end by the waterfall, but the active noise didn't distract Klara from soaking up every bit of sun she had left.

## 2.

"Alessio, are you still there at the Sandy Wharf?" Rakeef sounded tense.

"Yup Rakeef, no sign of them. I'm keeping an eye out for that Canadian girl too. She is lounging by the pool, catching some sun. You should have seen the other one she got into this morning. Something went down and Derk was involved."

"Really, could you talk with her for a bit, and let her know what we know so far. She's pretty up to speed with the whole investigation and was knowledgeable with the crime. Chand told me to let her be, but I want to make sure she doesn't get in any more trouble."

"Anything beats sittin' here waiting for time to fly by." Alessio ended the call and shut off the truck. Reaching under the steering wheel, he flicked a small toggle switch disabling the ignition in case of theft. His traffic unit looked as expensive as it was and was stripped of any exterior police lights, as Alessio had them moulded to the inside. With the kill-switch engaged, he left the truck, walked by the front desk, displayed his badge, and pointed to the pool.

"Hello, Klara. Officer Sufaletta, I don't want to alarm you but as I pull up this chair, just keep sunnin' yourself while I tell you what's been happening with Derk."

"What happened to Derk? Are you an undercover cop? I've never seen you before with him."

"I'm with the Northern Division, traffic mainly but I was brought down to help after that helicopter incident two days ago. I hope that doesn't leave a bad taste in your mouth over this week's violence. Barbados is, as you can feel, the Island in the sun, despite your chit-chat this morning."

"That girl is Florence Wickworth, my sister's maid of honor. She's flying out with me today, but hopefully not on the same flight. Did something happen with Derk? I thought he told me he wasn't working with your team today." Klara spoke with a slight bit of fear, still tanning with her eyes closed facing the sun.

"Well, a lot happened last night. I can fill you in, but only if you promise not to worry." Alessio looked for Klara to gesture and paused.

Klara faced him and gave the cue. "I'm not too worried. I've seen murder, counted over ten victims washed ashore, been on a bus crash, and now I'm heading home, so for the next forty minutes, nothing that you tell me will phase me. I'm a cop too just not in a division."

"Derk, would like me to take you to the airport, and be personally escorted because both of the criminals that we had in the holding cells, have escaped, and are at large, somewhere on the Island. I think we will be fine, but they might be trying something at the airport."

Klara sat up, "I'm a little worried." She stood and looked at him. "We should go now. I'll tell the front desk, that I won't be needing that cab." Klara moved past him.

"Do you have any bags?" Alessio began to follow her and glanced back at his parked truck, seeing some boys checking out the style and details. "I'll be right back Klara." He strutted out to the kids like a gangster.

"Is it too late to cancel that cab, I have a ride now."

"I'm afraid it is too late. They should be here within 5 minutes or so."

"Okay thank you, give them this for their trouble." Klara handed the girl her last US $10. She picked up her bag and wheeled it out to Alessio's unmistakable black truck.

Alessio had started the engine and revved the motor to make the muffler pop. The teens were gleefully entertained as much as seeing heavily dressed dancers with excessive cleavage at Crop Over. Klara opened the rear passenger door and used the step bar to hoist herself up, placing her luggage on the seat, then sat in the front, buckling her seatbelt. Alessio was already in the driver's seat, half hanging out the door giving a high-five and fist pump to his new admirers. He turned to Klara, who didn't display the same level of amusement, put the truck in gear and started his route.

## 3.

Travelling towards the Sandy Wharf was the cab that had dropped off the fare hours before, containing two men, tired, hungry, and armed. Oren had taken the taxi to one of the safe houses in a residential district on the edge of Bridgetown harbour. The house had little supplies but running water, a hidden room for sleeping quarters, and a duffle bag with assorted loaded, unregistered guns. He and Brett could only catch 2 hours of sleep apiece. They had a quick warm shower and used a coil of small US bills, a bit of emergency cash to eat two breakfast combos at Chefette. If their taxi had a traceable locator, they would dump it for a rental car transporting an elderly couple heading to the airport. Noticing that the cab had a dispatch radio, a call was overheard for a pickup at the Sandy Wharf for Klara Hockley. They decided to pass on the geriatric couple that might stop for the last souvenir for their entitled grandchild and take Klara instead. Brett laughed as he remembered the name and told Oren the history of Klara, saying that if Wodan had killed her in the first place, they would be in the clear. They set out with the taxi on route to the familiar Sandy Wharf location from last night to carry out their plan.

## 4.

Alessio had asked Klara if she had an enjoyable time touring around the northern half of the Island, talking about the North Point, Animal Flower Forest, Morgan Lewis Windmill, and antique chattel houses. He told Klara a brief history of the one roof and a shed design when he saw a taxi approach and slow down. Seeing no riders inside and a wide enough section of road for both to easily pass, Alessio flicked the lights and honked the horn to give the taxi the right of way. As the cab passed them, he watched the driver and passenger, then he turned to Klara and told her to hold on. He switched the truck into high 4x4, turned on the police lights and turned a tight U-turn initiating a chase. The taxi's acceleration zoomed ahead, creating a few car lengths of distance, then turned to Highway T, racing for Newton Road.

"Derk, It's Alessio! I've got Klara with me, but we are in pursuit of the two suspects headed north in a tan coloured Toyota taxi, my guess is that they're headed to the Tom Adams and to the airport."

"Is Klara, okay?! We'll catch up to you, and Chandler and Rakeef are both waiting at the entrance gates. I'll text them that you are coming." Derk spoke loud enough that Klara could hear him as Alessio dropped his cell on the center console cushion, ending the call. Just before Alessio was able to turn, a bullet struck his arm and flew past Klara's face close enough she heard it before exiting out her open window. She looked at Alessio and saw his arm pouring blood over his pants. He tried to look over at her then slammed on the breaks as the taxi came into view.

"Get down Klara. Head down, we're under fire." Klara began to scream and felt the truck lurch forward again before it slipped off the road into an open field.

Alessio was weeping a consistent flow of blood from his arm, with no time to bandage it as he was unarmed and under attack. He still had the police lights illuminated, and the 4-way hazard flashers were working when the truck came to a stop.

"I don't see them, Klara. It's okay. You can sit up again, but please be careful."

"Whoa, your arm! You're losing a lot of blood. Here use this to stop the bleeding." She offered her bikini top to use as a tie off.

"Please open the glove box by your knees and get out the first aid kit. There is a bandage of gauze in there that you will need to tie around my arm, to slow the bleeding. Can you see my cell phone too? I need you to call for an ambulance." Alessio's voice sounded dry.

"Suit and gauze first!" Klara opened the glove compartment and found the roll of gauze. Ripping it open with her teeth, she started looking for the cell phone. "Here, I got your cell phone," she looked up and let out a short scream. Oren had his arm around Alessio's neck and bare hand over his nose with a hand-sized patch of gauze, putting him into an unconscious state. Just as she was about to scream a second time, Brett grabbed hold of her mouth with a gloved hand and pressed a loaded handgun to the back of Klara's neck.

"Let me be perfectly clear here. You are going to cooperate and not scream. I'm going to move your stuff and sit directly behind you, with this gun on your neck. We just need to get to the airport like you do. If you do anything to try and stop us, you won't make your flight, and will wake up in a hospital if you are lucky. Am I understood?" Brett sounded as cold as a trained assassin.

Klara mumbled through his glove, "Yes." Brett took his hand away, and Klara looked for where Oren had taken Alessio.

"Just leave me here with him. He will die if you leave him here, and he didn't do anything to you. Take the truck, just leave me with my luggage, and this cop, and take the stupid truck!"

"Woah let's watch our temper there. We are going to take you to the airport as planned, and we will part ways in the parking lot. You don't want to be late." Oren used his sleeve to wipe the blood solidifying on Alessio's driver's seat. "There, there... just a little drive on the highway. You have your passport, right?" Oren put the truck into gear, turned off the police lights, released the 4-way flashers and reset the transmission back to two-by-four mode. As they drove away, Klara watched in horror the body of Alessio lying in the field, with his arm unbandaged roasting in the sun.

Feeling the metal barrel pressed to her neck was half the ache in Klara's heart. She had no idea if Alessio would live and was sickened at the calm demeanour of Oren resting his arm on the driver's windowsill as if he owned the police truck. Alessio's cell phone was in her hand, but she could not get past the screen due to his security settings, asking if someone was driving the vehicle and entering his passcode. Klara's phone had a different button layout, so making an emergency call would be impossible. Staring forward through the windshield, Klara tried to remove herself from the crisis that she was currently neck-deep.

Brett adjusted his grip of the gun pressed to Klara's neck and decided to up the struggle by firmly grabbing her hair and pulling it through the headrest. Hearing her wince, he whispered that it would be all over soon and chuckled.

"Why me?" Klara spoke out, breaking the silent hostage situation. "With all the death I've been through this week, you couldn't just hide out and steal a boat or a rental car and drive yourselves to the airport? Why kill that cop?!"

"Shut… Up…" Brett pressing the gun each time he enunciated the words.

Klara's phone began to vibrate, sending everyone in the cabin on edge. Klara looked down to see who was calling.

"Who the hell is that?" Brett barked from the backseat. "Do the cops know we stole the truck?"

"It's my sister." Klara held up her phone. "What do you want me to do?"

"Answer it and talk normal." Oren moved his finger to the answer button on the phone's screen and slid sideways to answer the call.

"Try anything stupid and you get thrown out of this truck, miss your flight, and maybe your life." Brett whispered from the backseat, pressing her neck, intensely gripping Klara's hair.

"Hi, Marcy, I'm on the way to the airport. Oh, you found a seat sale, Saskatoon to Toronto with a short layover in Winnipeg for Christmas Eve Day. Wow that's a decent price. Sure, go ahead and book my ticket, business class if it's affordable, but skip the extra meals, I guess we'll eat airport fare." Klara had spoken with no hesitation in her voice, and Marcy thought nothing was out of the ordinary; however, she assumed that Klara was tired and sunburnt.

Both Brett and Oren listened to her conversation but paid no attention to the gab, listening like junior high teachers for foul language in the cafeteria. Hearing no suspicious discussion, the remainder of the trip was pleasant for two truck hijackers holding a Canadian tourist at gunpoint on a cloudless day, minutes from the airport's turnoff lane.

# Chapter 30

# *ALESSIO'S PARTNERS*

**1.**

"Jones, turn now, and take that back road. Let's start the trace from where Alessio said they were headed." Derk watched as they passed the Sandy Wharf and continued north. "There is the hotel. Turn on to the T highway."

Jones was driving and trying to process the location that Alessio had described, watching out for potholes and the ladies walking with washing baskets balanced on their heads. He excitedly turned to Derk, "Is that their taxi, over there with the broken headlight?"

"Pull over, I think we've got something."

"Oh Jesus! Is that Alessio in the dirt? Who the hell is that?"

Derk pained to see through the windshield's glare but realized as soon as his uniform came into view. "Stop over there Jones! Call the ambulance," Derk opened the glove box and grabbed the standard police first aid bag, jumped out of the SUV, and raced to Alessio's side.

"Flo?" Derk squeaked. "Where's Klara?"

Jones came running over. "What happened?"

"What? Oh my God, Derk! These were those two guys from last night when you two took off. Whatever I'm over it! I knew something bad was going to happen. I was waiting for the bus this morning, and saw the truck zoom by, a gun went off and then I saw the idiot from last night grab this guy out of his truck and kidnap a girl. I'm sorry this island is nuts!"

"They have Klara. Jones call it in. They are heading to the airport."

Surveying his injuries, Derk checked for a pulse and began doing CPR. Jones joined and told him that the ambulance was on the way and should be here soon as they dropped off a nurse with a live organ for transplant and headed north. He worked on wrapping his arm and commented that the bullet went cleanly through, but he lost a lot of blood.

"Is he going to die Derk?"

"They can give him blood at the hospital." Derk harshly spoke as he was awkwardly performing chest compressions. "Come on man, stay with us." They began to hear the wail of the ambulance.

Jones used the air pump timed with Derk's compressions to get air into Alessio's lungs and continued until paramedics arrived and took over.

The paramedics did the usual checks when arriving at an unconscious body, then ripped open his shirt and prepared his torso for defibrillation. Putting the paddles over his chest and at his side, she called for clear and pushed the shock button. Jones and Derk sat back with their hands in the air, waiting for the moment to hear his heartbeat. The paramedics shocked again and checked his blood-oxygen levels.

"We have a heartbeat. Thanks for your help you three, he's stable. You saved his life. We'll load him up on the stretcher and get him to the hospital. We will need your help to lift, then we'll take it from here, again thank you for your expertise, you did everything right."

Derk moved to support Alessio's head, and Jones helped slide the board under his back, then lifted him and carried him to the back of the ambulance.

They ordered Flo to join them, hopped back into the SUV and took off north to the Tom Adams Highway.

"I swear Jones, If Alessio dies, and we don't catch these killers, he would have died for nothing. Call Chandler and see if they have seen them."

"They probably don't know they ditched the taxi and stole the truck." Jones dialled Chandler as they turned onto the highway.

Flo quietly spoke, "Derk, what are they going to do to Klara?"

"I don't know. These guys are desperate. They should just let her go." Derk groaned.

## 2.

Klara tried to ease the discomfort of having her hair pulled by shifting her hips forward and pushing her head back to the headrest. As she watched the airport coming into view, she tried to think of how she would get out of this situation. The guy with the gun to the back of her neck had the upper hand but did say that she would be able to catch her flight if she complied. *What the hell Derk, why did you get Alessio to take me to the airport.* Klara closed her eyes. *Jesus? Can you do something here?! Send a heart attack or stroke to either of these guys? Could you show me a sign?* Klara ended her prayer and opened her eyes to the parking lot. Seeing the familiar Police blue and yellow SUV off in the parking lane by the departures drop off, she unveiled a quick grin and gave thanks.

Brett loosened his grip on Klara's scalp, telling her that she kept her end of the bargain and did not think of anything stupid, like bolting from the truck at a stop sign or while driving. "And keep your seatbelt on. Don't be a brave victim!"

Oren eased into the parking lot and drove to the north-eastern corner to head around to the maintenance buildings. He instructed the others that the drop-off point would be suitable for everyone. Klara was to wait in the truck while Oren did a quick wipe down; Brett to grab the guns and close the doors before Klara would be allowed to leave.

Klara had to think fast; she didn't want to spend any more time with these two but didn't want any extra trouble. She hungered to survive and get home, so her only option was to sit in the seat and wait. Brett and Oren worked quickly, trying to get out of sight before an airport worker caused any problem.

"Excuse me, but you can't return your adventure rental over here, it needs to go back to the south parking lot," ordered a young adult with a clipboard and associate name tag. "That lot over there."

"Okay sorry," Oren offered. "Here are the keys, I have to catch my flight, and I don't have time to move it. I'm late." He tossed the keys in the air to the worker.

"I'm not a valet service or chauffeur…" The man received the keys and recognized the police logo on the keychain, "but since it is a sweet adventure rental, I guess I could return it for you."

"Thanks," Brett spoke, firmly tucking his pistol into the back of his jeans and concealing the gun heel from view. Oren had already moved towards the side door of the airport, so Brett lightly jogged after him.

The man opened the driver's door and was startled when he spotted Klara. "It's okay, I'm not going to hurt you. Have they done anything to you?"

"Those guys stole this truck from the traffic cop who owned it and had me at gunpoint."

He started the truck and slid it into gear, "I know it's a police truck, I saw the police force logo on the keyring." He carefully drove it away from the hangar and towards the police SUV on the other side of the parking lot.

"Thank you. They're right over there. What's your name?"

"Promise you won't laugh?" he tried to ease the mood and make her smile. "I know my name is special and named after some Saint," he began, "Francis! Something about starting something, do it if it's possible, and then you can do the impossible, but I haven't any idea about what that meant when I was told. My friends call me Franky."

"Thanks, Franky," Klara smiled relieved this kid didn't get hurt.

"Um, your welcome?" Francis answered.

## 3.

"Hey, Chandler isn't that Alessio's truck?"

"Yup, hold on though Jones is calling. Hello?"

"Chandler, stop looking for the taxi. They stole Alessio's truck and are at the airport by now." Jones spoke as Chandler looked directly in the direction of Alessio's truck.

"His truck is coming right for us, but who's driving is not either of our two guys. He turned over to park in the return rentals. Klara and him just got out, and she's waving a cellphone in the air. I gotta go Jones, just get here and we'll figure out what's next." Chandler ended the call and shut off the SUV. Rakeef had greeted Klara, who was now beside the hood explaining the ordeal.

Francis moved towards Chandler with his hands up, holding the keys as he spoke, "Officer? Here are the keys to the truck. The two guys went through the service doors near the maintenance hangar and seemed suspicious if you ask me."

"You did good, my man. You were lucky, those two are wanted on several murders here on the Island, and they are extremely dangerous. Thanks for bringing back Officer Sufaletta's truck.

Francis gave a quick nod, then jogged back to his office door. Klara explained, "I was held by gunpoint, and in the cab, the driver told the other guy to grab the bag of guns, but I didn't see him take anything out of the back seat."

Rakeef looked through the rear tinted window, then asked Chandler for the keys. He found a duffle bag with loose guns, two ammunition boxes, and a cleaning kit. In opening the door, Rakeef beamed, "Chandler, I think they forgot something. Look at these!"

As Chandler approached, Derk and Jones pulled into the lot and parked in a stall close-by. Jones went to the truck, looking over the guns and informing the other officers of the issues with Alessio.

Flo went over to Klara, who still seemed shaken from the circumstances. "You, okay?"

"Are you still mad at me?" cried Klara, "how's the cop that owns that truck?"

"Derk said in the SUV 'He touched Heaven, giving a high-five to his family that already passed, and then flew back to us.' The paramedics came, and we all heard his heart stop, but he fought and came back." Flo started, showing emotion.

"He is in the hospital now, passing Leroy in the hallway. Jesus, I need a rum." Derk wiped his nose, bashfully hiding from Klara.

"You don't need a witness statement from either of us right? We have planes to catch, you have a bag of guns, do I need to spell it out for you?" Flo stood beside Klara with her hand on her hip like she was ready for the rodeo.

"Ah no guns Miss. It's not like those America states that let you carry firearms" Chandler informed.

Derk stepped towards them, "I'll just quickly debrief with the others, you go on, and I'll meet you at your departure line. Are you flying with American Airlines or Air Canada?"

"Air Canada, then connecting to WestJet to get back out to Alberta."

"I'm on WestJet to Toronto then Calgary." Flo pondered if Klara had the better option.

"Okay, I'll meet you in a couple of minutes. I won't be long, and I want a goodbye from both of you." Derk winked at them and walked over to the enforcement crew.

## 4.

"Have you seen these guns? Look at this one; you could carry that like a cell phone." Jones conversed with Rakeef over the guns' size in their hands as Derk picked up one.

"We don't have any idea what they are holding, and based on the hardware we have here I will guess this may go down wrong. My vote is to leave the guns out the equation." Derk briefly paused, listening for any questions. "Alessio is in hospital, and Chandler has his keys, so when all is done and these two guys are back in custody, these are going to go into evidence and then get destroyed. No Guns." Derk looked each of them in the eye.

"Chandler?" Jones spoke up, "What are you thinking?"

"I agree with Derk. They have killed innocent tourists, and almost killed Leroy and Piper, then what they did to Alessio, and torturing Klara as she is about to leave her vacation and may never come back. We need to play it safe and catch them some other way. They are not from here. They're a different breed. Derk, I'm in." He zipped up the bag and shut the door locking the truck's contents.

Derk mentioned that he would meet them after Klara had got to security. Chandler told the group he had a contact that could get them through the security gates without detection. They parted and prayed that no severe issues would arise.

# Chapter 31

# *TWO TEAMS*

## 1.

"Over here!" Oren hissed at Brett when he came inside. A small shelving unit covered them from view so that they could discuss their plan and final arrangements. "Take this card. If you need immunity when you land, just present this and they will take you to a conference room with a private phone. When you get into that area, call the number on the back of the card. A member of the Shandwick Trust will arrange a pickup and take you to a safe house in a country of your choice, similar to the one we stayed in last night, only a few more luxuries."

"You sure this will work. How are we supposed to get on any plane without passports?"

"It will be a little challenging, but it is easy once you know how. First, we need to take another gun from the bag you brought, then we need to get some uniforms from the locker rooms, or knock a few workers out, and take their clothes."

"I don't have the bag."

"You're kidding me," Oren boiled with rage, "you left the bag in the truck?!" He waited for a response.

"Sorry, all we have is what we've got on us, I guess. You're a professional, improvise."

At that moment, Oren knew that Brett was useless, and he was on his own. *If Brett gets caught, I might be able to get off the island, steal his yacht...* Brett was staring at him when he realized his promise. "You said you were going to pay me for getting you out of jail. The least you could do while I wait for payment is bring the bag of guns."

"I'll transfer you the money, I promise. I'll make more if I'm out of here by tomorrow."

"I'll make it easy. Sign the yacht's title over to me, and we call it even. I'll make arrangements with the Shandwick Trust that I've acquired a new asset, and they will recover it for me. That is what I want in exchange for your freedom.

"Done. I will make the call once we get our plan set." Brett was honest, the *Assailant* was a prototype, and he had another more sophisticated ship in Belgium's Verbindingsdok port.

The plan was for them to split, using a fueling worker's uniform, keys, and fuel truck to gain entry and hide in the utility elevator of a large passenger plane. The other would have a similar cover of a baggage shuttle driver that loaded the checked luggage onto the conveyor belt into the aircraft's belly.

Oren decided on the luggage route, pretending to board a plane destined for any South American airport to evade police, then concentrate on plan B. Brett would be left with the fueling truck mission if he could handle it. They shook hands and parted into the hangar, one heading to the carts, the other hiding in the shadows.

In the security line, Flo stood with Klara as she was not feeling herself. The ordeal and stress this day had caused and the sounds of whining kids and passengers didn't help. Many were waiting in line up to check their cramped suitcases. She packed light for a reason, having been on numerous vacations with her family, the ease and speed of only having a carry-on with no duty-free was worth it. Klara was a bit lost and looked for the Air Canada wicket when a hand gripped her shoulder. She turned around and smiled.

"Feeling a little safer now that you are surrounded by tourists." Derk smiled.

"I'm not entirely sure, where is a place to sit down in this airport that has a quieter atmosphere?"

"I could pull some strings and get you up to the Sky Loft, where all the first-class highflyers rest their feet. I arrested some passenger up there once, for smuggling cocaine in her purse strap."

"I'd love that. I doubt that any of those people up there have been through a week like I have. And Flo had a rough night last night, so she deserves it too."

"Let me talk to my guy. Get your boarding slips, and I'll meet both of you by the Sky Loft doors." Derk gave Klara a hug and stole a quick kiss on her neck then disappeared into the crowd as she moved to the start of the Air Canada lineup, and Flo to WestJet.

**2.**

Brett tailed a worker that had filled up a large fuel tanker and went to the lockers for a quick snack and washroom break. When he closed his locker door, he brought his water bottle to fill up at the drinking fountain. Following behind the man, Brett waited until he was deep in concentrated work before striking him on the back of the head and dragging his body into the adjacent washroom. He chose a worker that was a little more heavy-set than he was so the uniform would be a good match and not too tight. Brett came out of the hangar's darkened area and lunged at the man, who did not have enough time to face his attacker. Brett slammed the gun heel on the man's skull with such force it knocked the worker's safety glasses from his forehead. He slumped forward, with a bright trail of rich blood mixing with the spilled water on the cement floor, then fell back and flopped his arms out to his side. Brett quickly grabbed his wrists and kicked open the door, dragging the worker into the washroom, then locking the door with ease. Within minutes Brett emerged from the room in complete disguise, with the fueling truck's keys in his overalls. He walked through the hallway and flicked the light switch off as he stole the full fuel truck.

Brett had also acquired the worker's wallet, cellphone, and car keys. In driving the full truck out of the hangar, he went to the side and turned on the cell phone. Brett tried a few passcodes and broke in as the third attempt gained entry from the fingerprints on the phone's surface. He called the number on the card that Oren had given him an hour before and arranged for a helicopter pickup off the runway's southern area. The voice on the call agreed that they would have a helicopter within the ninety-minute guarantee. Brett had said that the pickup would be for two and used Oren's code name, to which there was a long pause and then a click ending the call. Brett now had no idea if he was getting rescued or had to follow through with the original plan.

## 3.

Oren had made it to the luggage shuttle and put on a traffic vest and hard hat. His disguise was partially foolhardy, and in commandeering the empty shuttle cart, he was now seated with the warm air blowing by his ear. He loaded the cart's clasp clutching the entire luggage for a Rio Air 747 flight to Brazil. He drove the cart over to the luggage chute and began hoisting luggage from the racks to the belt. He performed the service without a care in the world, throwing suitcases upwards of eight feet to the belt mechanism. One bag zipped open, and the tourist's particulars were flapping in the breeze. Oren retrieved most of the belongings, but a black bra blew down the runway like an untethered kite. He placed the suitcase by the stairs and kept an eye on when the flight crew would board, so he could bring the bag on board and put it in the overhead compartments. He continued his load and stopped when the first pilot came to board the aircraft.

"Excuse me, this suitcase opened, and I would like to put it on board in the overhead bins, behind the first-class section where that oversize luggage area is. Do you know the one I'm talking about?"

"Yes, of course. The plane is open, I believe."

"Thank you, captain."

The pilot took off his hat and entered the plane. Oren ascended the staircase and carried the luggage to the tail-end of the aircraft, and on seeing the pilot seated in the cockpit, he pushed the opened bag into the overhead bin and slipped into the lavatory. Oren quickly undressed from his traffic vest and hat and waited, listening for the opportune knock so he could open the door and return to his free seat in passage to Rio. He had no gun so problems would arise if the police found him. He also hoped that Brett had found an escape soon, so if he became captured, the police would be busy, and Oren could make a clean getaway.

Flo, Klara and Derk arrived at the Sky Loft door with Chandler's access card. Jones and Rakeef had secured a table that the four officers could discuss the game plan, and were snacking on a platter of lobster nachos. Not making it obvious, Chandler had given the card to Derk in a washroom at the sinks, then joined with the other team members. Derk scanned the key card and held the door open for the Canadian girls to enter. They walked up the ramp, and loft steps to a serene resting area, equipped with a juice bar and two glass door refrigerators with pre-made fruit salads, yogurts, and a selection of coffee creamer containers. They found a table in front of a vast dome window overlooking the runway and ocean. A few patrons were looking in their direction, wondering how they could afford the status. Figuring they were a social media executive or e-commerce mogul; they went back to their fine wine and caviar.

"Thanks, Derk. I feel safer here, and I know how to get to my gate when my pre-boarding gets called."

"It was my pleasure, but we should take that picture in front of this window. Your camera might have a brightness setting to not wash our faces in shadow." He moved beside her and posed.

Klara tried to position the shot with as much focal length as she could, deciding on a close-up with the Caribbean Sea in the background. She tried to form a joyful smile, but emotionally she was spent. She took two pictures from slightly different angles and then put her phone in her pocket.

"I forgot to give you this earlier. It's Alessio's cellphone, from the truck." She handed the phone to Derk.

"Thanks, I'll make sure he gets it. I'll go check on him after we catch these two guys, and you are in the air back to your home. Do you want the goodbye hug now? Or when your flight gets called for boarding?"

"I would love one now, and then a follow up at the gate." Klara stood and leaned into him. Flo paid no attention and was checking her phone when they squeezed each other close.

Derk looked out the window and watched a plane taxi to the runway, imagining a vacation of his own, to visit Klara in Canada. When he saw a fueling truck drive by, he made no notice of anything out of the ordinary. He finished the embrace and looked Klara softly in the eyes.

"Try and enjoy the time here in the loft. Airports are full of people that are emotional, so you don't have to feel the need to engage a conversation with anyone. There is also a complimentary phone charging station by the magazine rack. You'll be fine. I must go now and form a general search party. I don't want to cause any panic, or delays. We'll get you on your flight, don't worry."

Derk thanked Klara for Alessio's phone and put it in his pocket. He looked back at her to give her a wink, but she sat and looked out the window at a baggage shuttle running an empty cart back to the main chute. Derk wished Flo a safe trip back, walked down the stairs and joined the table of his colleagues.

"Any nachos left?"

"What took you so long?!" Rakeef joked.

"Any ideas for the take-down?" Chandler looked at Derk.

"I'm thinking they have moved through security already, maybe they are in the baggage hangar hiding out." Jones offered.

"That's a good start," Derk said, chewing the remaining nacho toppings. "Jones and I will through baggage Rakeef and Chandler you two check the maintenance hangar for anything. I checked the departures board, and the next flights are the flights to Denver, and Rio Air to São Paulo. After the hangars Jones you should check the American Airlines flight to Denver, and I'll check Air Rio."

"The Denver flight has already called for boarding, so I'll go there first." Jones rose from his seat, "then I'll meet up with you by the hangars."

"Good luck," Rakeef and Chandler said in unison.

Derk turned to the others, placing Alessio's phone on the table. "One of you take this and pass it on to Alessio's family or the hospital. I hope he is stable, but I have no time to check. Please be careful. With any luck, no one else will get hurt. I'm bringing the hurt to them if they do anything to Jones."

Derk rose and walked towards the international gates, investigator badge in hand and approached Air Rio's gate.

# 4.

Chandler and Rakeef decided to check the maintenance hangar first since the other two were busy with planes. They threw the waste from their order in the garbage and put the tray on the stand. Chandler used the security card his friend had loaned him to gain full access to the entire airport and travelled towards the maintenance hangar's employee lockers. A man was seated on the bench by the lockers not in uniform, holding his head.

"Sir, are you alright?" Rakeef asked.

"I was filling up my water bottle and grabbing a bite from my lunch, when I felt a bang to my head, and I woke up in the bathroom. My uniform overalls are gone, keys, wallet. I'm not sure what happened, but I think I was robbed."

"Rakeef, stay with him and try and find an ice-pack for his head." Chandler turned back to the man. "Sir, can you tell me what your position is here in the hangar?"

"I drive the fuel trucks to fill up the planes."

"Very-well, I'll leave my partner here with you to help look over your head and check for a concussion. I think I may know the person who did this to you. I've been trying to charge him for doing the same thing to one of my team earlier this week in a cane field. She was knocked out too.

But look at the bright side, you'll be all better and ready for action after a well deserved day off!" Chandler placed a supportive hand on the man's shoulder then briefly stared at Rakeef, taking off in search of Oren.

# Chapter 32

# *PLAN B*

## 1.

Jones approached the staircase of the American Airlines flight thirty minutes away from taxiing and leaving on time. "Edgehill Southern Division. I need to do a very quick search of the passengers. Have you confirmed the manifest?" Jones looked at the flight attendant, "I know the guy's face. Eight minutes or less is all I need."

"Please hurry, I was about to close up the door. And we are going to do the safety presentation."

"I hope he is not on here." Jones moved past the attendant and took a brief look in the first-class cabin. Both passengers were busy with a neck massager, champagne flute and seat extension engaged, pampering the inflated ticket price. Satisfied that the area was safe, Jones focused on the main passenger class. Thankfully, passengers were all seated as he moved towards the back of the plane to the lavatory. A flight attendant approached and asked his intention, to which Jones flashed his badge, calming her discomfort. He opened the vacant lavatory door and saw the space was clear. He turned back to the flight attendant and said, "Have a great flight. I don't think the issues I was looking for are on this flight. Thanks for your time."

Jones continued to the front of the plane and thanked the front attendant, clutching the seat belt restraint with a life preserver around her shoulders. "I bet you hate doing that every flight."

"How could you tell?" she said sarcastically.

"All clear, thanks for helping me with my investigation. Have a safe flight." Jones gave her a firm nod and exited the door. He heard the door latch shut behind him and moved back towards the airport gate, looking for the Rio Air flight that Derk would be checking. He saw Chandler waving him down.

"Jones, I have a lead on Oren." Chandler raced over to Jones, breathless.

"I just checked the Denver flight and no sign of him. Usually there would be some crazy tourist drama on the flight, but they were all seated, so it was a breeze. Where's Rakeef?"

"Rakeef is with a guy I think Oren hit over the head. Then he took his uniform and hijacked a fuel truck, so he might be heading to whichever plane just landed to jump on board. I think we should head towards the middle gates because that plane," he pointed to a British Airways aircraft, "just landed and there is no fuel truck there yet."

"I want to check with Derk too, he's going to the Rio flight, so if we all are close together it might make it more official. Sometimes the South American pilots think we are checking them too."

"For drugs?" Chandler chimed.

"For anything." Jones laughed.

They made their way along the outside of the airport's baggage stations and saw Derk approach the concourse.

## 2.

The Rio Air flight was beginning to board the passengers of elderly age and those needing assistance. Children would be next on board, which would help Oren slip out of the lavatory as a child might have an emergency. The plane would transport four flight attendants, two pilots, and a mix of retired couples and families with young children still inexpensively able to fly. Heroic passengers, willing to take matters into their own hands, would not be on this flight, safeguarding Oren's escape. He opened the door, slipped into the aisle, checked his hard hat and vest into the overhead bin, and sat in row twenty-one, seat E. Adjusting for comfort, Oren was seated and trying to look inconspicuous.

A man came over to him and sat in seat B, followed by an older couple in Row 20, seats D and E. Oren had played this role before and was not this lucky, usually having to move seats, or sometimes sections several times before take-off. If luck would have it, Oren was not seeing passengers nestle around him; they were all filling up the front half of the plane.

The second boarding group was called, and families with small children, those travelling alone, and any other passengers requiring assistance were beginning to come aboard. For the time waiting for these new passengers to get seated, Oren pulled out the travel brochure from the seat pocket and held it partially up, blocking his face. A single parent with her pre-teenaged son was approaching row twenty-one, staring directly at Oren.

"Sorry, you are in the wrong seat. See here," the passenger pointed to her boarding pass, with her son looking at the seat markers.

"I'm sorry, I must have the wrong seat. My apologies." He held onto the brochure and moved to the aisle allowing the boy and his mother entry. They sat in E and F, allowing Oren to sit again in the row in seat D. He continued his interest in the brochure, occasionally looking up for either Brett or the police. Out of the corner of his eye he saw the police gather by the staircase. On to Plan B.

## 3.

Derk had met up with the two other officers and had a brief meeting on the tarmac. The plan concluded that Derk would continue to check the aircraft while Jones watched for any suspicious ground movement, and Chandler was vigilant in checking the fueling trucks. If they didn't find anything, they would meet back at this chosen location for their alternate plan. Jones began walking towards the baggage carts as Chandler asked a local crew worker which planes had a scheduled refuelling. Derk headed for the staircase to board the São Paulo flight. A slow family was moving onboard, struggling with a stroller, which Derk offered to help carry as their toddler was a handful. The father thanked Derk, and they moved a bit faster. When onboard, Derk gave the man the stroller and spoke with the attendant.

"Hello, I'm Investigator Warrows Police Force Southern Division. I need to do a quick scan of your passengers. I have a suspicion that you have a stowaway on board. Can I have a look at your passenger manifest?" Derk watched the flight attendant hold a binder flipping to the manifest page, "I know who I'm looking for, I just want to see where the vacant seats are, that he may be hiding in. You haven't seen any issues with passengers swapping seats?"

"Not anything out of the ordinary, there have been no outbursts. How much time do you need? We are ready for the main boarding call. We are at about 45% capacity from what I gather. Do you want me to hold them for a few minutes?"

"I would greatly appreciate that, thank you." Derk boarded and took a glance at the first-class cabin. Like the standard sweep Jones had performed earlier on his flight check, Derk saw no sign of either Brett or Oren. He turned towards the main class cabin area, which was still seating passengers. Adults were hoisting bags to the overhead compartments and youth stowing their carry-on under the seats ahead of them. Through the procedure, Derk and looked for his man but never found a matching face. It was when the woman seated three rows up from an occupied seat sat down when the passenger began to panic. He saw Derk was moving towards the back of the plane and had no way to move as there was only one businessperson with a briefcase between Derk and the plane's rear.

## 4.

Behind the businessperson going to his seat was an open section with emergency exit doors in the aircraft's middle. As Derk looked towards the passengers seated, he saw a man get up near the plane's back and charge toward the businessperson. Instinctively Derk bent down and watched the situation for merit to prepare for a take down. He hesitated for only a second, then clearly saw the passenger's face.

"Don't make a move! I have immunity!" the South American shouted, having all the passengers turn to look at the rising situation unfold. There was an eerie stillness in the cabin as collectively everyone drew enough air to let out a horrendous choir of screams. The man took the businessperson hostage, holding a pen to the man's neck, if the execution warranted, he'd stab him. Seeing the pen was a threat, Derk tried to calm the businessperson's terror-stricken eyes.

"Sir, let the man go and drop your weapon, don't ruin everyone on this plane's flight home, I don't know what the police have against you, but I wasn't looking for you. Just come peacefully and release the man you're holding. We can all get this sorted out." Derk calmly spoke, trying to deescalate the chaos.

"No!" the man shouted, and then the screaming began echoing through the cabin loud enough for a few passengers to exit and run down the staircase before Jones could run up the stairs to assist Derk.

"Derk, what's going on?!" Jones had moved toward the situation as Oren slipped off the plane. He had been hiding in first class and during the diversion swiftly exited when a few scared passengers fled.

Derk lunged at the South American grabbing the pen and toppling over the businessperson. He rose and detained the attacker.

"People, please remain calm!" called out a familiar voice. Jones tapped a double pat on Derk's shoulder that he had joined and would assist in the removal of the attacker.

People were screaming, with children wailing, creating a scene of pandemonium. Derk inched forward, maintaining eye contact with the businessperson, and trying to get the man carefully up.

"It's okay, everyone! It's all safe now." Jones shouted out over some high-pitched screams. He handed Derk some handcuffs and in reaching across he glanced out the window.

"Derk he's getting away!" Jones tried to run off the plane and warn Chandler that the drone helicopter was landing on the tarmac.

"Jones! C'mon man just stay put, you were trying to stab someone just now. There!" He closed the handcuff and quickly got off the plane chasing after Jones.

# Chapter 33

# *SWEET GOODBYES*

## 1.

"Chandler that's the helicopter that was chasing you!" Jones was running towards him and looking for the getaways if they were about to make a move. Chandler met up with Derk and Jones as he was the only one that could legally arrest Brett or Oren.

"Brett has to be in a fuel truck. Did you find Oren."

"We had a situation with a pen that some lunatic was going to attack some lawyer. He's in handcuffs. Wait, what about that helicopter? Jones are you sure?" Derk still scanning for Oren.

"That's the one."

Derk pained to say, "Brett's in a fuel truck? You sure?"

"I'm sure of it. He's gotta be trying to hide out and then slip on to another plane. British Airways just landed. Rakeef and I interviewed a worker in the maintenance hangar that complained about an assault and also stripping him to take his keys and overalls. He's still at large, wait!" Chandler pointed. "Is he in that one?"

The officers saw a fuel truck driving at a higher-than-average speed, and when the driver came into view, Chandler called out. "That's got to be him."

The officers stared at the fuel truck as Brett and Oren stealthily ran to the chopper's open door. With next to no effort, their escape plan worked. As the fuel tanker steered onto the runway to get away from the hangar, he noticed the helicopter begin to take off. Realizing that he was not a threat, the officers turned and gasped as the stealth helicopter was hovering over the sea.

Chandler watched his target make their escape, his heart pumping the adrenaline throughout his arteries, sharpening his focus. He pulled out his cell phone and called the detachment. "Piper, sad news. I don't know how we missed them, but they got picked up by that stealth helicopter and are headed north, it seems. Can you try and contact the neighboring island authorities to shut down any refueling attempts for that helicopter? I don't know when we will be able to catch them, but I'm sorry, not today like you hoped."

"Chand it's alright. We have enough to clean up and trust me when I say this, we're not equipped to handle these guys. We'll get Interpol on Brett's yacht. Everyone safe?"

"Yeah the team is strong. Jones should be a cop. We should fast track his training. He might be a good partner for Alessio."

Hearing Alessio, Derk chimed, "Ask her how he's doing?"

"How is he doing? Stable in hospital. Great. Alright Piper, thanks for the update." He ended the call.

"I can't believe they got away. I feel so cheated!" Chandler looked at Derk.

"We might need some coast guards, look!" Derk motioned to the thick black smoke coming from the far off helicopter.

"Do you think they'll crash?"

"They are too far out if they do. We'll never get out to them in time." Chandler said.

Klara watched the view from the Sky Loft and grew increasingly panicked when she saw the three officers running off the plane staircases. She figured it was either Oren or Brett but didn't care as everyone gathered at her window to see the smoking helicopter.

Derk, Chandler and Jones walked back by Rakeef as he patted them on the shoulder. "At least you got one attacker. A pen was his weapon of choice?"

"Yeah, the crazy thing is I can't tell if that was legit or a diversion. Oren might have been on that plane, and if not he's a trained killer, he beat us without killing us. So, I'd call it a win, especially with the fact that they may sink." Derk tried to lighten the mood.

"It's a good thing I didn't have to write up any injury reports. Banks is in order for tonight, right Derk?" Jones urged.

"Oh, I think the whole department should book a party cruise and let loose this weekend now that the criminals are off the island. Justice may still find them if they go down in the sea. They are getting farther out, and I don't know if the smoke stopped."

"I'm glad its over. These offshore criminals with their spy guys and big bankroll, I just want to work with the local jobs you know." Chandler, feeling heartfelt in his speech. "I was saying to Rakeef the other day that I need a little bit of a break from the force, I think. A hiatus or an exchange like Piper has."

Derk reached into his pocket to get his phone. "I gotta go say goodbye to Klara. Jones, you really need to find someone. Sheesh." Derk left the group and started walking back towards the gate doors.

"I'm serious guys I'm going to try and book us all a discounted party cruise so we can all relax and put our feet up. Might have to do it over a couple of weekends so we have enough people to run the department." Chandler chuckled with the men.

Klara had used the washroom when her boarding announcement was called. She gave Flo a goodbye hug and apologized saying that she'd see her at the future wedding planning days her sister would host. Seeing the officers retrace their steps, she figured the fugitives were either dead or arrested, and Derk would come for his last visit. She sat again by the window, watching the fuel trucks filling the aircraft and a pair of luggage carriers trying to recover the spilled suitcase that fell off. Derk approached her.

"I'm sorry if your flight is a little off schedule."

"I saw you were teaching some officers how to get the job done," Klara leaned in to start the hug. "You need a hug after all that police work."

They hugged with a firm embrace. Klara was not feeling right at the first meeting with the ordeal still in her mind, but now in the arms of Derk Warrows, she hugged back, hard and with purpose. She turned and kissed him, Derk returning the gesture and a little more passion than a simple thank you kiss.

"I'm really glad to have met you, Klara. Very unusual circumstances at the start, middle and end of this week, but I wouldn't have been able to do what I did this week without you. You have a real eye for investigating crime, and should make a splendid detective, if simple police work doesn't work out for you."

"Thank-you so much Derk! I know that Barbados is a beautiful island, and under the right conditions and tour guide, I bet it would be in my top ten vacation spots." Klara reached for her phone, slightly breaking from the embrace. "Put your contact info in here." Setting up a new contact and handing the phone over to Derk. "My flight is going to be called soon."

"Here, my sweet. Texting is cheaper than calling, you'll text me later tonight, after you are back in Canada? I have a few things to do with the station, and then get a bite to eat and have a hot shower. I know a day of travelling will be exhausting but please send me a text." Derk chimed.

Klara heard her gate paged over the intercom. "That's my flight. Thank you again Derk for everything. I loved our time together, but I have also been surprised at how calm I have been through this vacation. I got more than my money's worth at knowing that Kennedy's murder got solved before I flew off. I guess her body will be flown back to England and someone will take care of her things?"

"Usually, the family take care of the arrangements, but don't think about that, when you are on the plane, close your eyes, and think about the beach. Barbados will be here when you visit again. Hopefully, that will be while I'm still this athletic." He joked as his phone rang. He motioned to Klara to wait for a moment as it would be a short call. "Hi Gladys."

"Hi Derk, I don't know if you are busy but there was a call about some kids that broke into a rum hut, asking for cash. The store owner has one of them still there and probably needs assistance."

"All right Gladys, I'll be over in a bit, text Jones or Rakeef, no wait, Rakeef can deal with this, you and Chandler should take the night off. I'm going to head over to the hospital and check on Alessio."

"Ah, thank you. I heard about what happened at the airport. I can't believe they got away. Have a good night Derk. You are a lifesaver now. Alessio's awake from what I was told." Gladys ended the call.

"That was Gladys, and I guess now that all the tough stuff is over, it is back to business as usual."

Klara walked with Derk down through the Sky Loft door then parted with their last official kiss. Derk waved to her as she made her way to the gate and then turned to meet up with the other officers. Klara waited for the first boarding call, then approached the single travellers to board, feeling a little sad that her flight home would be alone. She made her way to her seat, knowing that the seat beside her would have someone that could tell her about all the adventures they had while in Barbados. Klara sat getting comfortable in her chair, gazing out the window as her heart rate rested. She opened her carry-on and pulled a little souvenir she got from the bridal store at Sandy Lane. She admired the little wedding dress cake topper and gave it a gentle rub. *Well, Derk, here's to a boring ride home. I didn't do many touristy things like go to the chattel village souvenir shop or snorkeling. I sure had fun.* She pulled out her phone as the flight attendant performed the safe use of the seat belt restraint system and flicked to the first picture of her and Derk at Dover Beach. She smiled and leaned back in her chair feeling something jab her. She reached around and pulled out a little box with a K in gold lettering. She opened it and gasped!

## 2.

The plane began to taxi, and the auxiliary air began to hiss. Passengers were putting in their earbuds, some reading, others starting to watch the inflight movies. Klara tilted the box to let the ring dazzle in the light thinking the distance between Derk and her shouldn't matter. The ring was beautiful, white gold with a large princess cut solitaire diamond encrusted with a dozen smaller dazzling diamonds. The size was perfect. *How did he slip that in my pocket?*

Klara tilted her seat to view the aircraft take-off and soar into the sky, caressing the ring that Derk gave her. She smiled as she saw the view of the beautiful island way down from her soaring height and made herself a promise to go back to Barbados—*the Island in the Sun.*

# Acknowledgements

There are many who I would like to acknowledge for the generous assistance they shared in furnishing this story. In the tender moments through the laughter and occasional tears of my youth to the cherished memories and patience throughout life, I wish many thanks to my family, with particular focus on Stephanie's guidance.

In Alberta and British Columbia, Coree, and John Girard; their daughter Rayna, and Coree's mother, Gwen Coleman. Dorinda "Dee" and Dave McCabe; their children Amy and Ian, Mia Rutledge, Marla, and Reagan Shumilak; nephew Ryker, niece Macy, Jennifer Simpson; her children Emmalee—one of my flower girls, Mackenzie, and Alex, Morgan, and Travis McMullan and many of the students I have taught over my career. I want to thank Tellwell and their team for helping me get my premiere novel published.

In Saskatchewan, Barbara and Ray Hoover, Jean Deyell, Graeme and Tanya Hoover, Miranda Maggrah; her children Carter, Zoe, and Owen—who were my other flower girl and ring bearer, and Hayden. From a professional side, my thanks to author George Watson's advice.

My travelling partner, confidant, and adventure seeker, who has been tirelessly by my side, a special thank you to my lovely wife, Sharleen.

To the Royal Barbados Police Force for the limitless job they do, to make and keep Barbados safe for Bajans and tourists.

And for you as well, dear reader, thank you!

# Author's Note

I worked for several months researching elements of the story to juxtapose actual world features and geographical locations with crime fiction. This story is a tale of fiction in the international landscapes of one of Canada's Prairie provinces, Alberta, and the Caribbean country of Barbados. *The Cattlewash Assailant* is, in my mind, a way to show law enforcements' tact in combatting fiction-based murderers; the crimes themselves, believable. Since I was not able to interview a police officer in Barbados personally, I tried my best to make the officers' dialogue as authentic as possible with professionalism. I hope a few copies make it to the Island, and it brings some happiness to the law enforcement community worldwide.

I hope that readers will enjoy its pacing; when they can visit Barbados's lovely beaches, historically classic landmarks, and the warm glow of the Caribbean sunshine, they do so knowing Barbados is beautiful and a pleasure to explore.

As a child, I grew up in a kind of bubble-wrapped Canadian society. Good values and safety protocols like *don't talk to strangers, don't eat anything off the ground (before I learned the 3-second rule), wash your hands with soap to make sure the germs go away*! I imagine you may have grown up in this *very safe time* too. I have lived in a big metropolis until I was eight, then lived in a small

315

village until I moved to Alberta in 2005, repeating the cycle of the big city and small town. I have often wondered what I wanted this particular crime story in the series to be about, recalling back to my years in elementary school, through my visits to Barbados as a youth and with my wife as an adult, reading, watching, and chasing the stories of criminal activity in my mind. It may seem odd, but I have pondered the thoughts of being on vacation without the comforts of home and having to deal with unexpected crises as they arise. I have always felt safe while on vacation in Barbados, renting cars, touring landmarks, shopping in grocery stores, tanning by the sea, and walking downtown in Bridgetown. I have felt eyes watching me, but that is usually to see *who I am*, not *what I am doing there*. With all this fantastic material spinning on the hamster wheel in my mind, I began to create characters that readers could relate to and give them a good-old-squeeze: Shady deals, fears of drowning, losing your passport, helping locate a missing person or watching a speeding car chase. In my personal history, I have been on vacation and witnessed some of these behaviours that have been floating around in my mind, which spurred me to pick up the pen and start writing.

# Photographic Credit

The photographs on the front cover, the back cover, the steppingstones, and the dedication page are taken by yours truly. The dedication page photo was taken in Ottawa while waiting for the fireworks display in 2000. My mother and father stood beside me as I captured that original candid shot with 400 Kodak Gold film on my Canon A1 SLR. It is my favourite picture of the two of them and my treasured photo that the world has never seen online, taken before the Age of Digital Photography. In creating a picture dedication page for my novel, I figured that now is the time to share and show them off to everyone with every copy of this book.

On a sad note, I took the front cover picture of Cattlewash beach, the steppingstones, and the Out of City bus stop sign near Ragged Point on the back, the day my mother passed on from her battle with cancer. After visiting by her bedside, I was down in Barbados to take pictures to show her after I returned a week later. During her sleep in the early morning of Saturday, July 16, 2016, she breathed her last, and my sister's post notified me through social media. I had no reason to panic, and since I was far from home, on vacation with a crisis of the loss of a parent, I did what my childhood thoughts as a budding crime novelist would do. I went out and snapped some breath-taking and unusual pictures to give my vacation some fresh air and to make my premiere novel. It was along that drive to Cattlewash beach, which ignited my manuscript for *The Cattlewash Assailant*.

When I found out she passed, I made the right choice to channel my loss into a positive treasured memory instead of laying on a hotel bed watering the pillows. I took that picture of the beach the same day she died— which was a decision I hold with extreme pride. It is on my wall at home and as my phone's wallpaper. Every time I see it, I treasure and remember that day as vividly as before. I hope you enjoy it as much as I do.

# Next Novel Excerpt

Here is an excerpt of the next book to be released in the Klara Hockley series that follows *The Cattlewash Assailant's* events.

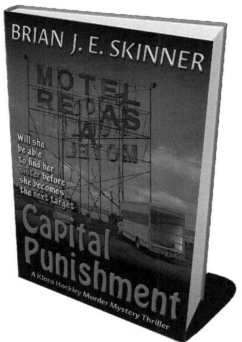

**Book cover not finalized.**

"I hate those frat boys!" Cassidy shouted as the floor mop resumed her attention. Grabbing the handle, she heard a loud thud. "Matteo? Are you okay?"

"What? No, I'm fine."

"Look there, at the window!"

With a custom chrome pipe coming out of the truck bed, the black diesel truck revved the engine, causing the windows to shake. Drunken cackling flooded the drive-thru lane. The boys sped away, leaving burnout tread marks.

"They're gone now. Cassidy it's fine." Matteo softened, seeing his regular shift partner was upset. He grabbed the final till with the count sheet and walked towards her flicking the light switch. He checked the street and parking lot through the lobby window, making sure the annoying bar crowd truck driver and their friends were clearly out of sight. "It's almost 2:30, we better get out quick, remember no overtime." He quickly called out to Cassidy.

"Just dumping the pail." Cassidy shouted from the back.

Through the front window across the street sat a parked fully electric truck with a stealthily, quieted muffler and a flimsy cheap tonneau cover concealing two frozen teenaged bodies waiting for an exchange. The driver reached over and toggled the modified headlight switch disabling the daytime running LEDs and taillights. Gripping the steering wheel with a black leather glove, the driver pushed the engine ignition button to start the electric truck. Undetected in the faint glow of the street, silently the beastly pickup moved, the frozen bodies resting peacefully.

There was no sound audibly louder than the humming of the streetlights until the two employees burst through the side door, quickly closing it snugly in the frame as the alarm chirped its countdown. Matteo lifted the garbage bags and walked with Cassidy towards their cars.

The truck inched behind them in the pitch-black alley.

"There we go. You work tomorrow, Cass?" Matteo chuckled as he fumbled with the padlock on the dumpster.

"Did you see me grab my keys? I thought I put them in here," Cassidy faced towards her Toyota Corolla, "oh, here they are Matt—" She froze.

"Woah man turn off the brights!" Matteo called out with a spooked and terrified voice as he strained to see who had turned on the LED light bars. As he spoke, he missed hearing the driver's window lower and a tranquillizing gun's dart whistle through the air penetrating his neck as it landed. Matteo awkwardly fell away from Cassidy's sight and collapsed by a pile of flattened cardboard boxes.

Cassidy had no time to scream as she held her hands to block the blinding lights. While the weak body of Matteo was struggling to defensively stand, the driver loaded another dart into the chamber and release his second dart with expert accuracy into the soft young neck of Cassidy Lemanski.

Dropping her purse and falling to the ground, her wrist flopped under her car, shaking her promise ring free and rolled along the uneven pavement to rest behind her passenger tire.

The lights when out, resuming darkness, and the driver opened the door peering towards Matteo. Seeing his eyes barely open, the driver reached over him and grabbed the carabiner of keys from his belt loop. Chirping the door lock of his Ford Focus, the driver put the keys into his pocket and continued slowly walking towards the tailgate. Releasing the gate and ripping the tonneau cover free from the closures, the driver pulled the frozen body of a teenaged boy sliding him to the edge. Lifting the stiff body with arms dangling towards the Ford and shifted it to the opposite shoulder as the driver's door opened. Swinging it wide, the driver placed the teenaged boy's lifeless body in the seat and fastened his seatbelt. Reaching into their jacket pocket, the driver produced a Bluetooth transmitter key fob and secured it on the keyring of Matteo Bridges' keys. With the door open and the teenaged driver safely buckled in, the driver returned to the drugged body of Matteo. Lifting his unconscious body and carrying him to the truck, the driver slid Matteo into the tight space which once held the boy and grabbed the feet of the other frozen teenager, sliding her for the subsequent placement.

Cassidy's body laid on the moist, muddy back-alley pavement, her face dirty and peacefully sleeping. She felt no sensation of the driver pick her up from the ground after collecting her keys and placed the teenaged girl. She was carried to the tailgate and flopped face-down, sliding her into place beside her associate; she did not feel the rough metal of the truck bed's jagged edges tear at her arms and face. She was shoved forcefully into the truck bed and bashed her numb skull against the frame when she slid to the front. With a bit of trickled blood weeping from her curly scalp, she slept beside Matteo as the tailgate clicked into place and the ragged tonneau cover draped over their bodies.

Casually walking over to the Toyota and finished the work of placing the frozen teenage girl's body in Cassidy's driver's seat, the driver fitted a duplicate transmitter to her keyring. They set a roll of taped tungsten filaments wired to spell the name—*Cassidy* in school-hand cursive and adhered it across the dashboard, firmly taping the wire in place. Satisfied that the job was complete and checking the handiwork of their body exchange, the driver shut the Toyota's door. Moving over to Matteo's Focus, they unrolled the second wired filaments spelling Matteo in the dash of the Ford. With both wired names securely in place, the driver walked back to the truck, flicked the headlight switch, and engaged the ignition. Reversing first, then backing out of the alley, the silent electric truck moved to the edge of the street and waited. The driver opened the center console and pushed the connection switch to the Bluetooth transmitters starting a 25-second countdown.

The pickup turned north on Preston Street, driving towards Gladstone Avenue to travel south to the Trans Canada Highway. As the truck turned under the highway overpass, the vintage neighbourhood heard the employee's cars burst. The explosive blaze ruptured the stillness of the early morning as thick orange flames, with the smell of upholstery foam and seared human flesh rising through the air.

The blast ignited a cascading fire of the vinyl siding on the nearby homes as bedroom lights flipped on. Sleepy parents clutched their crying toddlers as they exited to their front lawns.

Fire trucks were alerted and began to hustle to the out-of-control scene. The two cars of Cassidy and Matteo smouldered in the forest of flames of bubbling paint. The heat melted tire rubber encasing Cassidy's ring from her girlfriend. The bodies of the frozen teens were quickly thawed and began burning as sirens wailed through the early morning deserted streets.

The driver had watched the chaos of their recent work, rounded the corner approach to the Trans Canada Highway and drove up the freeway entrance. Both victims jiggled slightly at the racing acceleration yet were unaware that they would be going through the most excruciating torture of their young lives within hours.

Merging to the highway peppered with freight trucks, the driver smiled, knowing the next few hours with Matteo and Cassidy would send the Ottawa police into a puzzling nightmare of victims, unknown suspects, and a race to hunt them down before the media got a taste of the ruthless attacks.

In the pocket of Cassidy's jeans vibrated her cellphone, with her girlfriend's voicemail saying she cleaned the living room and made stove-top caramel popcorn from scratch, begging her to race home so they could watch the last episode of their streamed season. The call recorded the voicemail sending a traceable record of the Phone's

GPS location. The phone connected to a nearby hotspot and logged a description that the device was travelling southwest along the Trans Canada Highway. Cassidy's girlfriend sat on the couch, legs crossed and began nibbling on the popcorn, checking her phone for a response.

Sixteen kilometres away in the back of the truck bed, Cassidy's eyes opened.

# Book Club Questions

Use the following questions and activities to get more out of *The Cattlewash Assailant* by Brian J. E. Skinner.

1. Were you surprised that the author has a personal connection to the setting?
2. How did you feel about the author's choice in using a picture dedication for the novel?
3. What is the significance of the title of this novel?
4. In the Prologue, which character was the most genuine?
5. How did the author build tension and create a hardship for the main characters so early in the novel?
6. How have the scenes been created to help with the steady flow over a week's time?
7. Introducing the secondary main tourist character halfway into the story was an unusual way to keep the pace flowing. Do you think the author planned it this way for plot development?
8. What is a memorable passage that you enjoy in the novel? What makes you appreciate that particular passage?
9. Was the ending believable or too far-fetched?
10. Where are specific examples of alliteration found in the novel?

11. Did you know that the author created Basil's character in Chapter 19 after the author's uncle? What family member of your family has an interesting character?
12. What part makes your favourite chapter stand out to you, and why?
13. What surprised you the most about the book? Was it the plot, setting, pace, crime, or action?
14. Why has the author created characters for short cameos in this book in the series?
15. Were there any times when you disagreed with a main character's actions?
16. Was the book satisfying to read? Why or why not?
17. What provocative questions would you love to ask the author about this novel?

Activities with the Internet

1. Using a search engine or online map service, explore the locations in *The Cattlewash Assailant*. Which are real and which are fiction?
2. The author uses specific news stories about bravery, disaster, and dated events. Using a search engine or the event's local news website, research the reports to gain complete insight into the event. If the news stories are offline, hopefully, you learn something new in the process.
3. Using an online map service, zoom in to the map scale of Barbados at full screen, making a note

of the scale, and move the map to your home location and compare the size of Barbados to your local map's scale. If you live in Barbados, check Alberta, Canada, or the country of Belgium.

Manufactured by Amazon.ca
Bolton, ON

40595360R00196